SHEHKRii
-The Flame-

I.D. Martin
2019©

26BOOKS

www.26books.com.au

PO Box 1914
SUNSHINE PLAZA
Qld 4558
Australia

SHEHKRii
– The FLAME –

SHEHKRii

-The Flame-

(70,000 Words approx.)

I.D. Martin

Copyright © 2019 I. D. Martin

The moral right of the author has been asserted.
All characters, names, businesses, organizations and events in this publication are fictitious or if in the public domain used fictitiously and any resemblance to real persons living or dead is purely coincidental.

All rights reserved.

SHEHKRii
– The FLAME –

Acknowledgements
To Mr. Wilson & the Silver Mistress:
Instruction and inspiration
in that order.

Editor
Jessica E. Guzman
C.C.N.Y.

Cover Art
ZoZo

Adult Content Warning
This work contains violence,
sex scenes and 'strong'
language.

SHEHKRii
– The FLAME –

Also by I. D. Martin

The Travel Agency
(A novel)

Thin Skinned
(Anthology incl. the novella, Thylacine)

Thylacine
(Novella)

Coming soon

SHEHKRii - The Curse

SHEHKRii - The Tempest

SHEHKRii
– The FLAME –

Achievements

2018
Stringybark Short Fiction Award
(The Invisible Boy)
- Highly Commended -

2009
Aeon Award
(Pirate Copies)
- Shortlisted -

PROLOGUE

ROUGH TOR, BODMIN MOOR, U.K.

The man on the rock appeared to be squatting, perched precariously on the upper oblique face of the massive granite boulder. He was clearly visible from the nearly half a kilometer the group had to cross to get to the mound.

Three men and two women trudged the well-worn path with a mixture of emotions.

Dr. Neil Carlisle, the leader of the not-so-merry team was torn between anger at the mysterious stranger's impertinence and the hope of reprieve, which he was dangling in front of them. Carlisle had spent the last eighteen years, on-and-off, working around Bodmin Moor painstakingly measuring the ancient geomantic construction and with the help of military grade GPS systems and unique software, beginning to unravel its mysteries.

Then, suddenly, his funding had been pulled.

Two days after that catastrophe *she* had shown up and offered him a privately funded reprieve. *She*, Hilde Nordstrom – the softly spoken but very menacing 'consultant'. She, who now emerged from beside the giant boulder to meet them.

SHEHKRii
– The FLAME –

Looking up at the man, Carlisle said, "You shouldn't be up there. That's a valuable artifact and you'll damage it."

The man laughed softly, a deep, merry rumble.

Then he jumped.

Before Carlisle or any of the others could react, he landed a meter away with a soft thud and a slight bending of the knees. The fall had been nearly five meters.

"How the …"

"Now then, Doctor, is that the right way to be talkin' to your benefactor?"

Carlisle noted the slight brogue and became suspicious. The man was just over six feet, broad shouldered and forty something. 'Robust', was an understatement. The slightly longer hair and grey stubble gave him a rakish air.

"I don't care about your money. If you're some sort of New Age loony, we're out of here. I don't deal with wannabe Druids."

The man chuckled, "Doctor, the last *Druheidá* died eight hundred years ago and no amount of wishin' by the Romantics will bring her back. However, of all the researchers in this area, you have achieved the most. I want you to keep up the effort. You bein' a plural, of course – your team is unique. And what I'm offerin' is a package deal, minus one, but we'll get to that shortly.

"Are you still interested?"

SHEHKRii
– The FLAME –

Carlisle frowned. He glanced at his team. They were beyond good, even he knew that. And what would happen to them if this all fell apart?

Liam Cormac was his IT genius. A tall, wiry man who spent ninety percent of his time in front of a screen, he could work anywhere but had attached himself to Carlisle ten years ago and refused to leave despite continuous better offers from every other department in the university.

Bart Smith was the best field operator in most of Europe. Still a postgraduate, he should have his doctorate by now but was always up the side of some mountain digging or surveying or whatever it took for their current project.

Jasmin Bhari had only been back with him for two, no, three years and should also be a PhD by now. She'd co-authored almost every paper he'd published in the last fifteen years and they were all the better for her fastidious rigor and amazing imagination.

Then there was Brony; Bronwyn Petersen. Not an academic but the best secretary, project manager and all-round organizer he'd ever encountered. They wouldn't still be going if not for her.

He had to give them all a chance.

"Our work is almost pure research; no immediate applications. Why would you want to invest in that?"

"Knowledge is power, Doctor. And the understandin' of how the Earth works will be an emancipating little piece of knowledge for those among humanity willin' to listen.

The only thing holdin' you back right now is instrumentation …"

"Yes!" exclaimed Cormac. "Haven't I been telling you that for a decade, Neil?"

Carlisle gave him an exasperated look; this was an old argument.

"Doctor," said Hilde Nordstrom, and the word froze them all in place. A slight grin played across her face as she continued, "Cormac has been right from the start but the type of equipment Nathan is talking about will make your GPS system look like a tinker toy."

"Nathan?" said Jasmin.

"Nathan Chalk, at your service," said the stranger as he sketched a small bow.

"We can argue all night, Doctor. However, a demonstration should save us all some time. So, let me summarize."

He gestured around the tor and its broad view. "You believe and have partially proven that Bodmin Moor was a giant observatory of the *Celtoi*, which served to map the heavens and predict the weather. You've also documented a number of cultural finds that have devolved from your work. But it's the earth science you're interested in, isn't it?"

"Of course," said Carlisle. "If we can understand how they could be so precise we can use that knowledge for so much more. They used this area for millennia with extraordinary consistency. The knowledge is there. We just have to find it."

"You think of it as static, then, this grid, or *leys* or whatever?"

"Essentially, yes, but ..."

"You're wrong in that regard, Doctor. Let me show you why."

Nathan held out his hands, palms vertical and then whipped them straight down towards the ground.

With the exception of Hilde, all those present rose up off the grass. And didn't stop as they accelerated straight up for a few terrifying seconds.

***

The reactions were predictable, thought Nathan. *Every time I pull this trick they all seem to think they're balancing on a beam.*

As the sense of motion stopped and they leveled out, the little group stared at the grinning man who had ripped the fabric of their reality asunder.

***

"Before you all indulge the obvious, let's get to it, shall we. Among other things, I want you to document the geomantic pulse of Bodmin Moor and tell the world. It's not a static system, Doctor, but it has been severely degraded.

"The Romans deforested most of Britain for many a reason and timber wasn't one of them. The Earth breathes and where it breathes best there are signs. The *Druheidá* knew this and more importantly 'why'. The Romans sought out all the giant oaks that grew on the nodal points of the planetary grid and destroyed them. They were waging a war and symbols are important in war. Take out your enemy's symbols and you stand a good chance of winning.

"Here in Bodmin, things were a little more sophisticated but much of the ruination is Roman made; deliberately destroyed. Your instruments don't have the sensitivity to map the Grid and its variations because the signal has been weakened. Hilde will show you how to overcome that difficulty. Now, though, let me show you what you've been looking for."

Nathan held out a single hand, this time, palm up. Then he seemed to twist it, caressing the air. His hand became a slow fist.

"Look," breathed Jasmin, staring down.

Carlisle dropped to his knees, oblivious to the lack of ground under him. He saw it, saw it all instantly.

Everything he'd ever dared hope might be … WAS.

Golden lightning cascaded across the Moor a thousand meters below. The veins of it throbbed and pulsed strongest at Rough Tor but with other major points to the south and east. And all the little rivulets in between, they switched on and off. No wonder they had inconsistency away from the promontories …

He looked up, eyes moist, "How?"

In a soft voice that nonetheless terrified them all, he said, "It is given to me to heal the Earth and reinstate Her

SHEHKRii
– The FLAME –

Purpose. I could use some help and you lot have been elected. Except for one, eh, Bronwyn?"

She glared at him, an evil, rage-filled twisting of the face that transformed her into something to be feared.

"Heathen," she snarled.

Nathan snapped his fingers and Brony fell.

The others gasped but before they could protest, he said, "She betrayed you, Doctor. She was put in place, volunteered for it actually, so if you succeeded, her people could pull the plug before too much damage was done. Her superiors deemed you were too close to something major. All based on Brony's information."

"But she'll die," protested Bart.

"No, she won't. I will not allow it. She'll be conscious all the way down. The impact will shatter her in every possible way, but she'll live. And recover, fully. Hilde will arrange it. Then she can take my message to the priests."

"Which is …" said Carlisle.

"The yoke is being lifted. However, there is still a question unanswered. Will you accept my help? "

"If you can do this," said Bart, "what do you need us for?"

"Yeah …," said Cormac, softly.

"Knowledge imposed is a burden by any other name, Mr. Smith. I need you to discover what lies hidden. You're already very close. I will also protect you from the priests who finished what the Romans started and are none-too-keen to see the old knowledge rediscovered."

SHEHKRii
– The FLAME –

"When you say 'priest'," said Jasmin, "it sounds like a curse …"

"Indeed. I find facts, no matter how fanciful, preferable to faith. You can do so many evil things in the name of faith can't you, Jasmin?"

She blushed.

"What …" exclaimed Cormac.

"Leave it, Liam," said Jasmin. "Nathan obviously knows stuff about us all and will happily use it, I'm sure. Now, can we please get down from here? We've seen the light show and I for one need to change my knickers."

Nathan laughed and they began to fall but slowly now and in a wide spiral, which took in the neighborhood of the tor. The last of the energy signatures died away as they reached the ground. Hilde and Brony were nowhere to be seen.

Carlisle looked pointedly at Nathan, "How?"

"The energy grid I showed you …"

"Yes."

"It is mine to manipulate. I can work wonders, Doctor. But I'm only one man. And my purpose is to reveal the knowledge that will bring men together not splinter them into tribes. I'm not a tyrant, though; I need fellow travelers on the Path I walk."

Carlisle nodded to himself looking down briefly at the ground then raising his head turning through a full circle.

SHEHKRii
– The FLAME –

"I love this place. It's fierce in so many ways. Yet, when you stand here alone in the morning there's this sense of others all around you.

"All right, I'll do it; what happens next?"

"Hilde will be in touch, probably tomorrow. She'll deal with the interference you've suffered from and set up the grants system, which will keep you funded. You're going to have to move premises. Tell Liam to abandon his computers. Brony hacked them years ago. We'll provide a better system anyway. I'll keep in touch, Doctor, there's much to discuss, but Hilde and some of her friends will watch your back."

Carlisle nodded and glanced over at the others who were looking out over the moor.

"How will we …" When he turned back Nathan was gone. Given what he'd seen tonight Carlisle wasn't surprised. Grinning, he went over to collect the others and head back to their rooms. There were a few things he wanted to salvage.

SHEHKRii
– The FLAME –

CHAPTER 1

LONDON, U.K.

"HE'S ARRIVED, Sir Charles."

"Thank you, constable. Show him in, please."

Sir Charles Braithwaite was momentarily surprised by the man who entered the observation room a few moments later. He knew little of him except the name and age: forty plus and an old Swiss/German family on the father's side and an unknown African mother. Charles had assumed one of several stereotypes would apply.

This man was none of these.

This man was dangerous.

A touch under six feet tall, Braithwaite noted, *my height*. But noticeably slim. And very, very centered; combat balanced, if he was any judge, and he most certainly was. The man also had that rare combination in biracial offspring; his father's Prussian features and his mother's coloring.

The visitor surveyed the room quickly, leaving Sir Charles till last. Taking in the head of the Organized Crime Directorate at a glance he stepped forward and offered his hand.

"Johan Lutz, Sir Charles. An honor."

"Likewise, Herr Lutz," replied Braithwaite. "Thank you for responding at such short notice."

"I was in London on personal business, so the timing was auspicious. Please call me Joe. I am uncomfortable with honorifics."

SHEHKRii
– The FLAME –

"You're one of Interpol's most senior magistrates, Herr Lutz, I could hardly be so forward."

"I insist, Sir Charles. We have some nasty business ahead of us and I would value your trust. Formality gets in the way of that."

Joe focused and withdrew himself emotionally creating the sense of expectancy, which allowed the other man to accept a situation that might otherwise have taken weeks to establish.

Yes, very dangerous indeed, mused Braithwaite.

"Very well … Joe. In which case, we can, at least in private, dispense with my knighthood. Charles, if you will."

"Agreed."

Both men turned to regard the plate glass window before them.

"How was he captured?" asked Joe.

"Dumb luck, really. The drug dealers had a rear exit booby-trapped and our friend here tripped it on his way out; after he'd killed our undercover operative and some of the dealers. He had their whole load with him when the bomb blew out the door. So, we got five kilos of raw PCP and him."

Joe watched the man in question through the one-way glass. The prisoner was medium height and broad in the way of laborers or perhaps a wrestler but he prowled the interrogation room with a loping grace that spoke volumes for his reaction time and speed.

"French," said Braithwaite, "as near as we can tell. His ID is fake, but when he woke up he started cursing in Breton. We nearly lost him then. He had our people jumping through hoops before one of the nurses figured it out."

"It?"

Braithwaite cleared his throat nervously, "He can make people do what he tells them. Ah, here … you'll see what I mean."

A policewoman had entered the interrogation chamber to replace the water container. The prisoner froze and watched her for a moment, then barked an order. The woman hesitated, threw him a filthy look then quickly left. He swore in French. And kept pacing.

"Did you feel it?"

Joe nodded. "How did you overcome the compulsion to obey?" he asked quietly.

"The nurse I mentioned suffers from industrial deafness; wore a hearing aid. That seems to dampen the effect. The nurse sedated the prisoner before he got too far and then we fitted all our people with earpieces and played …"

"… background feedback to divert the impulse."

"You know what this is?"

"It's called Voice," answered Joe, "…and is a very rare talent. Not in the usual repertoire of criminal skills."

"Indeed. Which is why you're here. He had one of Kerenski's notebooks."

"How is it," asked Joe, glancing sideways at Braithwaite, "... that you know of Kerenski?"

"I was privy to Interpol's Class Three briefings last year, Joe. And I have an excellent memory. Is the good doctor still on your Red List?"

"Oh yes. He won't leave it until we have him. Monster!"

Braithwaite was startled by the venom in his voice.

"What can you tell me?"

Joe turned from the window and took a seat at the end of the room. Braithwaite joined him.

"Valentin Sergei Kerenski is a neurosurgeon. He worked for the KGB until one of Putin's purges scooped him up. The GRU was ordered to 'disappear' certain sections of the black research fraternity. Kerenski anticipated this and fled while his colleagues died."

"By 'black' you mean ..."

"Dirty. Very, very dirty." Joe shuddered. "Kerenski was into sophisticated interrogation. He specialized in subjecting prisoners to extreme levels of pain while under controlled narcotic stimulation. After a few days of this treatment, they found the absence of pain so traumatic they broke. The mortality rate was rather high, however. Kerenski dissected the brains to see what changes he'd been able to effect."

Braithwaite had gone white; all the blood having drained from his face. "The PCP..."

"Yes, undoubtedly."

SHEHKRii
– The FLAME –

Nodding at the window, Braithwaite asked, "So, what do we do about this?"

"I'll have a little talk with him, now," answered Joe, as he stood. "I'm immune to Voice and I may be able to trick him into revealing something."

"As you wish, but I'll have constables in there with you. I'm not risking your neck or my pension."

Joe grinned and Braithwaite felt suddenly he might have made a friend; a very powerful friend. Not simply by the status of position but by the way this strange man moved. When Johan Lutz had first entered the room, Braithwaite had intuitively known he was deadly by the way Joe held himself. It was a response the Englishman had developed as an undercover agent in Belfast two decades before. You learned to trust your gut if you wanted to stay alive. Braithwaite had done more than that. Now he watched his new friend walk confidently into the viper's den with little more than determined curiosity.

This will be interesting, he mused.

***

Joe entered the interrogation room after the three constables had positioned themselves behind the prisoner. He pointed to the chair and said, in the most common Breton dialect, "Please take a seat, Cousin. There is much to discuss."

SHEHKRii
– The FLAME –

The prisoner looked this new intrusion up and down, noting the expensive clothes, the casual elegance, the Prussian features and matte black skin.

"Half-breed," he spat. Taking a deep breath and standing very still, he roared, "Kneel to me."

The words echoed around the room and the constables shuffled briefly, one of them touching his earpiece. Braithwaite took a step back from the glass.

Joe laughed softly and turned to pull the chair closest to him away from the table. As he sat, his hand passed across his waist to undo his jacket. On the return, he deftly lifted a small dark stone that adorned his belt buckle and palmed it. He leaned back in the chair and placed both hands in his coat pockets, seeming to be totally at ease.

The prisoner was nonplussed. Momentarily bewildered at this mongrel's imperiousness he grabbed at the nearby chair and sat abruptly, glaring at the man opposite.

Joe said nothing. He made a fist around the stone in his left hand and concentrated on nothing but the sensation of contact with the little rock. Drawing a long, quiet breath he fixed it into the stone and then allowed his concentration to flow out over the man across from him.

The prisoner convulsed as his lungs suddenly stopped working. Breath simply would not come. It was as though someone had stolen it. His head began to swim and he grabbed the table to steady himself.

"Uncomfortable?" asked Joe. "Perhaps I can help." And he relaxed his grip on the stone.

SHEHKRii
– The FLAME –

The prisoner felt blessed pain course through him as his lungs filled greedily.

"Then again," offered Joe, "…perhaps not."

One of the constables stepped forward to help the man as he collapsed off his chair grasping at his groin as though viciously kicked in the balls. The policeman to his right placed a restraining hand on the other's arm and he stepped back.

***

Half an hour later in the executive lounge, twenty stories above the interrogation room, Charles Braithwaite said, "I don't suppose you're going to explain how you did that, are you?"

"Do you really want me to, Charles?"

"No, Joe. I can live with my curiosity unsatisfied in this case."

Joe laughed softly and sipped his tea.

"But what," asked Braithwaite, "do we do with the information? It's pretty thin. He knows nothing of Kerenski except the name and he works for the Twelve, whatever that is."

"Whoever. The Twelve are a dozen old men. I'll send you our file. They run a sort of cartel in Eastern Europe. Religious, somewhat …"

"I've never heard of them," said Braithwaite."

"It's unlikely that you would have. They're very obscure. But what are they doing with Kerenski's notes? That's the question."

"The prisoner, Andre Morvan, said the drugs were to feed the 'herd'. This is starting to sound like some sort of cult. Not something I want to be involved with. Morvan will go down for murder and major narcotics trafficking; I'm satisfied with that, but I don't want some fanatic chewing off my toes while I sleep because I threw his high priest in jail."

Joe stifled a laugh, "I'm sorry, that was quite colorful. But you needn't worry. I doubt Morvan is anything other than inconvenient now. We should report this to the security services for monitoring and I'll, of course, bring it to Interpol's attention. There may be some connection that neither of us is aware of. Your clearance will keep you in the information loop. I'll see to that."

"Thank you."

Standing, Joe buttoned his coat, briefly touching the small black stone that was now back on his buckle.

"I have an appointment shortly, so I'd better be away. Thank you again, Charles."

"A pleasure, Joe. Call on me any time."

"I may. I very well may."

WIMBLEDON, U.K.

Joe wandered about the sitting room while his host fussed in the nearby kitchen. The *bric-a-brac* of a long and full life was neatly placed around the room. Pictures of the couple who once called this place home were framed in everything from gold leaf to bleached timber. Thirty years of memories crammed into one small room. Frozen in place now by the husband's death. Joe pushed his melancholy away.

Alastair Bryce had been one of an extended family of unofficial uncles who shaped his youth and he missed the man still. But it was the wife who needed him now, even if her continuing grief wouldn't allow her to admit it. The lessons instilled by his mother showed Joe the weight that dragged Eddy down. The slight tightness about the eyes, the caution in every small movement, the shallow breathing and inattentiveness. Eddy had sunk into her grief over the last two years and showed every sign of staying there permanently. Joe was going to fix that.

Eddy Bryce returned to the room with a tray of tea and biscuits.

"Here we are. Sorry to make you wait, Joe. I haven't entertained in a while."

"No apology necessary, Eddy. My visit was unannounced after all."

As they both sat, Eddy's hand slipped, and Joe reached out smoothly to steady it.

"Fast as ever, I see. You haven't lost your tricks."

"No. But they're not tricks, Eddy. My little skills are very normal. I could easily teach you how to move much faster."

"Too old now, dear. We both know that."

"Never too old, Eddy. But that's not why I came. Are you sure you won't come to the dinner? Victor is very disappointed."

Eddy smiled wanly, "I really couldn't face it, Joe. All those reminders of Alastair. All those people wanting to talk about the 'good times.' It's too soon."

"Two years."

"Too soon."

"My mother will be there."

Eddy froze and Joe saw the woman she had been suddenly surface. "Really?"

Eddy had heard of Joe's mysterious mother for over twenty years but had never met her. The woman who had shaped this amazing young man was intensely frightening by her absence. But that made the fascination even stronger. Alastair had missed several opportunities as well and together they had spent many an hour speculating on who, how and when.

Joe held his breath and watched intently. The long-frustrated curiosity had hold of his friend and wasn't letting go.

"Well... maybe that warrants reconsideration. When did you say the dinner was going to be? And at the Ritz, to boot. Oh, all right."

"Excellent," breathed Joe as he reached for a teacup. "And it's Friday evening at 7. I'll arrange a car if you like?"

"No, no. I can make arrangements. Joanie from my shop will give me a lift if needs be. She's almost as persistent as you, Joe … at trying to get me to go out, that is."

"I've never met her, have I?"

"No. She's only been with me a few years and it's been longer than that since you were at the shop."

"Perhaps we should remedy that. Will you have lunch with me on Thursday? I'll pick you up and can meet Joanie at the same time."

"Oh … Thursday, no. I'm sorry, Joe. I have an appointment. One I can't refuse. Sorry"

"'Can't refuse' sounds serious, Eddy."

"Yes, well. Whitehall have been up to their usual stupidities and I have to go in for a grilling, so to speak. Although it is Andrew Pearce and I'll at least get a fair hearing."

"Sir Andrew Pearce - head of the tactical division in MI6. Eddy, what's going on?"

"Don't worry about it, Joe. It's nothing I can't handle. And as I said, Andrew is a friend. It will be fine."

"Nevertheless, some back-up is in order. I'll accompany you. And we will have lunch."

Eddy could see he had made up his mind and if she knew anything about Johan Lutz it was that one way or another he would accompany her to MI6 on Thursday. It might be nice to have some support just in case.

"Very well. And thank you. But let's make it morning tea. I know a little place in Westminster. It's quiet … and relaxing. Looks out over the river."

Joe leaned into the sofa with his tea. The old Eddy wasn't entirely back but this was a good start. And if he could get a word with Joanie they might be able to concoct some sort of plan to encourage her even more. MI6 was a worry, though. *I'll have to look into that,* he promised himself. Plus, there was his Russian friend to see on the same day.

Busy, busy, as usual.

LONDON, U.K.

"Your mother would not be pleased at this display of impatience, Joe."

Joe stopped pacing at this odd rebuke and regarded his companion. His chiseled, somewhat Prussian features squeezed into a slight frown. He smiled. "Since you've yet to meet her, I'll let that pass, Eddy."

"Nevertheless, I've heard so much about her over the years, I can imagine that your pacing would irritate her, as much as it is me. Please sit down. It's only been an hour."

Johan Lutz noted the wry grin tugging at the woman's lips and sat down. It was what came next, that concerned him more.

"I thought Pearce was an ally," he said quietly. "Why does he keep us this long?"

"Because others are watching and you know it. What's wrong, Joe? My troubles shouldn't be causing you and your father this much concern."

At the mention of his father, Johan let his tension drain away and accepted the full extent of his irritation.

SHEHKRii
– The FLAME –

Until now, he had hoped to avoid burdening Eddy with their worries. He grudgingly admitted to himself he should have expected her to detect his masquerade. In a low voice, he said, "Your problems are the tip of the iceberg. They indicate an official blindness, just at the time when the opposite is required. To have you involved doubles our concern. Don't these people have any gratitude? You shouldn't be submitted to this type of discourtesy."

"Times are changing," Eddy said, patting his knee in a grandmotherly fashion. At the same time, she noted a passing female official steal a glance at them. The other woman walked, unchallenged, into the inner office.

Muscular, thought Eddy, but with the body language of a soldier. A plain face but impeccable grooming. *Interesting that I haven't seen her before. Wonder who she is?*

***

The woman went straight to the senior secretary of the man who commanded this division. "Do you know who you have waiting out there?" she barked.

"Of course, Colonel Wethers," came the disdainful reply. "That's the Bryce woman. We've been told by ADMIN to give the 'old biddy' the treatment."

"Not her, you pompous idiot. The man. Tell Pearce he's been irritating Interpol's third most senior *Juge*

Inquisitor and while you're at it, ask him which one of the Orkney Islands he'd like his pension sent to."

The secretary went white with shock, almost jumped up and quick stepped into the adjoining office without knocking.

***

Eddy could hear the commotion behind the glass partitions, but was unsure of what it meant in this, all-too-proper place. "What was that, Joe?" she said, turning back to face the man.

"Are you sure you don't need a lift to Victor's testimonial tomorrow?" repeated Johan, also distracted by the unusual noises coming from within the offices.

"No," replied Eddy. "I'll be fine." She turned as the door was opening hurriedly and Sir Andrew Pearce stepped through. He nodded to them and walked briskly out. "Edwina, my dear," he began. "Please accept my apologies for this unforgivable mix-up. How can I make it up to you?"

"Whatever are you talking about, Andrew?" replied Eddy, in her best little-old-lady voice.

Pearce raised his eyebrows slightly at her obvious theatricality and stood a little taller. "Perhaps, we had best have you inside and comfortable, so we can discuss that," he said, ushering the couple through to the offices beyond the glass.

In the club-like studio Pearce called an office, he showed them to a leather-bound chesterfield and took a matching chair opposite. "Now that the audience is out of the way, Mrs. Bryce, perhaps you might introduce me to your escort and explain what is going on?"

While Johan's expression remained dark, Eddy Bryce's smile lit the room. Pearce felt a sudden pang. In her smile, he saw the classic beauty this friend had been many years before. And he recognized the toll, life's pain had taken, when only her occasional smile could show her inner self.

"Why, Andy, I think I've just scored a few points. You should be happy for me," she responded. Johan glanced at her, confused.

"It's a game we play, Monsieur," offered Pearce in flawless French. "Not with each other, but with the gossip mongers who haunt this place."

"The English and their games," replied Johan, also in French. Changing to English he continued, "Hasn't it ever occurred to you that no one else is playing?"

Pearce grinned slightly and shrugged. It was a very continental gesture and Johan smiled in reply.

Eddy intersected the exchange. "May I present an old family friend? Sir Andrew Pearce, this is Johan Lutz."

Both men nodded to each other and Pearce said, "An honor, Monsieur *Juge*," using the French honorific. "Now, what can I do for you?"

***

SHEHKRii
– The FLAME –

The senior secretary's stretched smile was starting to hurt. She held it for a few seconds after the group had exited the main office and then slumped into her chair and sighed.

"What was all that about, Lizzie?" said one of the nearby clerks. They had all been thrown out of routine by Pearce's agitation.

"We nearly had a major balls-up, that's all," replied the older woman.

"And what's a 'gerg?'" continued the clerk.

"It's French. It means 'judge'. Or sometimes 'magistrate'. And he's an important one."

"But he's… you know?"

"Yes?"

"Black!"

The look the secretary turned on her younger companion could have melted steel. "When was your last anti-discrimination seminar, Ruth?"

With an exasperated look, Ruth said, "You know what I mean."

"Yes, I do. Anyway, according to the file I pulled while he was in with Sir Andrew, his mother was African, hence the skin color. But, his father is Swiss. Some bigwig in the Red Cross."

"Oh!" said Ruth.

CHAPTER 2

"DRUGS, SISTER? IS that the best you can do?"

Brony ground her teeth fleetingly. She'd expected this from The Council, but it still grated. No sacrifice was ever enough. No explanation ever quite good enough. It was her perpetual penance and it always hurt.

"It's the best your experts can do, Eminence. Their facts tell this story. I am but the messenger."

A ripple of almost laughter ran through the group of men arranged in a semicircle around Bronwyn Petersen.

"Seriously, Sister, you were there. More than a messenger I think! What really happened at Rough Tor?"

"Memory tells me one thing, which is impossible. The doctors tell me another, which sounds plausible. I simply don't know, Eminence. If the drug explanation is correct, then it was almost certainly administered in the car on the way to the heathen place. Everything after that, in my memory, is suspect. It also implies the drug used was better than anything we already know about, which is why I've petitioned to capture the Nordstrom woman and interrogate her. And Carlisle and his team."

"That's under consideration, Sister," said another member of The Council. "What do we know of her, Sister? I've not read the background report as yet."

Brony suppressed a small shudder. Just thinking about her tormentor raised up memories of pain unparalleled in her experience. She swallowed.

SHEHKRii
– The FLAME –

"As you wish, Reverence. Hilde Birgit Nordstrom is Swedish and forty-one years old. She had a troubled childhood but overcame that to join the *Polisen* in her early twenties. She excelled in all fields but especially at interrogation. Seven years ago, she resigned and all records of activity since are blank. She became a ghost.

"She has never married but there is a daughter who would be sixteen now. The child disappeared when her mother resigned from the police force. Our contacts in the security services have no records of her. She doesn't appear to be an agent of any kind."

"And the man, Chalk?"

"Nothing, Reverence. No one living with that name corresponds to my experience."

The man referred to as Reverence made a quiet comment to the man on his right, who nodded and scribbled a note. He looked straight at Brony and said, "Sister, Carlisle and his people have vacated their rooms at Plymouth and we are yet to locate them. You know these people. Where would they go?"

At last, thought Brony, something to hunt.

"Scribe, yes Sir. They will need access to both ancient texts and high-end computer facilities. Carlisle has his own sources, which he does not share but these often have to be cross-checked against mainstream records. I can prepare a list of specifics, which would inform a detailed search."

"Excellent. Do that now, Sister, and bring it to me by the end of the day. If there are no other questions …"

SHEHKRii
– The FLAME –

A muttering of "no's" gave Brony her dismissal and she quickly left the reading room at one of many annexes to St Paul's Cathedral, London.

The Council rose and mingled as refreshments were brought in.

The man referred to as Scribe filled a glass with red wine and joined Eminence.

"You pushed a bit too hard, Peter. The psychiatric report indicated PTSD"

Eminence, aka Peter Mayhew, the undersecretary to the Archbishop of Canterbury, grunted. "You know my opinion of Sister Bronwyn. As a spy, she's automatically untrustworthy. A nun absolved of her Vow of Chastity ... *humph!* A fundamental conflict of interest, that."

"Personality politics again, Peter? It's clouded your judgment before and now we clearly have new players in the field. Facts are what we need."

"Yes, Scribe. I'll keep that in mind." Mayhew took his leave without courtesy and attacked the canapés.

Scribe was joined by Reverence, aka Keith Fitzsimmons, the CEO of one of America's largest Catholic charities. "Told you so," he said, conversationally.

Scribe grinned. "He won't indulge himself if he knows we're watching."

Another man in flowing Islamic robes strolled over.

"Mahdi."

"Gentlemen. Interesting development, this drug they're using, no?"

SHEHKRii
– The FLAME –

Scribe nodded, "Indeed. Without other examples, we can't be certain, but Bronwyn's experience suggests a significant product."

"We need to get our hands on it ASAP" added Fitzsimmons.

"Yes," replied Mahdi, "but there can be no loose ends. We need all the players in our net."

"The Bhari woman …" suggested Scribe.

"Ah … perhaps. If there is no progress in the next few weeks, I will activate our advantage. With your permission, Scribe, of course."

"Consider it given. Now, food! I'm famished."

The others voiced their agreement and navigated towards the serving tables.

Scribe circulated throughout the informal meal, a genial host. The tension in the room said something completely different.

The security staff watched with caution and just a little amusement. While any of the players here could easily have them individually and collectively wiped out, it was Scribe who scared them all. Each of the security team had been involved in the cleanups whenever Scribe indulged himself or dished out punishment. They were very secret occasions but someone had to tidy the mess.

The team leader pinged his crew's alert system. They were all just a touch jumpy watching the predators maneuver. Time to get back on point!

SHEHKRii
– The FLAME –

CHARTRES CATHEDRAL, EURE-ET LOIR, FRANCE

"How is it we're getting in here? We've been banned for nearly a decade," said Bart Smith.

She glanced back at the two men who lingered just beyond the crypt door. Pushing it fully open, she said, "Gift horse …"

Liam Cormac nodded. He could listen to Hilde's voice all day long. Her English was near-perfect but with just the hint of an accent to gave it a subtle, exotic flavor. It would be better if she wasn't so damned intimidating.

Shrugging, he smirked at Bart and walked through the opening, shining his torch to penetrate the pitch-black stair shaft beyond. They went quickly down to the ambulatory and headed for the area under the altar. Bart broke out half a dozen LED mini lanterns.

"OK," said Liam, "this is where you said we had to look. What now?"

"Now," said Hilde, "we go below. Direct your torches to the studs on this stone, please."

The men did as asked, a dozen questions popping through their heads simultaneously. Hilde squatted and held her right hand over each brass pin. The little ferrules twisted sharply then leapt into her hand. She collected all five in quick succession.

"What the f…" said Liam.

Hilde pocketed the metal pins then inserted a finger from each hand into the flagstone and stood up. Stepping to the side she squatted again and laid the lid down.

"What the f..." said Liam. "That thing must weigh over a hundred kilos."

"Torches down the hole, please, gentlemen," replied Hilde. "And start climbing."

Bart shone his torch and peered down. The stone lid had been resting on a brass-like frame and bolted to that was a slim ladder. He clipped his torch to a lanyard and shimmied down. Liam peered after him as more LED lanterns started to glow into life below.

"Show-off," he said as he gingerly angled himself onto the ladder and worked his way down the five or so meters of the drop. He glanced around adjusting his eyes to the gloaming and then sensed Hilde behind. He hadn't heard her descend. She gave him a gentle shove further into the cavern.

"Hey …"

His protest was cut short by what the lanterns revealed. Bart was frozen, staring up at the black, charred shape in the center of the roughly hewn chamber.

"A Venus," said Liam.

"No," replied Hilde, "this is all that remains of one of the Great Trees. She was two hundred meters tall and fifteen wide at the trunk before the Romans burned her down."

"What! Why? No, don't answer, we know." Bart exhaled a breath, his anger going with it.

"Yes," said Hide, "even then, propaganda won wars. It took them nearly a year to reduce her to ground level and a few months later she sprouted."

SHEHKRii
– The FLAME –

"No!" said Bart.

"Oh, yes. They were not happy, the Romans. So, they dug a pit and tried again."

Reaching out and caressing the gloss black side of the vaguely feminine shaped mass she continued, "And filled it with every incendiary they could find. The stump smoldered for months and this is what was left. Even the shape offended them. In final frustration, they filled in the hole and planted briars over the whole thing. A few centuries later the Druheidá excavated her and built a shrine. Another few centuries later the Christians knocked down the shrine and built a church."

She shrugged. "The usual story; one you're both familiar with, I think."

Cormac glanced at Bart, "So, why are we here?"

Hilde withdrew her hand. "You each have made an intellectual commitment to planet Earth. Time to meet the real thing and make your commitment more personal."

She reached out and touched the stump again and began to speak in a soft guttural language. Beneath her hand a golden glow sprouted and branched out in thin, lightning shaped filigrees, which grew in frequency and intensity until the cavern was filled with a deep golden glow that didn't so much emanate from the stump as from the air itself.

All the men's questions were washed away in the overpowering sense of presence, which seemed to press in on them from every direction.

"Welcome, Mother," said Hilde simply.

SHEHKRii
– The FLAME –

"Daughter, Sister."

The voice stripped Liam and Bart bare. Tears flowed instantly.

"I bring friends, Terra. They walk beside us on The Path and I would bind them to your Purpose."

"Indeed. They have the blessing of knowledge already. And, each in their own way, the will to stay true. *Uilliam* and *Son of Talmai,* welcome. How may I serve?"

"Wha ..." whispered Liam

"You have questions, I suspect," said Hilde with a small grin.

Bart cleared his throat, "Who are you?"

"Obvious but fundamental," said the disembodied voice, and the cavern flared into solid, golden light and each man knew instantly who they beheld. The effect faded away leaving them on their knees.

***

As Liam and Bart wandered off, still a little dazed from their experience below, Hilde closed the crypt door and turned to face the deep shadows of the nearby wall.

"Good morning, Monsieur."

An old, old man stepped forward, his walking stick gripped hard, "You should not be in there, you and your friends."

"None should have known we were. Yet here you are. How is that?"

SHEHKRii
– The FLAME –

The old man hesitated then said, "I heard the Lady call. It's been a long time."

"You heard ..." Hilde smiled. "Your lights are so dim, I can barely see you. And your accent, Breton but with phrasing I've only heard once before. How old are you?"

"One hundred and twelve last June. What do you mean lights?"

"What day of June, Monsieur?"

"Twentieth. A Solstice babe, my *mere* called me. What lights, child?

Hilde paced in a tight circle taking her closer to the man who clenched slightly.

"Oh my ..." said Hilde finally. She touched her throat and a small glow burst forth into the gloom. The man leaned forward, peering, and realized she had a necklace of sorts under her almost military clothes.

"What is that, chi ..."

"Nathan," said Hilde clearly with a chilling authority, "I need you."

"What ..."

He stepped from behind the woman, a tall man of middle years with eyes that held the threat of death. The old man shuddered, "Who?"

The man stopped, tilting his head slightly to one side. Then smiled.

To the old man it was like the shadows suddenly vanished and the warmth of the sun rose up within. He felt young again, reborn in the other man's smile.

"Nathan, he was born on the same day as you."

"Yes, I can see."

A voice like rolling thunder vibrated through him, making the old man feel even stronger. He stood straighter.

"You'd better get after our boy scouts, Hilde; before they bump into the less sympathetic. I'll have a chat with our new friend."

"Yes, Keeper. Be well."

"Be well, Hilde. Happy babysittin'."

Hilde stifled a giggle.

***

As she hurried to catch up to Bart and Cormac she felt The Biopulse below the cathedral surge as Nathan began the Returning ritual. *How can he do that,* she mused. He was present but only as a projection; she'd seen the effect many times. But now he was bringing the old man to his full potential despite his advanced age. The Pulse sang even louder and she realized that was the key. Terra had taken a hand. The old man was in for a few surprises!

She caught up to the men as they exited the enclosure to the side of the transept. They had thrown off the lethargy of their recent experiences and were in animated conversation. So much so they'd failed to see the priest who lurked in the wall's shadow, waiting.

He stepped into view and Bart stopped suddenly, caught out. The priest smiled a predatory grin, the light of recognition ablaze in his eyes. He drew breath to launch a blistering tirade.

Hilde was having none of it.

Bart glanced back, ready to take his cue from the woman when he saw her move. She was a blur, a ripple of darkness in the night.

Hilde stopped in front of the priest and slapped him. He staggered, barely keeping his balance. She slapped him again and he fell to one knee.

She bent down and whispered, "I know you, betrayer of dreams, curate of this hallowed place. Be gone before I wreak the Black Virgin's wrath on you and your coven of haters."

The priest scuttled backwards, rose and sprinted away, his cassock skirts held high. He looked back only once, absolute terror etched on his face.

Hilde turned to her charges; Bart was open-mouthed but Liam was grinning. Hilde cocked an eyebrow at the grin.

"Raised by his kind, I was," said the Irishman, "happy to see him get what's coming. You know him?"

"Yes. I keep an occasional eye on this place and those who live here. The curate is a hate-filled ascetic who revels in venom. I've wanted to do that for a long time. Now, let's go. We have work to do."

"Yes, Ma'am."

LONDON, U.K.

Andrew Pearce didn't return to his office after escorting his guests to the elevator. That little effort should set the tongues wagging, he mused. Instead, he walked down one flight to the Operations Section. Entering the director's outer office, he simply stood and waited for the receptionist to notice him. Andrew Pearce did not ask for anything.

The secretary flinched when she turned and saw who was standing at her desk. "He ...he's in. I'll announce you, Sir Andrew. Right away," she said as she scrambled to get out from behind the desk.

"Thank you," Pearce said to her retreating back. A reputation had its trivial uses occasionally, he conceded. The woman returned thirty seconds later. "Please come through, Sir Andrew," she said.

Pearce was escorted into the offices of Benton Colleridge, Director of Operations, MI6, and took a seat opposite the man's desk without it being offered. Turning slightly to regard the secretary, he waited patiently, until she realized she wasn't required and hastily left the room.

Colleridge watched this little play with growing anger. He had only just caught Pearce's mood as the man entered and had held his tongue until the door closed. "And?" he inquired.

"And the matter of the Bryce woman and the other externals is to be reviewed," said Pearce.

Colleridge bit back his reply. *Christ, this old fart knows how to get under your skin,* he thought bitterly. "It won't do any good, Pearce," he said instead. "The best you can do is a stay of execution."

"I know," replied the older man, "but that will be sufficient. Perhaps your patrons will be less generous in their influence when they realize how shallow their investment really is."

Colleridge surged to his feet. "Now listen here, you old has-been," he roared. "You do not come in here, in my own office, insulting …" Colleridge trailed off.

Pearce was softly clapping, as though at the theater, his expression cold and cruel.

"An honest performance at last, young Colleridge. I only wish the Minister could have seen it. But he will hear of it, won't he, eh! Your office is renowned for its rumors after all."

Pearce rose and faced the other man, squarely. Slowly, deliberately, he said, "The External Contractor's program is flawed. We all know this. But, to discontinue it because your accountants gave it a negative cost analysis is criminal negligence. The Externals predicted an increase in Eco-terrorism two years ago. And what do we now face; an increase in that very trend."

Shrugging, he resumed his seat. "I've just come from a meeting with Johan Lutz. Interpol has prioritized this issue. They want to know why one of our analysts, Edwina Bryce, had issued an alert recommendation ten months ago, which we did not act on; or pass on. That alert could have prevented the attack at Elche. You remember Elche, don't you, Benton?"

Colleridge also sat back down. "Yes, I remember," he said, sullenly.

"Good. Fix it in your memory, because it is the origin of future troubles," said Pearce. The other man's eyebrows went up slightly and his previously averted gaze snapped back to the older man.

Got your attention at last, thought Pearce.

"The bacterial soup released at Elche was the same type used at Calcutta, and at Woomera. The Americans are fully alerted. Paul Gareth is their primary target and they are preparing to launch a joint task force with the Australians. Low-key, of course, but would you care to hazard a guess as to who will be the liaison officer for the CIA in Canberra? Someone, I believe, you are familiar with." The silence dragged.

"Well!" snapped Colleridge.

"Henry Katz," said Pearce.

"Oh, Christ," breathed Colleridge.

"Precisely," said Pearce. "Chameleon extraordinaire. While you and your rationalist cohorts have been playing at 'cleaning house', everyone else has been working. This can't be swept under any financial carpet, Colleridge. If you want my help cleaning it up, I will expect prompt action. After all, as you are well aware, I won't be in the game for much longer." He rose and walked to the door.

"Wethers will issue a schedule by the end of the day. I'll expect your comments by lunch tomorrow," Pearce said. He turned and left without further comment.

"Oh, Christ," repeated Colleridge. Pushing his hair back over his forehead, he allowed himself a brief moment of self-pity. Then, spite took its place and he punched his intercom.

"Get me Kennedy. Now!" he snapped.

SHEHKRii
– The FLAME –

CHAPTER 3

JOHANN LUTZ SUBMITTED HIS papers to the second official. His impatience was not evident, but he was keen to put this day behind him.

In Russian, the clerk asked, "Do you have an appointment, Sir?"

Replying in the same language, he said, "Yes. At 2P.M., as verified by your Trade Department." The woman nodded and proceeded to make a phone call, confirming the details.

Joe considered the conversation with Pearce. The man was genuine enough and had made his position quite clear. As long as he remained in office, he would support Eddy. But, he had also made it clear he thought she should get out of the security analysis business soon. Eddy had tried to ignore him on that score, until Joe had pressed her.

Exasperated, she had said, "Well! Ganging up on me, are you? All right, I'll tell you the truth as much as I can admit, even to myself."

Turning to Pearce, she said, "You know what you're asking me to do, don't you, Andy? Retire. That's what. Retire. And what am I going to retire to. Alistair is two years gone and I still mourn him. If I retire, I'll have nothing to do but mourn. How long will I live like that? Well!"

Pearce had tried to answer, but it had sounded feeble. It was not a question easily answered, if at all. Eventually he had said, "Eddy, if you have to stay in the game why not get out of harm's way. Your journalist friends in Australia would gladly snap you up. A change of scenery and all that. And no more aggravation from Colleridge and his ilk."

She had not entirely conceded the point, but it had registered. Joe would speak to his father and find out more about this connection. Perhaps it would be what their friend needed after all; a change of scenery.

The clerk replaced the handset and said, "You may proceed, Sir."

"*Spasiba*," replied Joe.

He walked quickly down the indicated corridor to the guard waiting at its end and was escorted to an office several meters to the right of the intersection. Spartan by any standard, the office was, nonetheless, impeccably clean. A secretary ushered him through the foyer to the rooms of Vladimir Kalinin, the Deputy Director of Russian Military Intelligence for the Western Hemisphere. "Good morning, Johan. I hope you are well."

"And you also, Vladimir," replied Lutz.

Removing his coat and tossing it casually on the nearby settee, Johan took a seat and said, "To work, my friend. What do you want?"

Kalinin regarded his guest momentarily. He had cultivated a familial relationship with this man over the past ten odd years, but had not once made the mistake of taking him lightly. Others regarded Victor Lutz and his half-caste son as formidable idealists; flies in the ointment, so to speak. Kalinin was not one of these. If Johan Lutz was agitated enough to disregard the usual courtesies, then he had better step carefully. "As you say ... to business. In the matter of the slave trade, we are able, at last, to repay your father for past cooperation. In Bulgaria, there is a group that has come to our attention. You might be interested in them. They speak of themselves as Servants of the Twelve."

"We've heard of them," replied Lutz.

"Indeed ..." said the Russian, mildly surprised. "They've become more open in the last six months and our Serbian friends have been able to infiltrate their outer ranks."

After several seconds of silence, Johan said, "This is not new, Vladimir. The Twelve are a quasi-religious group who practice ritual torture and occasionally human sacrifice. Their influence is spread across eastern Serbia and parts of western Romania. They are very tightly organized and heavily insulated. We've never attempted penetrating them, since they are not in the Trade."

"You know more than I thought, Johan. I apologize for patronizing you. To the point, then. We have people inside their operation and they have been dealing with both Marouk and Gong-li ... in quantity. We can get into their pipeline," said Kalinin.

Johan eased himself back in his chair. *So, the Twelve were buying flesh. Was this the "herd" the man Morvan had spoken of?*

"If this is payment, Vladimir, it is gratefully accepted. If it is anything else, then, it is dangerous coinage."

SHEHKRii
– The FLAME –

Kalinin pursed his lips slightly and affected an air of injured pride. "Young man, I regard you as an adopted nephew. It is not proper for family to speak so to one another."

Johan smiled. "Uncle Vlad. Yes, it does have a ring to it! I'm sure my Interpol colleagues would be most amused by my family connections." He shifted his weight again and crossed one leg over the other to sit casually in his chair, regarding the older man with an impish grin.

Kalinin barked a sharp laugh. "That will be the day." Leaning forward he said, "Johan, if I thought giving you my word would convince you then you would have it. But, it is not the way our world works, eh. So …" he paused, removing a single page from beneath the valise on the side of his desk, "I give you this instead. It is a Memorandum of Understanding; typical diplomatic gibberish, but significant nonetheless, no?"

Sitting forward, Lutz examined the offered document. "Yes," he said simply.

"Good," said the Russian. "An understanding then. In this we are genuine. No games, eh?"

"No games," replied the younger man.

"Good, because the Twelve seem to be in the market for more than slaves. Several of Khan Bey's students appear to have been recruited."

"What! The nuclear renegade …"

Two hours later, when Lutz took his leave, they had hammered out a program of investigation and actions covering the following six months. Joe felt devitalized

SHEHKRii
– The FLAME –

after the strategy session. His father would be pleased. With just a little luck, they would be able to obliterate two of the major players in the international slave trade within a year. The void would be filled, but perhaps not to the same capacity. Perhaps not at all, if he called in a few outstanding favors. And the Twelve, what of them? He would speak to his mother tomorrow and see what she thought. This was more her province after all. If they were weaponizing as Kalinin suspected she needed to know - now.

***

As Lutz left Kalinin's suite of rooms, the old Russian leaned back in his chair and exhaled loudly, easing his considerable tension. His superiors did not trust Johan Lutz. They thought he was a spy. Kalinin knew better. He also knew much more about Joe's father, Victor, than anyone else. It was these secrets that convinced Kalinin he could trust this odd family. Their generation-long crusade against the slave trade had been seen at first as noble folly, then irritating altruism. But as Kalinin found out even more and watched Joe rise to the top of Interpol he had realized he had stumbled over genuine and very effective people.

In his putrid gray-on-gray world, this was welcome refreshment and he held it close. Besides, these days, you never did know when you might need to defect.

SHEHKRii
– The FLAME –

RASOVO, BULGARIA

Before his knuckles struck the heavy wooden door, the word "Enter" echoed through his skull. It was harsh and impatient. The Servant checked his hand at the last moment and pushed the door open, hurriedly walking the intervening ten odd meters to his master's elaborate desk.

"Viz …Vizier. An urgent matter."

The man who was once Aleksandur Danev peered upward from his desk at the Servant who was his secretary. Vasily was a valuable asset but a creature of habit and this annoyed Danev.

"Speak."

"Yes, Vizier. One of our French agents, Morvan, has been compromised. The British police captured him after he was injured in a drug purchase. Interpol have also shown an interest. They sent Johan Lutz."

"Half-breed scum," snorted Danev, sitting back in his chair and fixing Vasily with a penetrating stare. "Continue."

"Yes, Viz …Vizier. Morvan broke."

"What!" exploded Danev surging to his feet. "How dare he! He is Senior, is he not?"

"Yes, Vizier."

"How did this happen, Vasily?" Danev resumed his seat and glared at the other man.

"We do not know details but after Lutz left, the police knew Morvan's name and that he serves the Twelve. They don't appear to know more than that but we cannot be certain. Our contacts are very much at arm's length in England. The drug purchase was a matter of increased supply. The Herd number over two hundred now; otherwise we would not have sent him so far."

Danev glowered at his desk. Secrecy was essential now. They were so close to genuine production. So close to declaring themselves after the last few extraordinary years.

Looking up at his secretary, Danev said in a cold, deadly voice, "Vasily, see to it that Morvan is punished, but more importantly I want Lutz terminated. Make it ugly. I want Interpol distracted. You may go."

"Yes, Vizier."

Vasily scuttled out of the room as quickly as he could. His master's anger was legendary and while he was confident of his life he was less sure of his health should one of Danev's rages overtake them all. But he could not fail. If he did, his value as a Servant of the Twelve was not enough to stop his death being used as an example.

Morvan could be killed with relative ease. The British prison system was as entrepreneurial as it was corrupt. But Lutz. How to take out a senior Interpol bureaucrat? He must have bodyguards. Therefore, Vasily would need a team. And supervision by a Senior who could be trusted. No Servant would venture too far from the Grid. Grigor was in Germany. Yes, he would relish this.

Vasily hurried to his office in the old mansion, his head already filled with complex strategies for a nasty death.

SHEHKRii
– The FLAME –

LONDON, U.K.

Hugh Kennedy was unimpressed. The shop in which he stood waiting was deceptively ordinary. Browsing among the racks of electronic paraphernalia, he gauged visible dimensions against his own knowledge of the building, calculating a discrepancy of between four and five meters in the rear, left-hand quarter.

He waited until the shop assistant approached before making any mention of his appointment. The recognition codes were simple ones and he was casually shepherded into the workshop. "Your security stinks," he said, without preamble, as he passed through the workshop into the hidden space behind, which he now realized extended well into the adjacent building.

"I've no use for cloak-and-dagger, Kennedy. You know that. And I've never been compromised, so let's dispense with the pleasantries and get to work." The voice was cultured and female. The speaker made no effort to turn from her desk or otherwise acknowledge Hugh Kennedy, Chief Surveillance Officer for the Security Service. But an empty chair beside her, stood waiting. Kennedy held his ground. He would not be reprimanded by an elderly matron, no matter what her current clearance.

"My time is worth twenty pounds per minute. Can your budget afford this?" she said, swiveling in her chair to face the man. Edwina Bryce was fifty-six years old, and while the years had not been unkind, her face showed the price of time and pain. Impossibly casual, to Kennedy's eye, she was dressed in blue jeans and white cotton blouse, the only ostentation, an ornate silver belt buckle and matching choker. They had a vaguely African caste to them, he thought.

Kennedy remained unimpressed and unmoved.

The woman turned full circle and stabbed a button on the com-unit to her right. After several short rings, a male voice responded.

"Yes?"

"He's here and acting surly. Deal with it, please."

"Hugh, this is Pearce."

"Yes sir, what's going on?" replied Kennedy.

"Hugh ... your usual approach in this matter is, shall we say, inappropriate. Do not try to bully Mrs. Bryce. It won't work. You were told this, as I recall. Now sit down and get to work. If I'm disturbed again, I won't be pleased." The line went dead and clicked off automatically.

"You set that up," accused Kennedy, as he nonetheless removed his topcoat and approached the proffered chair.

"Of course," was the only reply. Bryce activated a series of keys on one of several ergonomic keyboards in front of her and the projection wall above the desk sprang to life assuming several disparate, projection windows.

"Where did you get a Tactical Display Net, Bryce?" demanded Kennedy.

"I invented it. This is the prototype. But, let's not digress. The material you've queried is loading now. What is it about my reports that upsets you so much you need a face-to-face meeting to resolve it?"

Kennedy watched, mesmerized, as the mini super-computer somewhere in this converted Wimbledon terrace house assembled and prioritized several dozen gigabytes of material and projected it onto the wall in front of him.

Dragging his eyes away he said, "It's flawed. I won't make operational decisions on obviously suspect material like this. The level of speculation is far too high and the factual components too low. We've paid tens of thousands of pounds for garbage and I won't have it. What I want from you is a complete review of your last three Trend Surveys. Your specific project work is not suspect, but I am recommending it be reviewed. Your input will be suspended until there's a positive resolution."

He sat back and regarded her with barely disguised contempt. Despite Pearce's backing, he knew she couldn't refute him on the Trend Surveys. Too many other sections had raised the same concerns. Besides, Pearce was due to retire within the year. This was common knowledge.

Input suspended was almost sacked, in his opinion.

She spoke as she operated her keyboards. "So, the new guard has found a mouthpiece at last. Don't interrupt!" she snapped as Kennedy drew breath to retaliate. "Your appreciation of history is sadly lacking, Kennedy. That's a fatal flaw in the Intelligence field. It irritates me to point out the obvious, but the whole focus of the Trend Surveys is that they are speculative. I might also point out, my long-term record of accuracy with those documents has been in the higher range for over a decade. If you and your operational colleagues can't prioritize your resources to take advantage of this material, I won't be held responsible for the wastage. Nor will the other analysts. Please look at the screen."

Kennedy's expression was barely below superheated, but he glanced reflexively at the wall and was instantly transfixed by what he saw. "How...?"

"How did I locate your supposedly secret South African investment account? Why, by following up on Nagel's Trend Survey Five Point Three. Your own people chose to ignore it, judging internal scrutiny was sufficient. I began a surface scan six months ago and followed it through for all liaison supervisors in the London, Madrid and Cairo offices. You are one of nine with undeclared resources, Kennedy."

"What are you going to do with this?" he said, a spiteful note creeping into his voice.

"It's already done," she replied. "However, your case has been judged benign. The letter of intent you buried in the Archives has been assessed and lets you off the hook, so to speak. The Survey predicted that also."

Eddy Bryce turned in her chair to face the younger man. She regarded him impassively for a moment. "Until recently, I thought of myself as a valuable member of the team, Kennedy. But lately, the rules and the players have been changing and I find myself wasting my time in defenses like this." She pointed at the man, who had recovered his composure and remained wooden faced, as she continued. "I've slapped you over the wrist on this occasion, but your influence is always going to exceed mine and I don't count today's fracas as decisive in any way. Consider this, however. What I've done to you today, I could be doing to our country's enemies if I wasn't 'suspended'. We are both on the same side."

Kennedy stared back openly for a few seconds. Then his expression hardened and he said, "I'll take your comments under advisement, Mrs. Bryce." Standing, he nodded to her and turned to collect his coat. "I'll also take my leave, now." Without further comment, he strode briskly out of her compartment. The assistant, who had shown him in, entered and looked at Eddy with a slightly speculative expression.

"A total waste of time, Joanie," said Eddy Bryce.

The young woman sniffed loudly. "Told you so, Missus," she said and returned to the shop.

Eddy rose and followed her out. "I could use a cup of tea," she said to no one in particular.

***

Eddy nursed her cup, sitting back in the deck chair. The rooftop terrace was one of her favorite places, despite the gray sky and cool breeze. The view over the tops of the houses towards the city was the London of Mary Poppins, and it pleased her to visit this comfortable delusion on a regular basis. More so since Alastair had been killed. Blind-sided by an idiot, drunken driver. So much a waste.

SHEHKRii
– The FLAME –

She choked down a sob.

She couldn't let her grief get the better of her this evening. That wasn't fair to Johan and his father. What a pair they were. And tonight, she would meet Joe's mysterious mother, M'La. She felt she must be at her best and steeled herself to deny, at least for a while, how much her husband's death had taken from her these last two years.

The testimonial dinner was going to be a significant social event. The Red Cross was throwing a major party for Victor Lutz. Unknown publicly, he was a dynamo behind the scenes. Nearly fifty years of dedication to the organization and a tireless activist against the slave trade.

Slaves! Who would have thought the trade still flourished?

She recalled how Alastair and Victor had met over twenty-five years ago. Alastair was Reuters' senior man in Rome and they had asked him to fill in at Prague for six months, after the murder of the chief editor there. His language fluency was the key to it, they found out later. The Prague man had run afoul of Romanian slavers, but no one knew it at the time. Until Victor showed up. What an education that had been.

They were both more than a little afraid of him for quite a while. More like a Norse warrior than a Swiss bureaucrat. And thus had started such a strange but wonderful friendship. They had befriended his half-caste son and watched him grow from his teens to manhood and beyond. And waged a war against the flesh peddlers.

Which was how Eddy had become involved with computers and the Security Service.

It had been Johan who had started it. Alastair had always relied on her methodical nature to track his diverse interests. Childless, by the cruelty of Fate, she had become an integral part of his career with a mind suited to puzzles and pieces of things. Something of a techno-phobe, she had always relied on an old typewriter, an extensive card system and almost total recall. Joe had badgered her for nearly two years to buy a PC and in a moment of weakness, she had relented. That was the end of it, of course. Once the machine was set up, she couldn't deny the obvious advantages and had immersed herself in the technology. It wasn't all smooth sailing, and soon she found herself writing her own programs and eventually designing specifications for new systems.

Which was when the government approached them.

Alastair would have none of it, of course. His neutrality was sacred to him. But, she was a closet patriot and couldn't refuse outright. Contracting had been the compromise that worked for all parties. Strangely, it had been Victor who finally brought Alastair around.

"You can't deny the heart," he had said.

It wasn't her heart, however, which bothered her now. It was the sour taste in her mouth that had become unbearable. Kennedy and his superior, Colleridge, were self-serving fools who believed their own lies. They infested the Service and would dominate it soon. And woe betide anyone who disagreed with them or said something they didn't want to hear!

She was upsetting herself again. Perhaps Andrew Pearce was right after all. Kennedy and his boss, Colleridge, were never going to accept her. She needed to get out of the game. Or take a long holiday. They had friends in Australia whom she'd not seen in a while, not since the funeral at least.

Greg Palmer had come all that way to help her lay Alastair to rest.

Maybe ...

CHAPTER 4

BRONY CONCENTRATED. SHE zoned out the constant clicking of the MRI and calmed herself, creating a sense of separation from now and what she had to remember.

She was fallin. Desperately flailing her arms and legs and starting to tumble. Her breath caught; she couldn't breathe! The air scratched at her face, her fingers hurt so much from the cold it felt like she'd been hit with hammers. And the ground was coming so fast ...

***

"Well?"

"One moment." The doctor watched as Brony was assisted from the MRI chamber. Once the door finally closed he turned to Scribe, "Yes, you were saying."

Scribe's expression could have frozen polar bears but the doctor knew his psychopaths and wasn't giving ground.

"Yes, Doctor. I was asking what the tests, all of them, indicate."

The other man glanced at his screen and several hardcopy charts roughly taped up on the control booth window.

"Her experiences appear to be real. The MRI, fMRI, EEG, P300 and NI spectroscopy all paint a consistent picture. She sustained those injuries. How she did is open to discussion but at this stage we can find not even microscopic traces of any hallucinogens."

"But the timeframe …"

"Yes! That's the fly in the ointment. The microfractures are barely detectable. For her to recover from that level of total skeletal damage in only a few weeks is simply not possible. Yet …"

Scribe began to pace. The doctor waited.

"Focused microwave induction?' Scribe barked.

"No. I have access to the latest data in that area and there are no correlating factors. Whatever was done to her is new. And terrifying."

Scribe snapped, "That's not an opinion I care to hear repeated, Doctor."

The doctor watched him for a moment before answering.

"With you, Mr. Prendergast, I concede the actual patient-doctor relationship. That involves a level of honesty I wouldn't normally indulge. If I'm concerned about this, I owe it to you to express that concern. I'm not one of your sycophants. And your threats don't impress me, so let's not waste time, shall we?"

Scribe smiled. A truly evil baring of the soul.

"You should be dead many times over, Doctor. But it is your fortitude that I value despite how irritating I find it. To business then. What do you recommend?"

"With regards to Miss Petersen, I'm at a loss to think of any additional testing that might be useful. I will give it further thought though, and if anything suggests itself, I'll let you know. If we could secure this Nordstrom woman I believe our interrogation techniques would get results."

"Yes. I look forward to that. Now, however, it's not an option. She's disappeared."

"Unfortunate."

"Our cross to bear," said Scribe and left without preamble.

When the door closed, the senior nurse dared to move from her corner and approach the doctor.

"Yes, Elizabeth; that WAS close."

"Why do you bait him so?"

"No other option. We're all still breathing because I stand up to him. And there's nowhere to run that The Council can't find us.

The nurse shuddered, "True, too true."

"I've had a thought, Elizabeth. Miss Petersen's bloodwork; there might be a clue there you can chase down for us."

"It was unusual. The pathologist speculated her blood had been filtered and enhanced. He had no other explanation for the high white count and red cell separation. 'The blood of a newborn,' he said."

"Yes, yes. What if there was a hallucinogen used in this little mystery and the traces of it were removed by that same filtration."

The nurse frowned, "That's a highly complex piece of blood chem ... I see, Doctor. I'll get to it immediately."

The doctor watched her go. She was the best assistant he had encountered in a decade and surprisingly, a very nice person. He wondered what leverage The Council had over her. His own sins were easy enough to find and manipulate, but he didn't really care as long as he had access to his work.

It would be nice to be out from under Scribe's influence, though. The man was certifiable.

PICCADILLY
LONDON

JOE WATCHED AS HIS PARENTS danced. They moved superbly. Both tall and broad shouldered. Quite a few envious stares bounced off them as they whirled past.

Strange, he mused. They looked like a loving couple who had spent their whole lives together. Yet it was only in the last decade that M'La had returned to Victor Lutz's life in any regular way.

The first dozen years of Joe's life had been spent with his mother, traipsing the world and learning so very much. Then as puberty hit he was, with some degree of ceremony, dumped in his father's lap for the next dozen. M'La would visit but it was essentially father and son against the world.

And that too had been good.

Very good, indeed. Victor's initial shock at finding himself a father had been interesting, too. Mother wasn't given to formalities that often.

Her companions tonight were a point in question. Patrick and Mira. Joe had never met nor heard of them before. Patrick had a slight Australian twang to his voice and was introduced only as Mira's friend. She, on the other hand, with the French colonial flavor, had the grave title of Apprentice.

To M'La.

The first of such, apparently. Still the weight of this didn't seem to bother either of the youngsters. Joe estimated they were late teens at best. Both seemed relaxed in this very formal company, he in a slim-cut tuxedo and she in a slinky thigh-splitting gown to rival the best. They danced and chatted with equal facility.

But Patrick was Unreturned. Of that Joe was sure. They shared this and Patrick seemed to know it as well. Joe wondered if he too carried a Stone–that wondrous little rock, which was both emergency communicator and mysterious enhancer of all things human. Hopefully there might be time to sound the boy out later. Now, however, the evening was winding down. Joe wondered where Eddy had got to. Andrew Pearce had shown up unexpectedly and partnered her for most of the evening. He had not been formally invited but that had been quickly rectified. The Englishman had shielded Eddy from the worst of the society gossips. He noticed the couple at the ballroom entrance apparently saying their goodbyes. He looked around and signaled to Patrick and Mira and began the preparations for leaving.

***

SHEHKRii
– The FLAME –

Eddy walked back into the ballroom wistfully. It had been a wonderful evening-something she hadn't expected. Andrew had been a treasure, a true friend.

But it was M'La who was extraordinary. Eddy thought she had been very brave when she had first arrived, before Andrew had made his entrance. But the stress of coping was taking its toll and it must have shown. As Victor was greeting her and about to introduce Eddy to M'La, the other woman had stepped forward and taken her by the elbow.

"Walk with me," was all M'La said and they left the vestibule to find a small private room. Eddy was unable to resist those simple words.

In the room, M'La had turned Eddy to face a large picture mirror. She stood behind Eddy and placed her hands gently on her shoulders and said, "Close your eyes," which Eddy had done without thinking. She had opened them again immediately, about to protest at these theatrics and found herself alone in the now-dimmed room, staring into the mirror. Before she could begin to speak she saw her reflection change dramatically. All the grief and fear of the last two years seemed to be there for her to witness. Its effects were debilitating to say the least. Eddy's reflection hunched in pain and seemed to shrink in on itself. Her face contorted and twisted. The life seemed to be wrung out of her.

Eddy watched herself, appalled.

SHEHKRii
– The FLAME –

Then it happened all over again, only worse, and her reflection crumpled to the ground, a shriveled, pathetic wreck.

"No," said Eddy to her reflection, with a vehemence that shocked her. She was disgusted with herself. At this realization, the lights seemed to suddenly spring back to life and M'La was standing behind her again.

"There's hope for you yet, Eddy," she said almost gently. Then in more commanding tones. "Back to Victor's party now. Or he will start playing the grumpy old man, which he does so well." She was at the door before Eddy could fully turn, holding it open.

A little dazed, Eddy walked out of the room leaving her grief behind.

***

The night was young, so to speak, and it had been decided they would walk to Knightsbridge and have coffee at the Yacht Club. Victor knew the manager, it seemed. Joe was pleasantly surprised. He had assumed they would all go their separate ways after the ceremony and its festivities and had been thinking of looking up Charles Braithwaite. But more time with his parents was a welcome surprise. Patrick and Mira apparently had a car and were departing to pick it up. Victor took Eddy's arm and they strolled off down Piccadilly. M'La imitated the gesture and guided her son the same way half a dozen paces behind.

SHEHKRii
– The FLAME –

"This is nice," said Joe.

"That it is, my son. Your father has done well and should be acknowledged. I am also pleased to have had the chance to help Alastair's widow. She was very quick. There's steel in that one."

Joe laughed softly, "Oh yes. And thank you."

"You're welc…" M'La's grip on Joe's arm tightened fleetingly and she said. "We are watched … with intent. Keep walking but a little faster."

M'La's free hand reached up and touched the black stone necklace that was part of her ensemble, a match for Mira's, Joe now realized. He heard a quiet tone and then his mother spoke in the coded language of his childhood. The tongue that usually meant some sort of action was imminent.

"Mira will join us shortly," announced his mother. "Swap with your father and take Eddy in hand, Johan. If you hear me in your mind, go to the ground immediately."

"Yes, Mother." Joe knew not to argue and smoothly orchestrated the switch asking Eddy an innocuous question about Andrew Pearce.

Behind him he heard his mother giving Victor an update. The old man grunted derisively.

Out of Green Park came five men, vaulting the hedge with ease. Dressed casually, looking like locals, they moved in, smoothly arcing out around Joe and Eddy. Joe felt his mother's mental touch and swept Eddy down to the ground.

SHEHKRii
– The FLAME –

Three coins doing near sonic speed raced above him and the heads of three of the men exploded. Their bodies toppled backwards. The two remaining were knocked out of their stunned disbelief by the sudden skidding noise of a car spinning to a stop at the curb, a perfectly executed maneuver by a gray BMW with a smiling young man at the wheel.

Mira stepped smoothly out of the car before it had stopped rocking and kicked the nearest man in the ribs. The blow was so powerful his body seemed to fold in on itself and cartwheeled over her exquisitely bare leg.

The last man standing turned and ran like hell and the shadows of the park swallowed him.

Joe helped Eddy to her feet.

"What was that all about. Oh …?" she said, seeing the bodies.

"Just the local thugs, I'm sorry to say," he replied as he guided her to the car. Mira held the rear door open. "We'll go the rest of the way by car."

The young woman tossed a small duffel bag to M'La as Victor joined them. All three slipped into the back and Mira retook the front.

"I'll join you shortly," said M'La.

"Take care," said Victor, as the car sped away, a still-grinning Patrick easily threading a course back into the traffic.

***

SHEHKRii
– The FLAME –

M'La stepped into the shadows cast by the park's trees. There was no one in sight for several hundred meters; a fact which suggested their attackers had back-up; observers, at least. Quickly she stripped off her gown and donned trousers and a light jacket from the duffel. The dress and shoes went into it and she strapped the bag flat to her back. A pair of light trainers replaced the low heels she had worn for the party. It was all done in seconds.

Still within the shadows she let her mind reach out, simultaneously following the imprint of the fleeing man and searching for the telltales of scrutiny that would lead her to the watchers. The man and his handlers were 'downstream'. He had looped into the park and then back out farther down Piccadilly. But there was another watcher– more remote and somewhat obscured. He was high and at least a kilometer away. And his signature was drifting. He had moved.

She stepped out into the dappled light and let her mind attune to its rhythms. From near invisibility in the shadows she faded into complete obscurity within the light. No one would see her even if they tripped over her. Turning towards the survivor who had just crossed the road she ran.

And covered two hundred and forty meters in six seconds, stopping abruptly three meters behind the man as he sidled into the alcove of a service entrance. He unlocked it and slipped in. M'La followed.

SHEHKRii
– The FLAME –

Three stories up, the man entered an apartment. It's living space looked back up the street. Two people turned to greet him.

"Did you fuckin' see that? What the bleedin ' ' ell is goin' on, ' ere, mate. They're all bloody dead, ain't they."

"Calm down, Benny. You ain't dead, is ya?"

"No. But what the fu …"

M'La seemed to appear out of thin air. The third figure, a woman, yelped and with the other man quickly stepped back. The survivor spun around, gulped and joined them.

M'La held up two coins, one in each hand. She had already determined which of these mercenaries had the most information, so she flicked her hands forward and the woman and Benny died. The man's soul fled, screaming. The woman didn't have one and simply crumpled.

"Tell me everything and you live."

"Tell you what?"

Another coin appeared.

"OK. OK. We was hired by a Bulgarian bloke, see. Name of Grigor. Don't know any other name but we's worked for ' im before, see. He wants the darkie done over bloody and anybody wot gets in the way. That's all. Set it up for us, ya know. Had times and places an' all."

The man's accent was beginning to grate on M'La and she seriously reconsidered her offer.

"Do you have to speak like that? Butchering your own language"

"Wot?"

"Never mind. Come here."

"No way, bitch ... sorry."

But the woman had disappeared again and was suddenly behind him cupping his jaw with one hand and his forehead with the other. The man, whose name was Matthew, Matty to his friends, screamed in anguish as M'La trawled through his conscious and subconscious mind, confirming his story and taking a firm image of this Grigor. There were a few things Matty had not told her and she took them as well.

She let him go and he dropped to the floor in agony. Walking to the door of the room she turned and said, "I've planted a compulsion in your brain, Matthew. You cannot report back to Grigor and will in effect actively avoid him. The alternative is pain beyond anything you've ever experienced or inflicted. If you attempt to harm anyone ever again, you'll be overcome with a driving desire to throw yourself off Big Ben. Considering what you've seen tonight, I'd strongly advise you not to test my words."

Matty rose shakily to his feet, clutching his head, but the woman was gone by the time he looked across the room.

***

M'La did not go immediately to the Royal Thames Yacht Club. Jogging effortlessly through the night streets of London she found a small, darkened office building off Grosvenor Square.

SHEHKRii
– The FLAME –

They were waiting for her as she arrived.

Shown immediately to the rooftop conservatory, she entered and approached a large stone slab in the center of the glasshouse. Placing her hand on its surface she imagined a man; a very special man who had transformed her life. As a sudden warmth flared under her palm she removed it and, unstrapping her pack, began to re-dress into her evening clothes.

Not far away the air shimmered and condensed as a translucent picture formed then suddenly snapped into solidity. Seeing M'La half-dressed, he said in a lilting brogue, "Oh. Excuse me, Em. Am I intruding?"

"Making jokes again, Keeper? -You can never intrude. And I think we both left modesty behind decades ago, eh?"

"Well, yes. We did meet in a brothel, after all."

"With Victor."

"Yes, indeed."

Straightening after putting on her shoes, M'La addressed the projection. "The Twelve have targeted my son. And Victor. I will not tolerate this, Nathan. The old fools, however, are your province and I felt you should be told."

The man's expression had deepened into an angry frown. "Six years ago, I caused a surge in the cluster of Biopulses they control when the parasites were sucking power from Terra. Three of them were destroyed. That should have been enough to hold them in place until we were ready to finish them permanently."

"Johan tells me they are buying slaves in bulk. And they do not apparently care who knows it."

"Things have changed."

"Indeed."

The image had begun to pace, a slow deliberate circle around the stone. "I will see to the guarding of your son, Em. You have other duties that must not be interrupted."

M'La sighed with relief, a weakness she would share with no other. "Thank you, Nathan."

"I'll be in London tomorrow evening. Take your leave within a few days and I'll keep watch till the danger is past."

"As you say, Keeper, so shall it be."

"Be well, M'La." The image faded away.

M'La gathered her pack and returned to the ground floor. The staff had called a cab, which was waiting as she exited the building. She'd had enough exercise tonight.

***

Half a world away on the island the Moro called home, Nathan Chalk meditated. His consciousness flitted around the globe following the lines of tectonic and magnetic stress, which held the world together. Each facet of his complex personality expanded to become a sub-mind of the whole, processing any and all information that came its way, channeling this back to the singular, dominant Nathan, suspended a few centimeters above a smooth black boulder wedged into the base of a small cliff on the west coast of Mindanao.

He had not assumed any of the classic meditation poses. No Zen or Yogic disciplines were necessary. The children who had gathered to watch simply saw a man floating with his eyes closed. They had seen this strange and delightful man do this before, so there was no fright in it for them, not now anyway. They just could not resist watching and knew that when finished he would tell them wondrous things.

Meanwhile, Nathan searched for indications of stress in the planetary grid. Ley lines, they had been called by others, but that term was but a shadow of the reality. The lines of energy and force were both constant and changeable, lasting for eons in some cases and mere decades in others.

All danced to the rhythm of a deeper drum, the will of this world.

Her tune.

And Nathan was both audience and occasional conductor of this global symphony. Now, however, he detected discordance in one particular place. Deep in the Balkans at the heart of the small empire, carved out by the old men who called themselves The Twelve, there was pain. But this was not new. The congestion had existed for a millennium and he had planned to relieve it soon. But the intensity of the discomfort had increased and now throbbed with the sharpness of new activity. Something would have to be done.

SHEHKRii
– The FLAME –

Briefly he surveyed the other points of stress that his awareness had detected. The major ones were few; the three around Rasovo in Romania, which he had just assessed; the still older single spot in the Himalayas; and deep in the jungles of the Congo, a double Biopulse; a new point of pain that had only begun to throb in the last few decades.

All would be healed. But which ones first? Nathan smiled inwardly. Despite his power, his knowledge, there was no surety to his destiny. Terra had made that clear at his awakening. Her world was in mortal peril and the complexities of ten thousand discordant years must be healed quickly, in a few short centuries. No constants, only variables; a mathematician's nightmare. But Nathan Chalk was far more that any savant and the power of his determination shattered rocks. He would not fail.

But his moment of focus was starting to show as the cliffs around him trembled in sympathy with his anger. He withdrew himself from his trance and dropped down into a crouch on his rock, whispering soothing words to the surrounding children who had suddenly found their fun threatened. Slowly their smiles returned and he told them a story of dolphins and whales and wonders beneath the sea.

When his story was finished, he shooed them home while he sat and mused on his rock. Freeing the Moro from the yoke of history was one of a dozen similar enterprises undertaken by the *Shehkrii*. These isolated pockets of humanity guarded, unknowingly, a rich genetic heritage that was needed out in the wider world. Half a century ahead, a very necessary cataclysm would drive the Moro away from these islands and their survival and eventual integration back into mainstream humanity was essential to Terra's plan.

Some of the Imams did not like this new influence. But bullies are easily dealt with and the Moro were beginning to see the sense in more ecumenical methods. Keeping M'La from decapitating most of the priests had been a bit of a struggle, though.

CHAPTER 5

RASOVO, BULGARIA

THE LABORATORY WAS NOT large but its dozen-odd occupants had all the room they needed and supplies were not a problem. Putting a test tube out of place or allowing a speck of dust to show, that would be a problem. Kerenski gave OCD a new, sharper definition.

Which was no real problem of itself. However, now Vizier was present in the laboratory and that was very rare. And dangerous. The technicians focused on their equipment intently and avoided any eye contact. Those who could, took samples to the incubation room and stayed there as long as possible.

Kerenski seemed oblivious to the tension.

"I have told you before, *Gospodin* Danev, I do not do 'wish fulfillment', I do science. And you have ignored me enough times to know the difference."

The technicians froze, as did Danev.

"Doctor," said Danev after a few seconds, "aim and achievement are never at odds, only separated by circumstance. My intention is to minimize circumstance. This is a point I have made repeatedly but you seem unable to grasp it. Or are you ignoring my concerns?"

Kerenski drew breath then checked himself. The look in the other man's eyes spoke loudly enough that even

Kerenski realized there might be a problem with sarcasm at this point.

"Danev ... Vizier, we are at odds over only one concept. In all other things, we agree, no?"

Vizier nodded.

"Thus, it is the question of quantity versus quality that separates us. To reduce this gap, my team and I need time. Your ambitions are retarded by time. I know this. We have achieved so much in the last few years, but without more time I can nether advance our knowledge of the Nectar nor devise more efficient means of production. My psychological profile is ..."

Vizier held up a hand, his expression stern. More technicians headed for the incubation room.

"Doctor, we have had this discussion. I do not enjoy repeating myself."

Kerenski sighed, looked around and signaled to one of the technicians who blanched and then approached cautiously.

"Medevco," snapped Kerenski, "what are the latest DNA results?"

"Doctor, Vizier!" stammered the man, "The profiling is inconclusive at this stage. We have indications of consistency for your profile, Doctor, but the numbers are far from conclusive. In addition, there are clusters of the same DNA combinations in the general population. Yet these are not always successful donors. Statistically we need ..."

Vizier's hand came up again. He turned and paced around the laboratory.

"Clear the room."

The technicians were gone in unsurprisingly short order.

"Doctor, your discoveries have made my ambitions manifest. My ambitions, fully realized, will re-establish not only your reputation but visit excruciating revenge upon your enemies. Why must we argue? Can you not focus on the simple task in hand?"

Kerenski's face took on a look that Vizier had rarely seen, a sneering, hate filled twisting that transformed him. A flicker of a smile twitched Vizier's lips at this reveal.

Kerenski didn't notice. "I will have my revenge, comrade. But it must be conclusive. Get me more people and double my laboratory space and I can get you faster result. But unless we make a breakthrough in the knowledge base I cannot offer an immediate solution. More technicians may produce that but …"

Vizier pressed his lips together and conceded the point, a rare thing for him.

"Very well. Speak to Vasily. He will get you more people and equipment. How long to see some benefit from that?"

"Once operational, if we can double our testing … six months to refine the profile, test it and then we can target donors. On current trends that would mean a fifty to sixty percent increase in production."

Vizier nodded and left without a word.

SHEHKRii

– The FLAME –

Kerenski shuddered. He was not oblivious to the danger posed by Danev, Vizier as the elderly maniac preferred.

Medevco poked his head around a door and Kerenski signaled him.

"That went well, Doctor. You are still alive."

Kerenski frowned then grinned. "It is a trial, Gustav, a real trial. At least the KGB were predictable. Vizier on the other hand ... he needs us but after; well, I trust you to maintain our exit strategy. You must save me again, save us all, perhaps."

"I will, Doctor. We cannot lose the work."

"No. Indeed not. The work is everything."

The others began to sneak back and the two men parted.

MONDRAGOE
BASQUE COUNTRY
SPAIN

Jasmin glanced behind, a quizzical expression fixed on her face. The local merchant waved and smiled as he took his leave. She skipped once to catch up with Neil and Hilde.

"Still confused, Jasmin?" asked Hilde.

"Yes. The Basque are notoriously insular. And Neil and I are very obviously not from around here. So ..."

"You're with me, which carries the necessary credit. Once we get you comfortable with the language, you'll be like 'family'. And then you can come and go with confidence and the community will watch your back. Perfect, no?"

"A little too good, perhaps," offered Neil.

"We all need safe harbors, Doctor. This is going to be one of yours. The Biopulse here is also unrestrained and you can test your new toys to your heart's content."

Neil smiled. The new instruments were a miracle. While the setup could be operated by a single person, it was optimal with a two-man team; one to control the three linked drones, which established an aerial sensor field and another person to direct that field's intensity and frequency. Everything he'd spent a decade developing with orbital satellites was now do-able with bits and pieces from Radio Shack.

Well, almost! The drones were strange little beasties. They had an articulated triple rotor configuration, not the usual quadcopter, and it was elevated above the circular sensing array, making the whole thing look like a thistle, in his opinion.

But the sensitivity... he'd never encountered anything like it. Linked, the copters could establish an E.M. field able to pick up the emissions from a digital watch fifty stories up; or the base rhythm of a ground vibration several kilometers long. What they could do with ...

Hilde stopped.

"Your offices are just around the corner. Why don't you retrieve the scanners and we'll field-test them some more? You're both close to proficient and I'd like you there soon so we can move on to other aspects of your new enterprise.

"I'll wait here, then we'll head up on the mound."

The other two glanced to the elevated, wooded park.

"There?" said Jasmin, "That's so ... obvious."

"This is an ancient community. Different priorities, different forms"

Neil nudged Jasmin. "Let's go."

Hilde grinned as she hurried to catch up. Their enthusiasm was infectious. Here in this particular place, this community, it was hard not to be uplifted. To be bringing Neil and his team into their journey was such a wonderful feeling. They were the first of the Unreturned to be directly incorporated into the Path. The first of many to begin the next stage of the strategy to prepare humanity for the terrible consequences of their own actions, and the steps Terra must take to rectify the damage done.

To have reached this point finally was exhilarating. To be asked by Nathan to contribute directly was uplifting in so many ways, too.

It was dampened somewhat by the Twelve and their new-found vigor. The three Biopulses controlled by the Twelve were in more pain and she knew Nathan ached to relieve it. Unfortunately, if he came too close his presence would be detected and the resulting turmoil would savage some, if not all of the nodal points, and it would take centuries to repair them. Time they didn't have.

SHEHKRii
– The FLAME –

Neil and Jasmin returned with a travel case each, the little wheels bumping and jumping on the ancient cobbles. Hilde smiled at the sight.

"Pick up the cases, please. They won't survive the stairs otherwise."

***

The little group humped its way up the knoll till almost at the summit, then laid out the cases and set up the equipment. Neil handled the drones and Jaz used a holographic tablet to monitor the readings. The sunlight didn't affect the images at all. She knew the basics of that particular problem, but was still amazed at how effective this new device had become. The patent alone would be worth billions.

She glanced at Neil and saw his 'concentration' face. It was so cute. She checked herself; *Work to do, girl. Got to get this right!*

***

Neil was feeling like a kid again. He should be doing Jaz's job but just couldn't resist flying the drones. The controls were conventional, with only a few additions, which let him focus on each machine individually or fly them as a grouped cluster. A small extendable dual screen showed his avionics while the other displayed the sensing net projected by the cluster.

He maneuvered to seventy-eight meters and refined the filter, selecting the optimal height. The drones adjusted themselves slightly a few centimeters lower.

"On point, Jaz."

"Got it. Can you engage auto-pilot?"

"I think so … yes. It's on. Let me set the rig down …"

He stepped over and leant in against her unselfconsciously. She braced herself automatically against him and moved the tablet so they could see equally.

The image showed a golden net pulsating over a lighter diaphanous recreation of the knoll. The fluctuations were rhythmic and steady. Neil touched an icon in the control bar and a second lower blue net formed, dancing to a different beat. The water table did not have the same frequency and was slower in its reactions, but every few seconds both webs seemed to syncopate and act as one.

More icons touched revealed more parameters, then Jaz began running different combinations and the linkages.

"This is amazing," he said softly. "Let's see what range we can get for the same accuracy?"

Neil picked up the rig and turned off auto-pilot. He glanced at Jaz as she adjusted the scanning limits.

"You should have the new height now. We're looking at a radius of just under two kilometers."

"Gotcha."

He adjusted the height to a hundred-and-five-meters.

***

SHEHKRii
– The FLAME –

Hilde watched with a certain pride. They were technically proficient now but just needed miles under their collective belt to be at ease with the equipment and not distracted by its novelty. Another few days and different locales and they should be there.

Then they could pass on the skills.

After that, things would really get interesting.

***

Jaz called out, "Hilde, look at this!"

She walked over to look at the screen.

"What's that, on the edge there? It looks like interference. Are we doing something wrong?"

"Ah … no, no. You're picking up regional effects. Send Neil a ping to go up to a hundred-and-sixty-meters."

Jaz tapped out the numbers and waited. The screen blurred and refocused.

"There you go, now …"

Hilde reached in and made a few adjustments and a new overlay intruded.

"Oh my God … you've, that's …" she swallowed. "Ground based E.M. signatures directly linked to atmospheric pre-conditions. This is a weatherman's wet dream."

Hilde laughed softly, the vibrations running through Jaz like a warm shiver, "Imagine what you could do with a satellite!"

SHEHKRii
– The FLAME –

Jasmin Bhari's eyes went very, very wide.

Neil side stepped over, "Wotcha?"

"Interconnectivity. And dollar signs. Let's see how high we can get."

They stuck with it for another hour, testing, experimenting. Eventually they were so proficient they didn't have to think about operating the equipment.

Hilde was well pleased.

"Enough," she said, "Let's take all this back to the studio and see what you can do with it."

They quickly packed up and headed back, picking up a late lunch on the way from a keyhole bistro.

At the studio, they shelved the equipment and joined Hilde at a large black slab in the center of the space. It hadn't been there before.

"What's this thing?" asked Jaz.

"Place your hands upon the stone."

"What?"

Hilde cocked an eyebrow at them both.

They did as asked and felt first a cool sensation, then growing warmth as a golden glow erupted beneath their hands. Jaz squealed and tried to remove her hands. She couldn't.

"Hey …"

"Relax and concentrate. Think of the data you've collected. All the possibilities it offers."

Jaz glanced at Neil and he nodded. They looked at the stone surface together and slipped into concentration trance.

SHEHKRii
– The FLAME –

After a few moments, an image erupted from the slab. Fuzzy at first, it soon focused and stabilized.

"Full spectrum," said Neil.

"Mmmmm …"

Hilde placed her hand on the stone, taking control and expanded the image of Mandragoe out fifty kilometers and up a thousand.

"Add the magnetosphere, Doctor."

A pale green pulsating haze bloomed into the image.

Hilde frowned and a red graph imposed itself on the image.

"This is the magnetic fluctuation by decade going back a thousand years; for this region. It's representative of the western hemisphere."

"Oh my …" said Neil. "Can you expand that to ten thousand?"

The graph shifted and reformed. Neil frowned, concentrating and slowly an equation formed in the air above the graph. The number at the end of it shocked him and he drew away, his hand still fixed to the stone.

"Neil," said Jaz, "what is it?"

"Polar switch," he said softly, "I know when it'll happen."

"And," said Hilde, "you'll soon know what to do about it. Now, I think, it's time for a break."

She tapped the stone and the images vanished and walked calmly over to the nearby bureau to boil the jug leaving Neil Carlisle staring after her in disbelief.

ST. JAMES PARK
LONDON

Nathan threw croutons to the ducks. Joe laughed as the little creatures swarmed their feet.

Sitting on the park bench they were soon surrounded by chattering birds. A couple passing by stopped to enjoy the embarrassing spectacle.

Raising an eyebrow at the spectators' audacity Nathan held up a hand and snapped his fingers. The ducks froze for a long second and then turned in unison and returned to the nearby pond.

The couple made a hasty retreat with Nathan's basso chuckle nipping at their heels.

"That will be in the evening papers. Those two are journalists. I recognized them although they don't seem to know me … fortunately."

"Don't worry, Joe. The story won't get past the junior editor. Now … where were we? You've asked Charles Braithwaite to hold off doing anything official …"

"Yes. He doesn't like it but is willing to defer to my judgment for the time being."

"Good. The less people involved the better, less accidental casualties. The Twelve are not bothered by collateral damage and tend to indulge themselves with object lessons if pushed. Let's keep your new friend in reserve, officially. Although, if he were to start something off the books … he would be well prepared when we did need him."

Joe smiled. He wanted to involve Braithwaite. There was a quiet confidence to the man, which inspired confidence.

Staring out over the small lake Nathan stood and Joe followed. "Give me your Stone, Joe."

Taking the large pebble Nathan held it up in front of his face. A sliver of golden lightning played briefly over the surface and then he handed it back to Joe.

"You'll have a bit more protection than usual until the present danger is over. Have it with you at all times."

"Yes, Keeper."

"You'll see me again when I've dealt with the threat. There may be some mopping up and we can utilize Braithwaite ... if you wish to involve him officially?"

"Yes, I think he's worth the effort."

"Excellent. Off you go then. You have a train to catch."

Joe nodded and took his leave. Nathan remained standing, drinking in the place and its spring exuberance then moved suddenly at a brisk walk heading northeast towards Green Park.

***

Piccadilly was its usual bustling self - all cars, people, and noise. Nathan strolled west along the footpath coming to the spot where M'La had thrown her coins. He stepped out of the pedestrian flow and leaned against the low wire fence, which bordered the park.

SHEHKRii
– The FLAME –

And stepped back in time to witness the attack on Joe from his very unique perspective. The vibrations were fresh so clarity was not an issue and Nathan watched as Eddy Bryce was swept out of harm's way and M'La dealt with the attackers.

He turned his awareness to the lingering impression that Joe's mother had detected. Locating the handler on a distant rooftop Nathan narrowed his focus and the man known as Grigor snapped into sharp relief. Nathan *saw* Grigor as he really was and fixed the ugly reality in place, sending part of his awareness out into the wider world of Now to locate the assassin.

As this process played out he moved smoothly off the supporting fence and resumed his stroll down Piccadilly. After a few moments, he knew where Grigor was and could easily have killed him with a well-placed thought or two, but there was a curious discipline to the man's mind, which Nathan determined to probe further and for that he would have to get close.

So, the hunt continued; always an enjoyable diversion, and there was new information on the Twelve on offer. The time was fast approaching when something would have to be done about those particular grumpy old men; something permanent.

***

Joe was a little nervous; not a frequent emotion, he acknowledged. But the idea, which had come to him as he left St. James Park, had stuck and he felt compelled to follow it. After several days maneuvering he had the two players lined up.

Now or never.

"Sir Charles Braithwaite, may I introduce Edwina Bryce."

They shook hands.

"Sir Charles."

"The notorious Mrs. Bryce. It's an honor."

Eddy's eyebrows shot up. Braithwaite released her hand and took a half step back. "Anyone who can get up Colleridge's desiccated nasal passages is someone I'm only too happy to offer a drink." He gestured to the side table, which had light refreshments.

Eddy snorted a laugh then caught herself. "Pardon me," she said. "I'm surprised you know Colleridge. He doesn't generally mix with the domestic services."

Braithwaite had been about to fill a glass with something richly red when he nearly dropped the bottle. And grinned viciously. "You've got the rub of it there, Mrs. Bryce. His prejudices have cost me good men and women. Enemy of my enemy is ..."

Eddy smiled and walked closer to take the now offered glass of Merlot.

"Call me Eddy ..."

Joe was worried. This was going far too well.

The loft warehouse was Braithwaite's off-the-books option, as discussed with Joe the day before. He had not been surprised the Englishman had this up his sleeve. In fact, he had been hoping for just this. Getting Eddy involved was both the key to success and the fly in the ointment. Joe was concerned her current sensitivity and circumstances would make her resistant to this big a gamble.

Apparently not!

Two young men who arrived at the top of the nearby stairs joined them. Braithwaite signaled them over. Joe joined the group and Charles handled the introductions.

"Mats Hendricksen; Brent Mersey; this is Johan Lutz and Eddy Bryce. For the record, you have never met either of them. Are we clear on that?

Brent nodded and Mats said, "Yes, Sir Charles. We're off the clock completely."

"And Jericho rules apply?" asked Brent.

"Yes."

"Jericho?" inquired Eddy.

"Total destruction, no prisoners. We are on our own," said Mats.

Eddy nodded, her face grim. "To work then, gentlemen. Let's not bore Sir Charles with details. I'll need performance *specs* on your baseline processing and activation speeds on ..."

Eddy directed the young men to the cluster of consoles and display arrays at the center of the loft and the three got down to work.

"That was smooth," said Braithwaite, with just a little awe.

"That's the Eddy I grew up with. It's so good to have her back."

"Did you see the looks on those two faces when I introduced her? They hid it well enough but I think my young guns are a bit spooked."

"Will that be a problem?"

"No. They're both very resilient. Too be honest, they're the best I've got. Particularly at this type of under-the-radar work."

Joe nodded. This was a good start. The plan he'd proposed to Charles two days prior had been based on an educated guess at the Englishman's motivations. Joe hoped Charles Braithwaite would be deeply offended by the specifics of the new development in the conspiracy, which Joe and his father had fought against most of their respective lives.

Organized slavery was real and a multi-billion-pound industry. Braithwaite knew this. His position and access ensured he did. But the Twelve's use of the Trade was exploitative on a scale above anything in normal experience. 'Human pill boxes' was the term Charles had used, in disgust.

Combined with the drug angle, he had agreed to Joe's proposal to start an intensive monitoring operation outside normal channels. The attack on Joe and his family at the Ritz had cemented the deal. Charles took such things personally, especially on his patch.

So, they'd plotted and planned. Charles had several properties where he could base the operation, especially one that didn't involve active agents. The loft was only accessible via a convoluted nest of passages with numerous safety valves. But, its nest of servers tapped into the information networks of London and the world in ways which impressed even Joe. From here Eddy and her young men could piggy back their inquiries via most of the major intelligence and media services of the western world, and more importantly, most of the corporate sub-web systems that laced through all of the above. Braithwaite had set up much of this parallel network as a matter of course. Decisively, however, it was his team, over several years, which had used this base to infiltrate the same systems used by government and corporations alike, and make themselves into the most effective detection unit the UK had ever seen. So good, in fact, that almost no one knew they existed.

Layers within layers within layers. Perfect for Joe at this crucial time.

Of course, as soon as he'd been able, he had casually laid his Stone on one of the control consoles and provided Terra with an introduction. She had been very pleased.

Then there was Eddy. Her benching by the British Secret Intelligence Service was galling although she accepted it as inevitable. Andrew Pearce's help had mitigated some of that, providing a buffer of sorts. Which unfortunately left Eddy with very little to do. Her shop ran itself and without any investigative contracts, Joe feared Eddy would slip back into depression despite his mother's intervention.

SHEHKRii
– The FLAME –

When he'd explained the reality of the attack at the Ritz, she had been at first offended by the lie then enraged when she realized the implications. So, a little manipulation later she'd agreed to meet Charles Braithwaite and see what he offered.

Now it was all going swimmingly. Joe was accustomed to more hiccups at the front end of a project like this.

Braithwaite seemed to sense his tension. "Joe, cool off. Go downstairs and see my people. They'll brief you on the 'labyrinth' security protocols for this place. Let Eddy whip my lads into shape and come back in a couple of hours. There should be something to show for it, I'm sure."

Joe grinned. He could use a good coffee and there was an excellent Italian bistro across the road.

CHAPTER 6

SOPHIA LOVED LONDON. It was a delicious rabbit warren and she never tired of exploring. It was also much cleaner than her first visit decades ago.

And the sun was out this fine Saturday afternoon, so she was enjoying the time off from guarding M'La's son, the delightful Johan. It was a pleasant and relatively easy assignment compared to the last few years in Australia.

She shrugged off remembrance and continued her window-shopping. Both her own sons had birthdays coming up and she was intent on finding them each something 'English'.

The scream was blood-curdling and the light crowd around her froze. Sophia moved a few meters to see across the road and down the alley the sound had come from.

A hooded man was pulling his knife arm backwards; ready to strike again, his victim slumped against the alley wall.

"Stop!" called a man at the entrance and started walking in. Sophia began moving but slowly so as not to draw attention.

"Ya want some o' dis?" shouted the attacker turning towards the man.

"Clear off. You've had your fun." The other man kept advancing as Sophia drew near. She examined them both in a glance.

SHEHKRii
– The FLAME –

The attacker was mildly high on cocaine and ready to keep fighting. The would-be rescuer was calm, alert but not agitated. Unusual.

She placed a hand on his shoulder and he froze in place. Sophia kept walking.

The attacker smiled, he liked sticking women, and slid into a classic knife-fighting pose, moving the blade from side to side - ready to strike. Which he did as Sophia was approaching.

She took the attacker's wrist in her right hand and moved it off line, turning her body slightly in the other direction. Her left hand came up and snapped the men's elbow and she released her other grip, whipping the heel of her right hand under his nose, driving the cartilage up into the brain.

The body collapsed straight down and Sophia continued through to kneel next to the injured woman.

The rescuer shrugged off his stasis and rushed up to them.

"I'm a doctor, let me see her. How did you do that, make me stop and kill him?"

"Full of questions, aren't you?" said Sophia. "Don't touch her. Your skills are not needed."

The young man hesitated. There was a command in the woman's voice, which he'd heard before in Afghanistan from the commandoes he treated in the camp hospitals. He complied and watched intently.

Sophia's hand against the woman's face told her the victim was a fighter but the trauma to her pancreas and large intestine was mounting and no amount of spirit would overcome that. Reaching beneath her blouse she released her Stone from its pendant and placed the small black rock under the woman's thyroid.

"Hold that in place," she said. The man complied.

Sophia reached under the woman's skirt and found the large arterial node on the inside of her thigh simultaneously applying pressure with her other hand to the similar point under the armpit.

The doctor recognized the points and the chakra at the thyroid and began to wonder what the hell was going on. Then the strange woman sang!

A low tone followed by a slow ululating rising pitch, then repeat. Before he could speak the stone under his fingers went freezing cold then suddenly warm, the sensation travelling up his arm and he knew!

Knew what was happening.

In his mind's eye, he saw the internal lacerations vibrate and reseal, the tear in the pancreas knit itself back together and the adrenalin pumping out of the cortex, slow. The pituitary started producing endorphins and the victim relaxed, groaning slightly.

"How?"

"Knowledge," answered Sophia, "properly applied."

She stood. "She's stable now but will need fluids and rest. Can I leave you to take care of that?"

"Of course, but …"

Sophia turned to look at the small crowd, which had gathered nearby. Three witnesses filmed the scene with their cell phones. She reached down and retrieved her Stone, concentrating slightly. The phones suddenly crackled and burst into flame, distracting the crowd and the doctor as Sophia smoothly walked out of the alley and back to her shopping.

***

Three hours, two croissants and several coffees later, Joe reached the top of the stairs, shielded from the loft proper, and was seized with sudden compulsion and regurgitated memory as he heard Mats and Brent approach, deep in semi-whispered conversation.

He had been eleven when his mother had shown him the trick.

"Pythagoras said it best," she had ventured, standing next to a tall tree, "All is number, number is all. He was referring to vibration." She had reached out and lightly touched the trunk with her fingertips and vanished.

Sudden panic was swamped with colossal curiosity, "How?"

Then she was back, casually drawing her hand away from the tree.

"If you concentrate your awareness down to only the sensation in your fingertips you will tune your physical vibrations to that of the tree. Others will see the tree, not you. Many cultures have developed this knack. The best of them was the Ninja of ancient Japan. Much of their reputation for stealth was based on this."

SHEHKRii
– The FLAME –

"They were *Shehkrii*?" asked a young Johan.

"Some. But the trick is learn-able by anyone with good focus."

It had taken him a week to find the mental discipline to do it at will. He hadn't tried it in over a decade but now simply reached out to the metal wall with his fingers and became the wall.

The young men stopped at the top of the stairs to finish their conversation.

"... Did you see?"

"Yeah! Amazing. No wonder they call her the Nasty Nanny. That's one seriously sneaky old lady. I don't want to be on the other side of the fence from her any time soon."

"No fuckin' way ..."

They started towards the stair again and continued their assessment of Eddy as they went. Joe waited a little longer then withdrew his hand. The sense of the weight of reality returned as though time had stopped while he touched the wall, and now it came back, trying to catch up.

He smiled. Eddy was well and truly back out of the pit of darkness she had entered when her husband Alistair had died. He turned the corner and walked over to Braithwaite who seemed to be sharing a joke with Eddy.

"How did you do that?" asked Charles.

"Pardon?"

"I heard you on the stair and my boys walked right past you without breaking their little chat. Like they didn't see you."

"Oh … ah …"

"One of your mother's tricks?" offered Eddy.

Joe nodded.

"Someone I'd like to meet, then," said Charles.

Eddy burst out laughing, the happiest sound Joe had heard from her in a long time.

"Only on your best of days, Charlie. Only the very best."

Braithwaite was smiling, too.

Charlie, thought Joe. *What have I done?*

And he had to be back in Belgium tomorrow.

WESTMINSTER ABBEY
DEAN'S YARD
LONDON

"Who are they?" asked Jasmin Bhari.

"They call themselves The Council for Interfaith Cooperation; mostly just 'The Council'. There are eight members. The three you see there are their leader, the tall one, Scribe. And Mahdi and Reverence."

"You're kidding!" said Neil Carlisle.

"No," replied Hilde, "I rarely do that. They, on the other hand, take themselves far too seriously. Hence the code names. They have taken one form or another since the eighteenth century. The current template has been in place for just over a hundred years."

Neil snorted and Jasmin put her hand out to calm him. They stood in the veranda of one of the surrounding buildings, deep in shadow, invisible to those below.

"And these are the ones behind Brony?" asked Jasmin.

"Yes. They cultivate their flocks assiduously and will not tolerate any distractions. Despite the drop in numbers over the last fifty years, The Council has never been more profitable."

"Is that all we are? A distraction?"

"A bit more than that. By marrying science and geomancy you would have impacted their bottom line by as much as thirty percent."

Jasmin took a half step forward, peering more intently. "It all sounds so very ... mercantile. Don't they believe?"

"Have you ever wondered, Jasmin, why the rise of the evangelical movement has equated prosperity with grace?"

"Oh."

The three men under observation began to return to the Abbey proper, flanked by over a dozen guards. Neil found a wooden bench and sat down. Jasmin sat with him.

"Why?" he said, the single word carrying a withering weight. He seemed to shrink in on himself.

Hilde watched, seeing the years of effort slip away from the man into the depths of depression. Seeing the woman who secretly loved him hover between anger and despair.

"Because you succeeded, Doctor. You scared them shitless."

Neil's head came up as did his spirits. "I've never heard you swear, Miss Nordstrom."

Hilde laughed, "That was profanity, Neil. If you want blasphemy I'm happy to oblige."

The couple smiled and Hilde saw the momentary retreat into darkness vanish as they both sprang back. She'd chosen her words well. Now, to cement the deal.

"The Council has been jittery for over a decade. The New Atheism they can deal with by just ignoring it, but it's the pagans they really fear. You will usher in an alternative resurgence that will swamp them. Which means The Council might have to come out into the open. That's the stuff of nightmares for an organization, which has always … always worked in the shadows."

"All we want is the truth," said Jasmin.

Hilde raised her eyebrows but said nothing.

"Yes, I know. Naive. OK, what now?"

"Now, we get back to business. You've seen your enemy and that's sufficient. I'll give you our files on The Council and their proxies so you know who to avoid. When your work reaches a certain critical mass, there will be some strategizing to counter The Council before you publish. The loose cannon in the ruling group is called Eminence. He may very well have put a price on your heads despite Scribe's instruction to the contrary. If that's the case, we'll arrange an accident."

Jasmin laughed, "I like you."

"Thank you."

Neil stood. "We're going to have to be mobile, aren't we?"

"Yes. You are all moving targets now. That's an adjustment only. The big change is attitudinal, which means you're going to have to share, Doctor."

"What. I don't know what ..."

"Give it up, Neil," laughed Jasmin, "… we all know."

"Know what?"

"Your secret source; up in Scotland. Bart saw you in Glasgow over a year ago, when you were supposed to be in Paris. Then you suddenly had the answer to problems which had been bugging us all for six months. Wasn't hard to figure out."

Carlisle looked devastated. "I promised ..."

"Things change, Doctor," said Hilde.

"Yes, yes they do," he replied glancing out to the Dean's Yard. "All too often."

***

"Simon."

"Yes, Scribe."

"Reverence wishes to review some of the financial numbers, assist him."

"Yes, sir."

"I'll take my leave, Keith. I want to keep an eye on Sister Bronwyn. I have high hopes for her efforts. And we need a quick result in those matters."

"Yes. If it's a drug …"

"Indeed. The Messiah Project might actually work."

He turned and left, leaving his senior secretary and Reverence, Keith Fitzsimmons, alone in the annex. Alone if you didn't count the security melting into the walls.

"Well, Simon, let's get cracking, shall we?"

They walked over to a nearby desk and the secretary opened the laptop, which never left his side and called up a complex schematic of financial transactions.

"The current overarching spreadsheet, Reverence; what specifically are you interested in?"

"Right! I have concerns about our East Euro territories. There's been fluctuations in the revenue streams for several years. I'm not convinced it's cyclical. I think someone is skimming. More than is acceptable, at any rate."

As he spoke, Simon refined the spreadsheet focusing on the Eastern Orthodox Church and the Chechen Republic.

"Mahdi," said Simon, "has expressed some concern about the Chechens. Our investigations so far suggest a small group of families is funneling money to one of the fringe separatist groups. It's not very sophisticated. Rectification is underway."

"Yes, I'm up-to-date on those matters."

Simon manipulated the screen again.

"Reverence, our analysis over the last three years shows nothing outside statistical variance. Perhaps if you could give me a starting point for your concerns."

Reverence scratched his chin. "Right, the pattern of revenue fluctuations suggests to me that someone is taking from the front end; extracting funds before they're counted. Look at that item there, the parishes in Bitola, Macedonia. The take from four of the five principal areas is down against the population *stats* yet those are prosperous regions which should have higher yields.

"The demographic profile clashes with the revenue stream, especially when it comes to corporate donations. Who's the operational bishop in that precinct?"

Simon called up a territorial personnel page. Pointing to the screen he said, "Bishop Pandev is the official controller."

"Who's on his team?'

Another few key strokes showed a group of five individuals.

"Alright," said Reverence, "full confidential investigation on all of them, their families and their immediate associates. Assume they've established some sort of arrangement with donors, which involves a double shuffle. Especially look for donors who've changed their pattern of contributions sometime in the last five years.

"I also want to see a layout of our return investments in those areas. Look for increased wastage figures. If I'm right, whoever is doing this will be trying to skim coming and going. Extend the profile over the whole territory. I want a progress report by the end of the week."

"Yes, Reverence. I'll see to it immediately."

THE HAGUE, BELGIUM

Johan Lutz replaced the telephone handset in its cradle with great care. He didn't want to react to what he had just been told. Or what it implied.

"Well!" said his father, exasperated after sitting for almost twenty minutes, watching his son quietly listen on the phone.

Joe took a calming, deep breath. His heart slowed, his other senses amplified. And he relaxed. Like a tiger, before it strikes. Victor saw the signs and decided to wait patiently. *The boy is a force to be reckoned with,* he thought with pride.

"The information Vladimir provided has been confirmed," Joe began. "In the last two years, the Twelve have purchased at least a hundred and eighty slaves from Gong-li and Marouk. Mostly young. No one over thirty. There's more, Father, but we need some privacy to discuss it." He stood as he finished and looked around the office. Interpol's *departmente* within the administration building of the International Court of Justice in The Hague was extensive and well appointed. Joe considered the value of secrecy and the risks involved in making this an Interpol case.

"Let's walk, Father," he said, gathering his coat.

Ten minutes later they stopped in a nearby park, shielded from direct surveillance by low trees and a children's playground. Victor was near bursting with curiosity.

Johan said, "Vladimir has been very busy. His Serbian agents have had little trouble documenting the Twelve's activities, and their information has opened a can of worms in Moscow. Do you remember Valentin Kerenski?"

Victor grunted an assent. "Animal," he said. "I thought they did away with him."

"Unfortunately, not," replied Joe. "It seems the manic doctor had a Romanian assistant who shepherded him out of the USSR and into the hands of the Twelve. They have abandoned their usual secrecy, Father. It is not a good sign. And then, there are the atomics."

Victor looked hard at his son. "You are sure?" he said simply.

"Vladimir is. Three he knows about. Small warheads bought on the black market."

"They are planning a coup. Now is the time. But what are the slaves for?" said the old man in frustration.

"Test subjects, perhaps, for Kerenski's mind drugs," speculated Joe.

"No. There are too many," said Victor, standing up straight with his hands behind his back. He stared into space momentarily. "There's a piece of this puzzle we don't have. Your mother needs to know these things. Perhaps she can work out what that missing piece is."

Both men held the silence for a few moments, considering. Eventually, Joe also stood. "I wonder how Eddy is doing?" he said.

SHEHKRii
– The FLAME –

Victor laughed. "From what you've said, 'very well' would be the answer. Braithwaite is a fine man."

"I didn't mean it like that!"

"I know. But that's the way it is. Now to more important things, I need good coffee, son."

Laughing softly, both men started back to Joe's office.

***

Grigor watched from a hundred meters away, his vision and hearing enhanced by concentration, his thoughts as black as a pit: *After I kill both father and son I will return to London and find this 'Eddy' and deal with her also. She was undoubtedly the old woman present at the failed execution. Any friend of my enemy is my enemy.*

That failure still mystified Grigor. His vantage point had been less than ideal, obscured by the trees in that damned park but the team was expert and should have dealt with the task easily. Instead they had faltered and disappeared. Cowards! Hiding for fear of retribution. He would deal with them as well, once the Lutz bastard was properly butchered. And his father. And Eddy. And anyone else who stood in the way of The Twelve's ascendency.

Wiping a small drop of drool from his chin, he moved smoothly into the surrounding crowds and angled closer to the two men who now had started their return journey. There was a small connecting alley they had to traverse in a few hundred meters: with a blind spot. Grigor quickened his pace.

CHAPTER 7

THE BRITISH LIBRARY
LONDON

OFFICIALLY THE BASEMENT resource center didn't exist. Brony liked that. It suited how she saw her mission. People really didn't know what was good for them. Time and time again, they proved that maxim.

Guidance was what they needed and it was her privilege to be part of that. Keeping out of sight was a necessary deception. And occasionally fun! Secrets had always fascinated Bronwyn Petersen.

It had all started in high school. She hated the nuns who taught her and loved the attention of the boys. Then she'd been caught in the store room with Clive Badham; with her knickers down and … she blushed at the remembrance.

Sister Veronica should have expelled her but instead she'd taken Brony to the courtyard balcony and asked what she saw. Sister made it clear her future hung on the answer, so Brony frowned and started to describe in detail what she saw. Sister prompted her a little and before she knew it, she was spilling all her friends' secrets as well as her enemies'.

"Good," said Sister Veronica and then proceeded to psychoanalyze half a dozen of the people Brony had picked out - three friends and three enemies. She tore them down to a collection of petty spites and hormonal flushes that had teenaged Brony blushing till she felt she would burst.

"Now, Bronwyn, you know yourself better, don't you? For example, with just the right word to Diane, you could have her scratching Marcie's eyes out. And the next time Dylan calls you 'fine' you know he's on a bet with one of his mates."

Blush was replaced with cold anger.

"Show me more. Pleeeease"

"All in good time. When you earn it."

So, her recruitment had begun. First to the sisterhood and then to The Council. Veronica was not a Council operative as such but a gifted recruiter for *higher purpose,* as she put it. Brony's libido had never subsided despite all the tricks she'd been taught, but she loved the life of manipulation and secrets and knowing her sacrifice made a difference. When they offered her a dispensation on the vow of chastity she almost fainted. It was the best of both worlds - purpose and libido were both satisfied. And the natural allure she knew was hers became another weapon in God's arsenal. She used it carefully. Or so she told herself. Occasionally guilt surfaced but that disrupted her focus and she squashed it back down quickly.

Now she was in her element. Even if it was part of the empire carved out by Eminence.

She much preferred working for Scribe, but the investigative archive built secretly under the great library was the best asset they had, in Brony's opinion even if it was Eminences' brainchild. She could tap into just about any server in the world from here, including the upper levels of the intelligence services. Going deeper required 'permission'. But if you could get it, well ... the world was your oyster.

Fortunately, she didn't need permission for what she was trying to do now. Carlisle and his team had abandoned their rooms at Plymouth, but she had facial recognition worms inserted across the U.K. and the E.U., and would have them identified soon. They seemed to have gone to ground because there were no hits to date, but they had to surface soon. It was simply not possible to stay concealed for long.

She had back-ups in place, regardless. They all had their foibles. And Scribe had told her privately the Bhari woman was not who she seemed, so they had leverage there if needed. Brony hoped she got that chance; she hated Jasmin with a passion. The woman was a wanton, taking and abandoning lovers as though they were candy, all the while adoring Carlisle. Such a hypocrite!

When Bhari had returned from the U.S. she had been more than accommodating, adapting to the office organization Brony had created. But slowly she carved out her own corner of the group and her security measures were near perfect.

And Carlisle changed. His growing dependence on Brony shifted and the obvious attraction between Bhari and himself became the new normal. Brony's plans to seduce Carlisle were thwarted. She took her frustration out on a local lad but the spite didn't subside.

Scribe entered the basement and everyone stood.

"Back to work, please." Privately he was more commanding and Brony felt a small flush rising.

"Yes, Scribe," echoed around the control area. He joined Brony in her corner work zone, well away from the other occupants.

"Well, Bronwyn, how goes it?" He took a seat beside her.

"Slow, sir. They are obviously hiding. If *facial rec* and financial records don't give us something by tonight, I'll initiate behavioral tracking. The profiles are finished now and I can load anytime."

She finished in a rush and took a deep breath.

Scribe smiled patronizingly and said, "Behavioral?"

"Yes, sir. They each have personal foibles that should register as a pattern. May I elaborate?"

"Of course."

"Well, over and above the background on Miss Bhari, which you've alluded to, she subscribes to a unique set of websites; a mixture of strategic foreign policy commentators and conspiracy theory provocateurs …"

"Show me."

"Oh, ah … yes, here we are."

Scribe leaned in. Brony detected mint in his breath and flushed again.

He sat back. "Interesting. That pattern alone suggests something. Can you see it, Bronwyn?"

She looked back at her screen. *What am I missing?* she mused? It was the sort of thing an investigative journalist would be involved with, a mix of the serious and the silly. The discussion boards were filled with gibberish and acronyms; code words for every nut ...

"Oh dear!"

Scribe chuckled, "Yes, Bronwyn. Miss Bhari is very well connected. But ultimately, we'll use that against her. Has she logged in to any of those sites since the group went to ground?"

"No, sir. Not with the ID's I'm aware of."

"Adjust your search parameters to look for, say sixty percent of those sites accessed within Britain in any two-hour period, then target those locations."

"Yes, sir."

"Now, the others?"

Brony typed a few quick strokes and her profiling matrix came on screen.

"Carlisle travels to Scotland regularly. He has something or someone up there that is his little secret. We all guessed early on but he thinks he's rather clever and goes to elaborate lengths to conceal his destination - in the west by all accounts. It's probably a mistress but my investigations haven't isolated any specifics as yet. It's in the Fort William area, I believe.

"The others are mundane. Cormac favors particular Italian brands of clothing and uses several high-end electronics suppliers for his equipment. And Smith is a tea freak."

"Pardon?"

"Sorry. Bartholomew Smith is a beverage snob. Very odd recipes of Chinese and Indian tea. Give him half a chance and he'll pontificate for hours on them, eh."

The half joke fell flat and Brony slunk into her chair.

"Mmm … start those searches now Bronwyn, regardless of the facial recognition process. And re-visit Dr. Carlisle's Scottish adventures. Get a team on that. I'll upgrade your operational authority to smooth the way. I would really like to know where he goes."

"Yes, Scribe," she said meekly.

The man rose and began to pace.

"Your doctor suspects whatever drugs were used on you, Bronwyn, were flushed from your system during your recovery."

"Drugs, Scribe."

"Yes, Sister. You were subjected to horrific injuries then repaired. Along with that, somehow, the illusion of your meeting and fall were imposed. Both processes are outside our current experience. Whatever was used is potent in a multitude of ways.

"We must locate these people and their resources, if nothing else than to prevent them using those resources against us."

"And it would make the Messiah Project viable," added Brony.

Scribe stopped and looked directly at her.

"Yes. Turbulent times are coming and if we can present a divine leader at the right moment, even for a short period, we would expand our congregation fivefold."

SHEHKRii
– The FLAME –

He sat back down next to Brony and she inhaled the minty essence of him, shifting a little in her chair.

"This is why, Bronwyn, locating Carlisle and his people is so important. Not just the drugs, but the alternative philosophy they represent. Combined, both those things are a seductive distraction to unthinking peoples. We cannot allow them to interfere with our holy purpose."

"I understand, Scribe. I will not let you down."

The man reached out and laid his hand on Brony's arm. "Thank you, Sister. Your efforts are appreciated. I would be pleased if, in future when we meet in relative privacy like this, that you call me "Miles". Sir and Scribe are so formal, don't you think?"

Brony nodded, mute and red as a beetroot. Scribe chuckled, rose and left.

She collected herself and felt her flush turn to pride and determination. She was favored, therefore, she was worthy. It meant so much, that simple touch!

She turned back to her screen - focused, determined. Loading her search profiles, she remembered a few additional things about Carlisle and Smith and added them into the mix. Scribe's favor was paying off already, she told herself.

Her internal email pinged and her upgrade came through. She flushed again. Typing furiously, the personnel requisition was quickly processed and she arranged a meeting with the group who would track down Carlisle's dirty little secret.

SHEHKRii
– The FLAME –

She hoped the woman was ugly!
And old.

THE HAGUE
BELGIUM

Nathan Chalk lingered, admiring the park's delicate subtlety – a work of true genius. *A gardener's life for me,* he mused, lost in thoughts of his childhood and the manor houses of western Eire. No urgency bothered him as the assassin bore down on Victor and his son. He strolled towards the alley as the two exited its further end, oblivious to the killer frozen in place a few meters behind.

Nathan paced around the man, noting the beads of perspiration as he fought to throw off the stasis. And the hooked knife now visible at his side. He stood two paces in front of the killer and released him.

Grigor did not hesitate and whipped his knife forward in a slashing lunge that should have disemboweled. The stranger had not moved yet his strike had missed by centimeters. He stumbled off balance but corrected quickly and tensed for a counter stroke, projecting his thoughts outward, attempting to smother the man and freeze him in place. The resulting pain was so intense Grigor dropped his knife, clutching compulsively at his temples and then fell to his knees in agony.

Nathan reached out and grasped the man's head with extended fingers. He made no attempt at subtlety and Grigor convulsed in pain beyond description.

SHEHKRii
– The FLAME –

"So, the Twelve have grown in power," said Nathan softly as he released Grigor and turned away. The assassin quickly got to his feet, the memory of pain causing him to hesitate.

Glancing over his shoulder, Nathan said, "I don't need you anymore, Grigor Patrascu." He flicked his hand at the man, a casual backhanded slap of little seeming power. Grigor was swept away by a wave of brutal force and hit the alley wall with a sickening crunch.

Nathan turned to leave the alley and found a mother and son at its entrance. The woman was looking around undecided on which direction to take, in thrall to Nathan's lingering, latent suggestion that the alley was inaccessible. The boy, however, was staring straight at him. Nathan approached the pair and bent on one knee to look the nine-year-old directly in the eyes.

"Say your name, young man."

"Wim, sir."

"You are destined to walk the Path, Wim. When your blood surges I will return to show you the Way." Standing, he regarded the woman for a few seconds. "Your mother suffers, does she not?"

Yes, sir. Her breath ... it is not easy for her."

Nathan reached out, touching the woman's cheek. She froze in place momentarily, then restarted her distracted search for direction. Glancing down he said, "The tumor is gone and will not return. Tell her this soon. It was in the left bronchial cluster, if she asks."

"Yes, sir," responded the boy, smiling. "Sir, your name …"

"Nathan."

"Thank you … Nathan"

He started tugging at his mother's hand and she looked down and began to walk off. The boy glanced back but the stranger had gone.

***

Joe was feeling nostalgic. Victor had not long left the office and he was remembering how good it had been to see his father every day. It was something that hadn't happened in a long time.

Suddenly, Nathan strolled in.

No one seemed to notice and Joe reminded himself they probably didn't. He stood up.

"Keeper."

"Sit, sit, m'boy. I've news for ya. Sittin' is probably better. Look up this name for me, if you please; Grigor Patrascu."

Joe was worried. As he accessed the Interpol network he remembered the warning his mother had given him long ago. When Nathan Chalk's brogue thickened, it indicated he was angry, very angry. The man used the exercise to control himself. Concentrating on the clichéd tone and phrasing helped him hold his more destructive urges in check.

Or so she had said.

"Don't worry, Joe. I'm not going to level any buildings. Watching Victor leave reminded me of how much your family means to me and to have that threatened … well, I am Human, after all."

Joe didn't know where to put himself, so he concentrated on the information on his computer screen. "Is this Grigor going to be a problem?"

Nathan laughed, a mirthless sound. "Not any more. However..."

As the other man left, Joe moved his Stone onto the phone console and called Charles Braithwaite. The little rock would ensure the conversation was private. He quickly sketched out the story Nathan had just revealed and asked Braithwaite to take whatever precautions he felt appropriate. Joe was sure to add that shutting down their operation was an option. Charles declined but assured him the necessary safety measures would be moved up a notch or two.

Joe called in one of his assistants and quickly made arrangements to return to London. It was not ideal and would draw attention, but he could not be passive if the Twelve had singled him out. Nathan had guaranteed his family's safety, as well as increased surveillance in a general sense. M'La and her apprentice would move into his home in Seville.

But a moving target was better than a static one, so back to London. His friendship with Braithwaite and Eddy's return to normalcy were things he was determined to protect.

Before he left he rang his wife and they spoke for an hour with many interruptions from his children. *"Never forget the important things"*, his mother always said, *"not even if you have to step over bodies to do it."* He wished she was here now, not merely on her way.

RASOVO
BULGARIA

The screams were becoming repetitious. The torturers must be getting lazy. Vizier turned from the balcony. The view he had been contemplating was harsh, as befitted this place in the hills behind Rasovo. Now, he must see to the herd and the milking.

As he re-entered the upper room of the ancient country house, the handful of black robed men hesitated in their ministrations. The subject of their attention lay strapped to a bizarre contraption in the center of the room. She whimpered like a wounded animal.

"You are losing her."

"Yes, Vizier," they all mumbled and returned to the process at hand. All except one; Vasily, who stood to the side of the group monitoring an array of medical equipment and taking notes. Vizier strode over to him. "Well?"

"Slow, too slow. She resists repeatedly. Three times they have had her to the threshold, but she will not go over," whispered the man.

"The Ephrin levels?" said Vizier.

SHEHKRii
– The FLAME –

"Adequate, but there is insufficient dopamine. The mixture is …"

The room was split by a shrill scream that ended sharply in a gurgling retch, "… not even sufficient for training purposes."

Vizier turned from the man. In a harsh commanding voice, he said, "Kill it and start again. Don't call me until you have a more useful donor." He swept from the room as one of the men slashed a surgical knife across the woman's throat.

The torturers stepped away from their work, some sighing with the stress of failure. Their leader spoke to one of the Seniors hovering nearby, calling for refreshments.

Vasily watched absently as the corpse was removed. Kerenski's methodology had been followed meticulously. There were no doubts. It was the test subjects who proved the stumbling block. As they had acquired more slaves the failure rate had risen.

Then there was the London report. The Lutz hit had failed: Grigor did not know how but he would rectify the failure personally. He had better.

They were expecting a fresh shipment from the slave trader, Marouk, in less than a week and Vizier would brook no problems, no delays. But Marouk was whining about the Serbs infringing on his territory. *Life was never this complicated in the old days,* bantered Vasily to his pessimistic self. Grigor he could trust, but Marouk…no. One of the newly elevated Servants was Greek. *Yes, I will send him to Athens to keep Marouk in line. Yes.*

SHEHKRii
– The FLAME –

Suddenly he stiffened as another mind joined his own.

***

Vizier reclined on the chaise, savoring the aroma of the small glass of clear liquid he held in front of his face. Such power in such a small space, he marveled. What a fool Kerenski had been to deny himself this wonder!

A neuro-accelerant, 'The Nectar' was a far more eloquent term. And it had been he, Aleksandur Danev, who had discovered it, courtesy of Valentin Kerenski. When the Russian had become a liability in his homeland, it had been a Servant of the Twelve who had swept Kerenski and his assistant away before the GRU assassins could catch him. And brought him here to Rasovo to continue his work. Test subjects were no problem and within two years they had the Nectar.

Powerful hallucinogens administered during torture carried the stressed human brain into realms of awareness undreamed of by modern science. And if the subject were killed at exactly the right moment, the residual chemicals in the brain tissue could be extracted. Kerenski, however, had little interest in the product itself. He was obsessed with the 'science'. More fool him!

Vizier sniffed the glass again, smiling thinly and then downed the contents in a single greedy quaff. The spasm that shook him passed quickly and he sat forward, focusing on the air in front of his face. His mind expanded and he saw the air move with its many rhythms, felt the heave of the Grid beneath his feet and its struggle to be free of them. With consummate satisfaction, Danev reminded himself that nothing of worth was attained without struggle.

His tolerance for the Nectar was superior to any who had tried it. But rationing was essential to maintain order. And supply. This latest of his monthly doses kept his powers sharp. They could spare no more. With the quarterly ration available to the twenty-odd Servants and even a yearly one to the more numerous Seniors, their stocks were barely enough. But with the increased supply of the new donors they would overcome these difficulties. Danev was determined to see this done.

Six years ago, his three co-rulers had perished in the ritual; their bodies sucked dry of life and liquid. And he had assumed the ultimate position. The Nectar was new to them at that time, but only he had shown serious capacity to use this glorious substitute. The narcotics they had previously relied on to access the Grid prolonged their lives but ravaged their bodies. The Nectar had no such side effects. At ninety-three, Danev felt like a youth again. And the slaves they purchased to provide the Nectar also provided an outlet for his newfound vigor. He smiled in remembrance of a hundred rapes. *What is not taken, is not earned*, echoed through his thoughts and his smile deepened.

He stood and sent his awareness out to encompass the Grid; the zone contained around three nodal points in Bulgaria, Romania, and Serbia, which made up their

SHEHKRii
– The FLAME –

empire. He felt out the minds the Twelve controlled, found the key officials that ensured their safety and the cadres of militia who were loyal to their order. A thousand years of struggle and careful planning had crystallized in him. The Sufi outcasts who had originally formed their cabal around the three nodes of power and set them on this path seemed to writhe in his collective memory and Danev let out a growl of satisfaction. He felt the Masters, the eleven other members of the Twelve acknowledge him. They were gods and he was foremost among them. Soon, they would declare themselves. Soon, they would have enough Nectar to stay permanently in contact with the Grid and a new empire would emerge in the world.

His reverie came to an abrupt end as he realized their current problems with the donors must be overcome. He sat down and focused, joining his mind to that of Vasily and together they attacked the problem of the stubborn resistance these cattle, his herd, had acquired of late.

CHAPTER 8

LONDON

"WHY SHOREDITCH?" asked Joe.

"Ah," said Braithwaite. "I could say hiding in plain sight, which is true enough but after the fact. The reality is we're within a kilometer of five major network nodes and have properties over or adjacent each of them. This place pulls all of that together."

"Ah ... but this one isn't one of the five?"

"No."

Joe had been back in London for a day and a half. He'd shown his face in a few places it would be noticed and then disappeared. The plan was to pop up every couple of days in somewhere random and in between get the real work done. He was due in Cardiff tomorrow night.

Eddy waved them over.

"Hello, Joe. I wasn't expecting you back this soon."

"Things have changed. I need to be mobile. How are things here?"

"Good, good. I have Charlie's boys almost up to speed."

Mats and Brent grinned without looking up.

Joe noticed a few changes. There was a bank of servers off to one side that pulsed and glowed with an eerie light. Beside these was a makeshift cradle with the biggest single television he'd ever seen. It was divided into twelve parts but otherwise blank white. Eddy's operational setup, Joe mused, having been in and out of her shop for several decades.

"Right! Mats, if you will, a summary, please," instructed Eddy.

Hendricksen grunted and swiveling around he slid, with tablet, over to the screen cradle and activated the set up.

"OK. We've done intensive searches on both Morvan and Patrascu. Those are ongoing but there's a little bit of anomalous data starting to surface. These guys are very well set up. None of the usual flags came up on the standard two layers of searches. Eddy's algorithms, however, did a few funny things to that data and we started to get hits. The follow ups confirmed the dodgy path."

"Examples?" asked Joe.

"OK. Starting with Morvan; he's got form going way back for low-level stuff: assault, extortion and similar, but he's been off the usual radar for almost five years. Digging deeper we found an impressive net of aliases and blind credit card accounts. Someone picked him up and gave him access to a range of services, which stepped around the organized crime monitoring systems. He fits the profile of a high-level courier. There's also indications he's been used as an enforcer but that's circumstantial at present."

Mats made some adjustments and Grigor's face filled the multi-screen.

"Patrascu, on the other hand, is an out and out thug. Lots of form in the past but clean for over seven years. Brent's been concentrating on him."

Mersey turned from his station and, also using a tablet, started splitting the screen into different views.

"Give me a mo', OK, here we go. This bloke is a nasty piece of work. Eddy's profiling system has tagged him all across Europe for the last few years, and everywhere he goes people die or get maimed. I'd like to think he's just a psycho but his patterns are too organized. Eddy, you want to do the honors on the financial angle?"

She rose and walked over to stand beside Mats. "Thank you, Brent.

"Joe. I have some reservations about all of this. We've not started from first principles and nor have we challenged our assumption that these two men are connected to the Twelve.

"Having said that, there is no doubt they are part of a very organized group, and the systems which support them are well concealed. The financial entities are many and varied, mostly small businesses, occasionally charities, all with enough vagueness in their finances to make precise tracking impossible. The only common denominator is geographical. Most of the support systems originate in Eastern Europe. Not all, but most.

"That's as much as we currently can report with confidence. There's some overarching work, which is just starting to produce patterns but we'll need more time for that."

Joe let out a breath. This confirmed quite a lot, but didn't give any new directions.

"Overarching?" he inquired.

Mats eyebrows rose briefly followed by a wry grin.

"I saw that, Mr. Hendricksen," said Eddy.

"Mats," said Braithwaite in a quiet, flat voice.

Eddy laughed softly. "Charlie, it's OK. We disagree, Mats and I. On this only, for the moment. And it's early days. To answer you, Joe, I see bits of a pattern with Patrascu. It resembles the serial killer profile. He's been targeting something but we don't know what, if at all. Do you remember the work we did in Prague all those years ago with your father? It's similar and that turned out to be selective slavery, mail order brides of sorts. I really hope I'm wrong."

"So do I, Eddy," replied Joe. "Are there any connections to the information supplied by Kalinin?"

"No," said Eddy. "Nothing to suggest Morvan or Patrascu have been anywhere near that side of things."

"OK. So, anything you need from us in the short term?"

"Well," said Brent, glancing at Braithwaite.

"Yes?"

"We need field operatives to run down a lot of the bits and pieces. Without confirmation, you know, sir … accuracy and all that."

Braithwaite snorted. "Only too well. You doing anything particular in the next few days, Herr Lutz?"

"What!" exclaimed Eddy. "Your mother will kill me if ..."

"Actually, Sir Charles, I've been a little bored lately ..."

And the two men wondered off in conversation, totally ignoring Eddy's spluttering protests. Mats and Brent studiously avoided eye contact and hunkered down over their keyboards.

"Cowards," muttered Eddy.

***

An hour later the men stood, shook hands, and Joe departed, waving to Eddy who was standing at the multi-screen watching a series of inputs flicker through some type of analysis. Braithwaite followed, stopping briefly to the side of the woman.

He placed his hand gently into the small of her back leaned in and said, "Please don't worry. I won't let anything happen to him." Then he too was gone, leaving Eddy equally concerned about both men and secretly thrilled at Charlie's touch.

***

The FSB senior analyst was nervous. One did not enter Vladimir Kalinin's domain with anything other than extreme caution. The old bear had survived more purges than anyone living, which was really the point.

Which meant in reality, he had probably killed more enemies than anyone living.

Or so the conventional wisdom went.

The secretary announced him and he entered the inner office.

"Director Kalinin, an honor. How may I assist you?"

The old man laughed, "Well said, major. I see you have a stomach, unlike many of your comrades."

"I wouldn't know about such things, Director."

"Which is why you are here, major. Your discretion has kept you alive. And will continue to do so, I trust."

"Let us hope so."

Kalinin laughed again. A little fear was useful, always. Too much and everyone just told you what you wanted to hear.

"Major, sit and tell me about Kerenski."

"Oh …"

"Indeed. The GRU failure to succeed based on your intelligence got your career path diverted …"

The major laughed, not a happy sound.

"… and brought you to the attention of people like myself who value ability over bravado. So, fear not, major."

"So you say, Director. But that maniac is one of the few truly evil people I've ever met. I am reluctant to revisit the experience."

"Even if it could mean his death?"

"You know where he is?'

"Da."

SHEHKRii
– The FLAME –

"And you can get at him?"

"With your insights ... perhaps."

The major swallowed. "Very well. What do you wish to know? My files are quite comprehensive. I assume you have read them."

Kalinin nodded, "Yes, several times. They are very much 'what, where, and when'. I want to know 'why'."

"Ah, I suspected as much. My superiors didn't feel the same way."

"No, they only wanted someone to blame. I am not them. Pour your soul out on my desk, major. If for no other reason, it will make you feel better. And even if there is nothing there that I can take advantage of, I do reward effort."

He swallowed again. "Very well. Kerenski is as close as I have seen to a pure psychopath. He also has a specialized genius level IQ in chemistry, all things biochemical in fact.

"Unfortunately, he knows and accepts this about himself and can control his urges. He channels it all into his work. Without that he would be a mass murderer."

"As I understand things, major, he has already killed dozens."

"Yes, but that was science, Director."

"Ah ... please continue."

The major nodded. "Very well. Let me see ... Yes, he was identified in his late teens as a rare talent, and the KGB recruited him to their research division. His impulses got the better of him several times but this was covered up, because his work was ground breaking. He is fascinated by pain, in others, of course."

"Of course."

"Yes, and his ability to manipulate pain response is truly extraordinary. Where scientific measurement stops, he appears to have an instinct for what can be achieved beyond those thresholds. His experiments have led to significant improvements in our interrogation techniques. Much time has been saved, for example, in breaking spies and traitors who refuse to talk.

"Also, his work has contributed to improved pain management techniques in our hospitals."

"Not that Kerenski would care, I suppose?" asked Kalinin.

"No. When told of it, he merely shrugged and changed the subject. In fact, I suspect it disappointed him based on the observations of his associates."

"Speaking of which," said Kalinin, "some of those appear intensely loyal. Gustav Medevco, for example."

"Those that attach to him share his passions."

"Ah. You seem repulsed, major."

"As you say, Director, 'what, where and when'. I have documented the excesses and their devotion to do harm is truly frightening. And disgusting."

"And yet, you persevere, major?"

"They are predators, Director. I am bound to restrain such."

"Indeed. Please go on."

"As you wish. He has no family affiliations. If there is anyone he cares for, it is unknown. He does not seem to need or pursue relationships. As long as he has work, he is satisfied. Medevco is his longest serving acolyte, assuming he is still alive."

"He is. Anything else, major?"

"I can elaborate on what I've just told you for hours, but it is only more detail. There is one thing, though.

"Yes."

"Kerenski seems to take criticism of his work badly. Challenge his results and he will argue for hours without heat. But imply there is anything morally wrong with the work and ... well, there have been incidents. No proof, though."

"I see. And what of Vasily Radu, his rescuer."

"Ah, on him we have much more information. He is a criminal, of course, but a brilliant strategist. However, he hasn't been seen for a number of years."

"He hid himself away in Romania but is still very active. Please go on, major."

"Yes, of course, Radu was, is, we're not sure, a member of the Cojocaru crime family. He is Moldovan but related to the family on his mother's side. He rose through their ranks as a young man and was considered part of the inner circle. He was not the typical thug one would expect from that ilk. He has always been adept at long-term planning and the subtler forms of coercion."

"Kidnapping and blackmail?"

SHEHKRii
– The FLAME –

"Indeed, director. He disappeared from our usual monitoring systems approximately seven years ago. We became interested in him because he facilitated Kerenski's disappearance in Ukraine. The GRU nearly had him but the attack squad was mysteriously incapacitated at the last minute."

Kalinin nodded, seemingly lost in thought. The major waited.

"Very well," said the old man at last. "Please keep my secretary apprised of your schedule. I expect we will talk more soon."

The other man rose and nodded. When he had left, the secretary entered unasked, eyebrows raised at his superior.

"Dimitri, don't be like that."

The man laughed. "I was merely curious, Vladimir. The major's presence in London just when you needed to talk to him is very convenient, no?"

"Fortunate, yes, but not unusual. This diplomatic posting is yet another punishment the poor man must suffer because of the incompetence of others. He is separated from his family deliberately. I think we will do something about that. I need people I can trust in St. Petersburg. See to it, please."

"Da, Vladimir. At once. However, I have some concerns."

"Radu?"

"Yes. He is protected. He was exposed in the original Kerenski operation but all our efforts to hunt him down since have been diverted. Our operatives in Serbia and Romania refuse to have anything to do with him. Fortunately, his interests are opaque and he hasn't caused us any problems. Which is to say, he is an unknown. I do not like unknowns."

"You are so organized, Dimitri."

Both men laughed. This was an old conversation.

"Very well. Intensively interview the major before sending him home. Set him up with a security detail and a research unit when he arrives in St. Petersburg. Use him to start an oblique investigation into Radu's zones of influence. Nothing direct. We will share that information selectively with young Johan."

"And be ready to act if opportunity presents itself?"

"Exactly. I am most concerned about the nuclear material. An opportunity to retrieve that would be a small coup, indeed."

"Yes."

Smiling, Dimitri left to start his hunt.

MONDRAGOE
BASQUE COUNTRY
SPAIN

Neil placed his hands on the stone. It was early morning and no one else was around.

He wasn't sure if it would work without Hilde present but he wanted to try without witnesses. After a few moments of nothing it went cold for several seconds and then the familiar warmth flared, rising up his arms.

He imagined the model they'd worked on yesterday and ever so slowly it oozed out of the stone.

"Concentrate, Carlisle," he murmured to himself.

For an hour, he experimented with the device, first digging down into every parameter he could think of, coming to understand the mountain region intimately. Next, he expanded the model, segment by segment until he had planet Earth in all its magnificence floating in front of his face.

For five full minutes, he collected his thoughts, layered them and prioritized until he had what he hoped was the appropriate mental image and then released it into the model.

The result snapped into place and he stepped back, away from the stone, shocked beyond any rational thought. What he had just seen terrified him.

Then he noticed the model was still there, above the stone, rotating slowly. His hands were not in contact.

"How did that happen?"

"I allowed it. And you've earned it."

The voice was soft and female and it came from everywhere. Neil's head snapped around guiltily, expecting an audience.

"It's just the two of us, Doctor. You're late, by the way. Jasmin did this last night."

"Damn. Always one step ahead."

"Always. Now. Your model is a touch off. The deep ocean current retardation is not quite as bad as you predicted."

SHEHKRii
– The FLAME –

"Who ARE you?"

"My image is right in front of you."

"Really?"

"Yes. Most refer to me as Terra. The name is not as derivative as you might think. But that's a story for another time. I believe Liam and Bartholomew have already spoken of their introduction to me."

Neil swallowed. "Yes. Introduction is barely an adequate term. You're a goddess."

"Hardly. Any explanation of me is always going to be rooted in science. Unfortunately, for you, it's a knowledge you haven't accessed yet."

"And yet, here we are."

Terra laughed, a delightful peel that made Neil smile.

"Yes, here we are. What does that tell you, Neil Carlisle?"

He frowned; yes, what did it tell him.

"Things are bad?"

"Oh yes, things are very bad. My plans, the schemes of four and a half billion years have been thwarted. You and your friends have been recruited to do something about that. It's much more complicated, of course, but in a nutshell, that's what's happening here."

"Why me? Why us?"

"My Beloved has already answered that question."

"Associates? Company on the long journey? Pardon my skepticism but I've seen so much in the last few weeks that I have to wonder why you need us at all. You have so much technological advantage …"

"Jasmin said you would be like this. Do you think I'm going to let just anyone play with my toys, Doctor? Place your hands upon me again. Get the full version. Jasmin did."

"Ha!"

He did it anyway because at heart he knew this was about intuition, not logic. And if Jaz had, well, good enough!

Half an hour later Jasmin found him laid out on the floor next to the stone. The Earth image still floated above the slab.

"Neil!" she rushed up and sat lifting his head into her lap.

"He's stubborn," she said.

"Oh, yes. His overload threshold is almost as high as yours."

Neil groaned and sat up.

"Hell's bells! That was amazing. Why do we need to talk when you can do that?"

"Burnout, you idiot," said Jaz. "Your brain must still be fried."

"And only my Beloved can endure full communion."

"So, this is not the real you," said Neil, standing up with Jaz's help.

"I am but a splinter of a much greater tree," said the stone.

"Compatibility," offered Jaz.

SHEHKRii
– The FLAME –

"Yes. We need to be able to communicate. I facet myself to my audience as needs be. Now, Doctor, you have seen the future. What do you think?"

Neil cricked his neck, shaking himself slightly. "Well, the model tells me magnetic reversal is going to happen a lot sooner than most would want. On top of which, global warming is accelerating. Things are really, really bad."

"Yet?"

"Yet … your toys! With them we can predict when and where. We can anticipate, maybe even mitigate what's about to hit us square in the face. Have I got that right?"

A soft laugh echoed from the stone. "My Beloved chose you well. You do not need to ask anymore, "Why me?" do you."

"No," said Jaz with heat. "Get over it, Neil. OK?"

"OK, OK," he said raising his hands, "I'm not as quick as you. OK already."

Jaz laughed, "Good. Now what?"

"Now," answered the stone, "we get down to business. There is a lot to do but, first you must plan."

CHAPTER 9

Neil watched Jaz leave the café and drifted his mind back to the first day they met. She'd bailed him up outside Emmanuel College to berate him about a paper he'd submitted for review. Her Masters tutor had given it to her to 'play' with, apparently.

She was livid.

He was fascinated. It was winter and they were both bundled up in heavy clothing. Her eyes shone like beacons out of the shadow of her parka hood and coffee-colored face. Eventually, what she was saying penetrated his hormone daze and he realized he'd just stumbled across someone truly important.

She ripped his paper to shreds.

And then they rewrote it together and the journey began. Her commitment to the social sciences was as strong as his to the natural ones, and they shared a bond which merged the two.

A waiter approached and offered him another cup of coffee. They chatted briefly in Basque and then the man withdrew. Neil was still stunned at the language training Hilde had forced on them.

Two hours it had taken. Two hours!

Jaz had gone first. Hilde had sat beside and opposite her and taken her face in her hands and begun to speak in the local dialect. Every few sentences Jaz had to repeat whatever Hilde said. That was all for two straight hours and then she was fluent.

SHEHKRii
– The FLAME –

Then Neil had tried. It was a fuzzy mess at first, but eventually he saw the pattern. Hilde got them to focus not on language but sound. He repeated the sounds until syntax, cadence and breath were all in synch, then she started over and somehow with the sounds right, the meanings began to follow. The last half hour was spent on vocabulary.

If someone could bottle the methodology they'd make millions.

The headaches started a few hours later, but Hilde helped with that too and they were right within another hour.

Now, Jaz disappeared from view and he felt a little trip in his stomach.

Damn, I'm a kid again. He wasn't sure what to do about Jaz. They'd known each other for nearly twenty years and the attraction had never waned. But he'd put that on the shelf that first day back in Cambridge; you don't fuck your colleagues! Or at least you didn't if you were Neil Carlisle.

Now, though, things were so different in so many ways. Not just the crazy adventure they were on, but the fundamentals of the team he had relied on for the last decade. Liam and Bart were in contact every few days but he missed them both. He watched them grow over that time and knew them as friends and almost family. They'd been his rock when his marriage had dissolved and he wasn't entirely sure if he would still be alive if they hadn't been around. Jaz had quite rightly kept her distance at the time and they'd avoided the sympathy trap.

He still couldn't credit having made the marriage at all. Especially since his ex-wife had managed to drain the trust fund left by his parents.

He stopped himself. Old news and the bitterness it stirred up were pointless. What to do about Jaz?

He had to take her to the Library. It was long overdue. She'd yell at him for keeping it secret but that was only fair. She'd trusted him with her secrets and he'd not shared his. Time to fix things on that score, at least.

***

Jaz entered the studio and looked around, a huge smile in place. This was magnificent, she felt truly at home here.

Which was seriously weird since she absolutely shouldn't! Now that she could speak the language, what a buzz that was, the locals were all asking where she came from and who her family was.

Her old cover story came in real handy. But it was an inclusive curiosity and she made an effort to participate. They were shocked she didn't have children, though.

It was a question, which had never come up. She had made the decision long ago: no family. And besides, since she'd met Neil she knew she was on a crusade, and despite her history, family responsibility was always going to get in the way.

SHEHKRii
– The FLAME –

Maybe she would regret it all when she was old and frail, but right now, there was just too much fun to be had.

Starting with this place.

The building was old; all brick, plaster and heavy timbers but punched through with new openings and raised platforms, glass partitions and exposed ductwork.

The Stone was still there and she smiled again.

Terra, it called itself. Wow!

You're not in Kansas anymore, Dorothy.

Not that she cared. "Take it as it comes" had been her motto since she ran away from home, and it had served her well.

And Neil was on the verge of finally being happy despite the ever-present vein of cynicism, which he used as a defense mechanism, really. He wanted to embrace everything that was happening but couldn't shake the suspicion it would all be taken away.

Not that she blamed him; so much had been taken from Neil Carlisle.

First his family. Mother, father, brother and the brother's family, all wiped out in a plane crash.

Then the bitch of a wife, Peggy Mantell. The social butterfly had swooped in, charmed him naked then, with the family lawyers had taken his trust fund, the last reminder of how much his own family cared. Neil wasn't super wealthy, but his parents had left him with a good living wage out of a sizeable trust. At least he'd had sense enough to split off a small portion so the research could keep going. She'd been quite annoyed about that, the conniving Peggy had.

And then Brony. Jaz had never taken to her but certainly hadn't seen the deception coming. They'd worked well enough together to get along. She had, however, seen Brony maneuvering to get into Neil's pants. He, of course, didn't have a clue, nor did the other boys.

Maybe it was a girl-thing, Jaz surmised. She had been ready to have words with the other woman when their funding at Plymouth had been pulled. And Hilde had shown up.

And all the rest.

She shook herself. Nostalgia wasn't usually her thing but they'd all been upended in a major way and it was, she supposed, a way to cope.

Fuck it! I need a good shag, that usually fixes things.

But she hesitated. There were plenty of good-looking men in town and casual sex was not a problem, but … She really wanted to sort things out with Neil. Her libido could wait.

That thought prompted a wondering. What was Brony up to? Probably still in rehab. Now there was a woman whose libido had a firm grip on her short and curlies; a masochistic nymphomaniac, if there was such a thing! She was a mess.

Jaz glanced around again. What had she come up here for anyway? Spying the laptop on a nearby desk she walked over and sat down, placing her hand on the black dome nearby. The 'toys' Terra referred to were pure joy.

SHEHKRii
– The FLAME –

She concentrated and the computer sprang to life and opened the file she had mentally visualized. Neil's presentation appeared on the screen. Hilde said Jaz would be elsewhere but she so wanted to be there when he gave this speech. It summed up so many things; all the diverse circumstances, which had brought the four of them together.

Neil had come through the Earth sciences, determined to expand the human database, as he called it. Liam was into weather and using his amazing computing skills to better predict and protect. And poor old Bart, the failed geologist. Or so he said. Four years drilling for oil for a multinational had turned him into a dedicated conservationist and brought him into Neil's orbit.

She was the odd one out, of course.

Sociology and political science were her passions. She ached to know why people hated so much. And by inversion, how to stop it. The happiest peoples she had ever encountered were almost always those involved in low-tech community projects. Hippies, greenies, disaster rehabilitation professionals. Neil's long-ago paper on bringing local communities onboard as scientific observers had caught her eye immediately, but it was so badly written and so ... fucking high-handed in attitude ... she nearly had a meltdown after the first chapter.

So, she'd hunted him down and torn strips off him in the middle of some street in the middle of Cambridge.

He was so attentive. And he didn't get his back up at all. She'd never encountered anyone like it before.

And that was that. She had to work for him.

Now, it all came together in this speech. But it was a draft and needed work. She focused and lost herself in the flow of ideas trying to figure out how to make them hit home in the best possible way.

***

Hilde ran.

It was her way of relaxing so she could think quietly, alone.

Broken field running, some called it. Here in the mountains it was more like broken rock running.

She loved it.

Her life four months ago was rather sedate. She was established in Sydney, Australia, and had set up her daughter to study at an arts-based college near their home in Glebe. Hilde helped with any of Paul Gareth's projects in the great southern land or throughout South East Asia. It was erratic at times but not all that demanding and allowed mother and daughter an important growing period. Although lately, Hilde had come to the pleasant conclusion that her daughter, Astrid had achieved a level of self-reliance, which didn't require much attention from her mother. The girl was a treasure. And her father was easily able to visit several times a year so things had become very domestic.

Hilde reached a dry wash strewn with large roughhewn blocks of granite the size of small cars.

SHEHKRii
– The FLAME –

Without breaking pace, she bounced from one to the other seeming to float down the gully.

Nathan must have known she was getting bored because he pulled her out of all that and dropped her into sooty London to shepherd Dr. Carlisle and his little team. A change is as good as a holiday, he had said.

He was right, of course. She looked forward to returning to her daughter's life on a regular basis but helping these people had invigorated her. They were on the edge of so much, swamped with information and new concepts, yet they kept on trying to adapt and do better. It seemed like a small victory, just four people, but … so much hinged on what they did in the next few decades.

It felt good to make this particular contribution.

She wondered how long it would take Neil and Jaz to 'get together,' as the English called it. Their attraction and more importantly, the respect they shared was obvious. That they had never pursued a sexual relationship seemed very odd to someone raised in Sweden. Especially someone who could see emotion as easily as any color. Bad timing, perhaps. She expected things between them would work out soon. They were much more relaxed around each other than a month ago.

Reaching the bottom of the gully she turned left on a small dirt road and headed back to the town at what most people would consider a flat-out sprint. Hilde was yet to raise a sweat. She waved to the few farmers who were out and about. Most of them were used to her excursions and waved back.

Liam was due in Mandragoe soon to start his computer training and establish a working group. She was keen to participate in that process, but had to get Jaz and Neil to Spain and Scotland respectively in the next few days.

Delegate.

Yes, that was the word! Peter and Sophia were already in that part of the world. She'd ask them to help out and remain here in the mountains a little longer. The air was so sweet and she hadn't enjoyed running this much in years.

Yes, she would delegate.

TILBURY, U.K.

"Remind me why we're here," said Charles Braithwaite as he pulled his coat closer and shivered.

"Patrascu has been here four times in the last two years."

"I hate the cold."

Joe looked pointedly at Charles who grinned back. "Reminds me of my undercover days. They were hard, hard times."

"I can only imagine."

They waited behind a row of forklifts as the last of the storehouse workers completed their sign out procedures and locked the tall gates to the compound. Security was due on site in forty minutes, but Braithwaite's earbud would warn him if that changed. Brent was monitoring all relevant systems.

SHEHKRii
– The FLAME –

They waited another five minutes before moving to the office door.

"Shit!" said Braithwaite under his breath.

"What?"

"This is a biometric security system. Serious stuff. My usual tools won't get us in. Damn! I wonder why they have this ..."

Joe touched the throat mike he wore. Charles had insisted they both be 'kitted' up, so they had earbuds, throat mikes, clip cameras and light body armor.

"Mr. Mersey," said Joe. "Is there anything you can do with this?" Joe angled his camera at the lock panel.

"Sorry, Joe, no. Not without a couple of hours of research. We don't know whose parameters are programmed in."

Braithwaite shrugged and turned away. "We'll have to work out a different angle."

"Maybe not," said Joe as he fished out his Stone and placed it on the panel. He concentrated on an empty, open feeling, not trying for specific instructions just a general sense of release.

Braithwaite watched, fascinated.

***

Peter Tan and Sophia Theophoulous watched from half a kilometer away, crouched on top of a stack of shipping containers.

SHEHKRii
– The FLAME –

"Good thinking, Joe, very good," murmured Peter. Sophia smiled briefly. "Did you expect anything less?"

"He's never tried that sort of thing before. Always a gifted improviser, is our Johan."

"M'La does tend to bring that out in everyone ..."

"Oh yes."

Peter stood suddenly. "Did you hear that?"

"Five o'clock, two hundred meters?"

"Yes. Voices and a scuffle. Let's see ..."

Peter's eyes unfocused and his right hand rose up slightly. After a few seconds, he turned to Sophia and said, "Local gang, out to see what they can lift. Do you mind?"

Sophia grinned. "No, I need the exercise." She took two quick, skipping steps and launched herself over to the next stack of containers. Peter returned to his observation of Joe and Charles.

***

The door clicked open.

Charles raised his eyebrows.

Joe shrugged and entered the office.

"We have to talk about that, Herr Lutz."

"Maybe. For the moment, however ..."

Charles nodded and turned to the office proper. *Hardcopy or computers,* he mused. Touching his throat mic, he said, "Brent, I'm placing your Infiltrator now. Quick as you can, please."

"Yes, sir."

SHEHKRii
– The FLAME –

He put a small box next to the office server and pressed a switch. "Right, Joe, let's skim the paper files while Brent works. That should take about five minutes. I don't expect to find much in the stacks but you never know."

Joe nodded and they each set to work, quietly rifling through the office.

Three minutes later one of the office computers sprang to life. "We're in, Sir Charles," observed Brent Mersey. Both men clustered around the screen.

"Running the search program now," said Brent, almost as though speaking to himself, "… nothing, nothing … hit! There's those dates … Yes! Sir Charles, I'm scooping up everything attached to those transactions. We've also inserted a clone program, which will copy the server and local drives and any off-site backups and give us all future activity. The Infiltrator needs another fifty seconds then you can leave. Their security is on its way a bit early. You've got ten minutes, maximum."

"Thanks, Brent."

They returned to the files until a soft ping sounded. Charles scooped up the little box and Joe closed the last cabinet returning the office to a tidy state.

Closing the outer door softly, Charles said, "Hope that was worth it."

"Yes. We should know soon." Pulling his coat closer he added, "It is a bit cold, isn't it? I'll be glad to get warm."

Charles chuckled. "This is mild really. You should try …"

SHEHKRii
– The FLAME –

***

Sophia landed silently on the stack directly above the gang of six young men, who had now stopped and were arguing about whether to keep trying to find unlocked containers or mug the first person they met. Joe and Charles were angling away to the south, but could easily fall fowl of these amateurs.

She stepped off the stack and dropped down behind them, landing with only a slight bending of the knees. Several of the men saw her appear and drew breath to shout. Sophia stepped forward and pushed the nearest two into the group. Most of them fell like skittles, the others were gaping.

She slapped the closest who cartwheeled in place then skipped over to the next. A tap to the solar plexus doubled him up like a gymnast and she nudged him with her hip to place him against the nearby container. Several of the fallen were getting up, so she simply walked forward quickly and swatted them just above their respective ears and soon the whole group were unconscious. She turned one over so he wouldn't dislocate his shoulder.

With a glance and a sigh, she leapt straight up to the top of the stack and headed towards Peter who was on the move tracking their friends.

***

SHEHKRii
– The FLAME –

The loud group had spilled out of the pub with no warning. Four grumpy, angry drunks! Straight into the path Joe and Charles were beating back to their car.

"Wotcha lookin' at, mate?" slurred the nearest man as Joe pulled up short. He squared his shoulders, spilling what was left of a dark ale.

In the blink of an eye, Joe hit him in the nose with a left hook that came snapping up from his hip and wrapped his hands around the man's head to prevent him falling back. He dragged the man forward and kneed him viciously in the groin. Maintaining a grip, he stepped slightly to the left and pushed him behind.

"Incoming," he said quietly to Charles without looking. There was a soft thud heard behind him.

"Step back, Joe," said Charles in a quiet, deadly voice.

The remaining men were just starting to react as Sir Charles Braithwaite appeared from behind their mate and his attacker and removed a silver gun with an obvious silencer from his jacket and held it across his chest, ready.

"Hard times, friends, 'ard times," he said in a deeply Irish accent. "Wouldn't want 'em to get any 'arder, would we now."

The men began to back up and out onto the road. Joe and Charles walked away, careful to keep an eye on the group, who were now attending to their friend.

Touching his mike, Joe said quietly, "Brent, get an ambulance to the Oak and Barrel on Dock Road, please."

SHEHKRii
– The FLAME –

"That was quick-thinking back there, Joe. A little savage but well done."

"He was about to glass me. I could read him easily. Drunks are so predictable."

"Where did you learn to box? That was one of the best left hooks I've ever seen."

Joe laughed softly. "I'm not much of a fighter. I've no aptitude really. And no motivation. But I did have a good teacher."

***

A hundred meters behind and a block over Sophia gave Peter a soft elbow in the arm.

Peter smiled. He had been Joe's teacher when the boy was ten years old, imparting at least basic self-defense skills in a youngster already deeply committed to non-violence. While Joe considered himself inept by comparison to his teacher or his mother, he was in fact Olympic standard, although he rarely used the skills.

Where he excelled, however, was in reading physical intent and of that in particular, Peter Tan was very proud.

CHAPTER 10

SHOREDITCH
LONDON

EDDY WAS IN EARLY. SHE'D TAKEN half of the previous day off to rest, after two double shifts in a row. Brent and Mats were due mid-morning following similar efforts over the last week. They were close to something big and she wanted some time to herself for reflection. She should be dog-tired but there was an energy about what they were doing, which she hadn't felt in a long, long time.

And then there was Charlie.

She still couldn't credit how she felt, how she had reacted. Flirting at her age!

But it was more than that. When they'd first met it was like a switch being flipped. She knew him by reputation, of course, but the reality was exhilarating. Everything she'd loved in Alastair but with sharper edges; a more dangerous combination with some of her own fierce patriotism. She'd heard Joe remark about the 'old' Eddy being back and it rang true in ways which made her angry at the two years she had spent mired in self-pity. Alastair would not have stood for it.

So ... let's see where this thing with Charlie went.

In the meantime, there was a mystery to be unraveled. She set up her split screen display and ran a custom program, which flashed all of their previous work around in a series of rhythmic patterns. She let the data-dance take over and immersed her subconscious in the display, losing track of time as the program slipped into an endless loop.

***

Brent found her at her desk several hours later, furiously scribbling notes and bubble diagrams.

"That looks interesting!"

"Possibly. Where is everyone, please, Brent?"

"Ah, Mats is right behind me and Sir Charles and Joe are due in a couple of hours. Why?"

"Good. That should be enough time. Take this and get cracking."

She handed him a sheaf of paper, which he took and started scanning.

Then mumbling, "Why didn't we …"

Mats arrived and Eddy silently held up another handful of paper, which he also took while glancing at them both. Eddy kept scribbling.

Mats also started mumbling to himself as he sat down and activated his workstation. Brent was already typing furiously.

***

Joe arrived first and was ignored for a full five minutes as the other three concluded an animated discussion about things which Joe knew he'd never understand.

SHEHKRii
– The FLAME –

Eddy finally glanced at him and her radiant smile was worth the wait. Charles walked into that and was a little nonplussed.

"What did I miss?" he said cautiously.

"Smugglers!" exclaimed Brent. "Fucking good ones. Sorry, Eddy."

"Don't be," she answered, "I agree."

Looking at Joe and Charles, she said, "Grab a seat, gentlemen, and prepare to be amazed. We finally have something concrete."

Joe and Charles retrieved chairs and rolled them over to the multi-screen.

"Right," said Eddy, "there are caveats, the usual ones about statistical accuracy, *et cetera*. And while we have Tilbury's server *en masse* we only have general access to the data of the other organizations connected to it. But we have a verifiable history and a behavioral profile."

The screen had rearranged itself, directed by Eddy's tablet. She stood behind the two senior men as they scanned the display, trying to follow the now-slowing cascade of information.

"Seven years ago, an organizational genius named Vasily Radu began infiltrating a certain type of business in Eastern Europe. Radu came from a militia based in Moldova but has a very low profile. Specifically, his focus has been transport businesses, which had contacts or contracts in the West, usually family run with solid finances and hardworking, intelligent people who built up profitable enterprises.

SHEHKRii
– The FLAME –

"Radu would kidnap a family member and leverage his own people into the business then set up a special department, which modified trucks and containers so they could move a lot of small things anywhere they wanted."

"Law of averages?" asked Charles.

"Yes," said Mats, "this is where the genius of it comes in. They must have had data on every route used because the dodgy goods only moved at times of lowest risk. That was the only priority. Plus, the anti-detection measures. These guys could teach our customs people a thing or two."

Charles glanced at Eddy who nodded gravely.

"Anyway," she continued, "the bulk of the movement seems to have been inward, from the West to the East. We have records of narcotics, arms and ammunition, electronic and industrial equipment and medical supplies. Increasingly that last has ramped up by three hundred percent."

"How long?" asked Joe.

"Eighteen months," answered Eddy.

There was a long silence as Charles and Joe absorbed the information. Charles asked a number of logistical questions and then fell silent again.

"So," interrupted Mats, "we have a small, tight organization with established and stable lines of supply. Two years ago, however, things changed, eh, Eddy."

She grinned. The two young men Charles had supplied her with were pure gold. It had only taken them a few days to adapt to her working methods and now the three of them were a potent unit. It had been a long time since she'd worked this way and the thrill of it was something she'd decided not to give up. MI6 was probably never going to come around so if she didn't screw things up with Charlie … maybe.

"Yes. They've been expanding their profile in the medical technology area; integrating the high-tech transport businesses they already controlled with specialist cytotoxic and cryo-isolation services.

"Joe, they have access to lead shielded containers ..."

"Oh crap ..."

"Indeed. The really interesting thing is the people, however."

Charles glanced around at her again and grinned. This was something he was passionate about and had regaled her with on several occasions. 'Follow the money and know the people' was a mantra for every serious investigator, but so few of them were really good at it. Eddy was one of those and he'd expressed a gratifying appreciation of things she had never been able to convince MI6's senior analysts of.

She returned his smile with a little flutter in her stomach. *I have to get this man into my bed soon,* she mused, *before the chance is gone.* That thought must have shown because Charlie, bless him, blushed and turned away.

Eddy cleared her throat and continued, "Two years ago Radu sent Grigor Patrascu to Bradford to smooth out a few bumps relating to a business they'd bought into, west of the town. It's a specialist funereal service that repatriates deceased émigrés to their country of origin. It's mostly Islamic but they also help Chinese families. They specialize in traditional burial services for cancer victims. The business doubled its capacity in the first year after Patrascu's visit."

"Who'd he kill?" asked Joe.

"Several family members of local government inspectors. Looked like accidents, of course."

Joe grunted.

"The assistant manager of this firm is the cousin of the operations director of a company in Zagreb, which was one of the first Radu infiltrated. It facilitates transport to the Middle East of sealed caskets from all over Europe, including the UK. The Bradford business is something of a local institution. It's got very strong community ties and has been a voice of moderation for a decade. The local M.P. is a patron and the Immigration Minister's photo is on their reception wall.

"Now," said Eddy, "this is where it gets really evil. Associated with the funeral and medical businesses is a group of charities which make random donations. These include scholarships to get disadvantaged youth into employment, refugee assistance programs and random donations for traditional funerals. From the data we have, many of those last coincide with smuggling runs. There's identity fraud involved and outright substitution; all of it very smoothly handled. No one could have even suspected this without the encrypted information you retrieved from the Tilbury server. That appears to have been some sort of regional hub.

"And that's about it, gentlemen."

Charles stood and paced. Speaking to Joe, he said, "Imagine messing with the people who get your granny buried in the old country. You'd have everyone against you. It's brilliant cover. How are we going to get an undetected foot inside that place given they've almost certainly got security as good or better than we found at Tilbury?"

"I might know someone," answered Joe. "He speaks the language, all of the Aramaic languages actually, and has a track record with Islamic communities. Can charm the birds from their trees, according to my mother. Name's Zarre, Bijan Zarre."

Eddy giggled then stopped, "Sorry. I've met the 'Prince of Persia'. Charming doesn't even get close."

"When?" inquired Joe, surprised.

"Long ago. Ten years maybe. Victor introduced him to Alastair, and we all had dinner in Rome one beautiful summer's night. The waitresses were fighting over him."

Joe laughed. "That's Bee all right."

Charles stood once more and faced them all, a frown creasing his face. "So, am I correct in summarizing that Zagreb is the transport nexus. Anything this organization wants goes to Bradford or one of their similar firms in … where, Bonn, Rotterdam or Lyon, and is packaged in shielded containers then trucked to Croatia, which is the only European country that allows air transport of this type of cargo. Croatia, which is conveniently close to Romania?"

"Correct, Sir Charles," said Brent, "but consider the reverse. What happens to those specialized containers, the coffins and *medivac* canisters once they've done their job? They go through decontamination and are returned to source ..."

"Jesus H Christ ..."

"Exactly! Two-way traffic, all signed off," exclaimed Mats. "Radu is a piece of work in all the right ways. And six months ago, they expanded into the US. There are supervised trials underway as we speak."

"Damn!" said Joe, letting out a long breath. The others all looked at him.

"Even with my Interpol contacts and Sir Charles's influence, it would take us months to get any action on this information. And that's optimistic. No one will want to believe Vladimir Kalinin's information about the nuclear material. They'll procrastinate forever."

"Which brings us back to the original concern, Andre Morvan's 'herd'," interjected Eddy.

"How so>" asked Charles.

Eddy glanced at her tablet. "We found this in Bradford."

The screen showed a single page of text, ostensibly an instruction from the funeral company's HR department seeking new employees. Particular emphasis was placed on the psychological 'attributes'.

SHEHKRii
– The FLAME –

"This," said Eddy, "is a serial killer's wish list. It's what I spoke to you about before, Joe. Patrascu and others presumably are hunting a certain 'type' for their herd. Youngish immigrants mostly. Children who've assimilated into western society but still have strong family connections; high achievers with something to prove.

"You know the sort, Charlie. The intelligence services recruit from here for their information analysts. They're too fragile to be field agents but they make for great commentators, they see different angles." She glanced reflexively at Mats who grinned back.

"Why?" asked Joe.

"Second last paragraph, third and fourth sentences," answered Mats. "It's true enough."

Joe read out loud, "...under extreme stress these individuals will shatter psychologically but not break, leaving a functioning personality but with profound neurological changes. They should not be subjected to undue 'responsibility' ahead of time.

"Why is responsibility emphasized?"

Charles snorted, "It's code for handle with care; sedate and transport."

Joe's face darkened as the implications sank in. "Kerenski," he muttered.

"We need to get inside Bradford," said Eddy. "Soon."

"Agreed. Joe, when can your friend Bijan get here?"

"I'll start making calls." He rose and walked to a quiet corner of the loft.

SHEHKRii
– The FLAME –

"We'll organize hardcopy and summaries, Sir Charles," said Brent. Charles nodded and walked over to face Eddy.

Quietly, he said, "Despite all of this and what comes next, you and I need to have a talk." His tone was neutral but ever so slightly expectant.

Eddy looked deeply into his eyes and breathed, "When?"

***

Two hours later only Mats and Brent were left at the loft.

"That was interesting!"

"Oh yeah," replied Brent. "Hope it works out. Sir Charles could do with somebody solid."

"Really?"

"Yeah. He's been divorced for nearly a decade but the bitch of an ex-wife is still causing trouble. Tried to turn his sons against him; just can't let go. She's a lawyer!"

"I'm a lawyer. Well, graduate actually, and it sounds like you've been reading files you shouldn't have access to."

"Would I do that! No, I just listen; especially when the higher-ups are gossiping."

"Ah … What about Eddy. You think she's up to it. She's a year older than him, you know."

"Doesn't look it. Neither of them look their age, do they? Now who's been reading files they shouldn't."

Mats snorted a short laugh. "Hope it doesn't mess up the work thing. Christ, I've had a good time this last week."

"Oh yeah … cross your fingers."

NEW BERN
NORTH CAROLINA
U.S.A.

The view was extraordinary. Bart Smith couldn't get enough of it. He didn't study rivers as a rule and was used to being up mountains or down ravines.

Out in the middle of the Neuse River, so far from shore … it was intoxicating.

The man standing beside him had done it for most of his sixty-plus years.

"Look sharp there, Mr. Smith," he said. "You're starin' off into space again instead of watching your screen."

Bart laughed. Try as he might he could not get Will Abrams to call him by his first name. And he was easily distracted.

He glanced at the tablet in the crook of his arm. "We're on course, Will. No worries. This thing almost flies itself once you set the right parameters."

"Don't tell that to the boy, now. He wants to have a go at the damn thing."

Bart turned and looked aft. Will's third grandchild, ten-year-old Bradley, was standing in the stern of the boat, one hand locked on the guardrail and his head angled up, mesmerized by the thistle drone Bart was using.

Maybe, he thought. It couldn't hurt and the drone had pre-sets, which made it almost impossible to crash.

The tablet pinged.

"We're in the track," said Bart, excited.

"*Rightoh*, then," answered Will. Raising his voice, he said, "Sarge, get ready."

"On point, Skip," answered Tom Parsons, the first mate. He turned from the wheel and watched the drone as it moved forward and slightly to the left of the fifty-four foot Bertram, which Will used for charters. Bradley dashed from stern to bow following the drone. As Tom trimmed his course, Bart glanced back at Bradley who had joined their other passenger at the bow.

She was tiny, virtually the same height as the boy. Her name was Thuy Pham and Hilde had assigned her to guard the group. She said almost nothing and went where she wanted, so sure footed on the big boat you'd think she had suction cups on her shoes. Tom Parsons was scared of her, which was saying something.

Will and Tom were veterans of the war in Vietnam, two very competent old soldiers. Tom had been Will's platoon sergeant and spoke fluent southern Kinh. He had married a Saigon woman named Nhung so when Thuy showed up, there had been extended introductions and much formality. Will was sure Thuy's accent was Australian.

Later, Tom confided in them his wife called the other woman 'shadow dancer', an epithet, which translated to 'assassin'. They were all a little cautious after that.

But Thuy had taken Bradley under her wing and tended to always be nearby when the boy was doing anything remotely dangerous. Will had noticed and approved and if the Skip was happy then it was OK.

Bart turned back to his tablet. It had taken three days to survey the river from New Bern to Pamlico Sound and prepare the flow profile he had been sent to find. Now they were in the sweet spot, the zone of maximum subsurface power. He stowed the tablet and went to the rear of the boat. Lifting an array of tinkling metal cans attached to a long rod, he gently placed the rig over the side and let it sink, holding onto a long lead with a claw anchor and another with a buoy and signal flag. Once the anchor lead was fully extended he dropped it and the buoy and returned to his tablet.

Will stepped over to look.

"How long?"

"A minute, maybe less. It stabilizes quickly. Ah ... there we go!"

Bart tapped a few times to get his screen rearranged.

"Oh my ..."

"Good?" asked Will.

SHEHKRii
– The FLAME –

"Very. Power output is at maximum calculated value. If that stays within fifteen percent for twenty-four hours, then we have a project."

"You sound relieved. Did you have doubts?"

Bart sighed. "Yes, many. All our tech is new. You have to assume something is always going to go wrong."

"Equipment is a bitch."

The tablet pinged again and Bradley let out a cry as the drone swooped down to the rear of the boat and hovered a few meters away from Bart, its job done. The boy followed almost as quickly, his face expectant.

Bart grinned, called up the control screen and handed it to him. He turned slightly and Thuy was there; close. Bart started a little then smiled and nodded, stepping around the small woman who moved next to the boy.

***

As they were leaving the dock, Thuy noticed Bart glance at his tablet; an email had arrived.

The young man scanned the screen and then seemed to miss a step. Thuy made a subtle signal and handed off her shadowing of Bradley to another member of her team and waited.

Bart bent over his tablet a little closer and then wandered to an unoccupied part of the dock, lost in thought.

Thuy followed and watched his mind churn. He was alternately troubled and ecstatic.

SHEHKRii
– The FLAME –

"Good news?" she said, close to him.

Bart twitched and almost dropped the tablet. Laughing slightly, he said, "Don't do that!"

Thuy smiled. "You seem troubled, Mr. Smith. I'd like to help."

"Bart, please. One 'Mr. Smith'-sayer is enough. Troubled is the wrong word; overwhelmed is probably better." Holding up the tablet, he asked, "Do you know about the message I just received?"

"No."

"It's from Liam. Something we've been working on for a very long time is about to go public … I never thought I'd see that. And, well … it's all a bit emotional."

"Planetary Management Theory," said Thuy.

Bart turned and looked at her. "You know about that?"

Thuy laughed, an almost girlish sound. "Bart, I live it, every single hour of every single day since my Return. And you have bathed in its waters at the Biopulse, Chartres. Why are you so reluctant to accept what is obvious?"

He looked at her again, head tilted.

"I'm a scientist. I can't be anything else. Taking things on faith is just not right."

"You have a wealth of empirical data."

"Yes and PMT will pull all that into a cohesive whole. But what lies underneath all that. Terra and you and Hilde. And Nathan, especially him. It all seems like fantasy."

"And you worry that the otherworldly aspects will undercut the science?"

"Yes."

Thuy grinned. "I have a niece who is all logic and rigorous argument. She's a terrier. Yet she shapes the most delicious puzzles out of endless numbers and takes immense joy in the art of doing so. You are a geologist, are you not?"

Bart nodded.

"At the center of the Earth, geologists speculate there is a super dense core of metal, which spins in a sea of molten rock generating our magnetic field, one sufficient to repel the Sun's radiation. It's so strong that at the ionosphere it generates electrical storms which could fry a city, no?"

"Yes. It drives the weather and therefore life; so?"

Thuy laughed again. "That magnetic field vibrates at frequencies which modern science has yet to produce instruments capable of measuring. Frequencies within frequencies, layers within layers; from the center of the Earth to its outer atmosphere and beyond. And it has done so for billions of years. A vast, stable network of oscillating energies, which control a biosphere, the rarest of stellar entities …"

Bart's mouth hung open. He closed it as Thuy stopped talking.

"A living planetary mind …" he breathed.

SHEHKRii
– The FLAME –

"After Chartres," he said, "I had a vague idea that She, Terra was infused throughout the land and water. And air. A construct of the leys. But … the whole planet?"

"Science, Bart, science. The planet lives because physics works. Our explanations of it are still infantile but also, still valid. We just have a lot of catching up to do."

"We can't put this into the Theory. There's no proof."

"Not yet. But one will lead to the other as instrumentation develops. You'll live to see that."

"Will I?"

"Indeed, you will. For the moment, however, we have a community at hand to foster and build."

She gestured towards Will Abrams who was patiently waiting at his pick-up to give them a lift back to town.

Bart smiled and started to walk. "I need to talk to Liam. He's the gadget man. Maybe we can come up with those instruments a little early."

"Maybe."

***

The next day there was a meeting at Nhung's café. She had what she called a tasting-room, an alcove at the rear where she kept and served exotic teas. Bart had been thrilled when he found the place. He nursed a cup of his favorite, Iron Goddess of Mercy, and called the meeting to order. There were five people present.

Thuy hovered nearby in the shop proper.

SHEHKRii
– The FLAME –

"These numbers are extraordinary," said Morris van Grinsven.

"Seven percent above your best *specs*," said Bart.

"Yes. And with no operational stress; it's all because of the location, you say?"

"Yep. Will is going to monitor for the next three months, but there's no reason to believe the variances will be anything other than minimal. And that's based on your current test data, not ours, so …."

Morris scratched the side of his cheek.

"This puts us years ahead of our current program. I'm stunned."

Bart laughed, as did the others.

"Nice to get one up on private enterprise," said Captain Jimenez, from the nearby Marine base.

"Ha," answered Morris, "do you still want the power feed or not?'

"Now, now gents," said Will, "we're past this, aren't we?"

Both men grinned. The banter had always been friendly.

"I still don't get that part," said Peter Sholten, the local business representative and Will's friend.

"The base is laying the cable and taking the feed, but it's supposedly not a government project. Can't some jerk in Washington just step in and take all this away?"

"No," said the Jimenez, "Morris's company has the patent on this type of piscine turbine and is leasing Marine Corps facilities as part of a Department of Energy co-share program. The Federal Government gets rental revenue and licensing options while maintaining oversight. The *tech* itself and the research data are always property of the company. If this works ... the cost savings are massive. Department of Defense is very interested. They're looking at shaving up to ten percent off their bottom line."

"Only ten ..."

"Defenses' budget is in the trillions."

"Oh ..."

Bart cleared his throat. "And once the test data confirms the viability, New Bern has the option along with Cherry Point Marine Base to set itself up as completely self-sufficient. The power supply will even work during hurricanes. For that alone ..."

"Oh yeah," said Peter and Will together. They had both lost property and more to the seasonal devastation that plagued the Carolinas.

Morris had been running some calculations on his laptop and said, "Oh!"

"What?"

"Ah, if this is right, we can start that program in less than two years."

"Holy mother of ..."

"Hang on, hang on," said Sholten, "I still don't get how this can happen so fast. I'm not against it, mind."

Van Grinsven swiveled his laptop, so the other man could see the screen. A timeline was showing.

"We and our U.K. parent company have been intensively trying to commercialize this technology for nearly a decade. Renewables are clearly the only option for long-term power."

"But …"

"It's not easy. No one's willing to cut us the slack needed for R&D. Not without buying out the whole package. The military don't have as corporate an attitude as others."

Jimenez laughed.

"And Bart's company has the investment structure we need. That, combined with the DOD option, lets us very quickly iron out the bugs in the *tech*, establish statistical performance and document a test project. Bottom line is, we can get to first base in just a few years and then license the system. That's where the effort literally pays off."

"But it's not one size fits all, is it …"

The discussions rambled on for another half hour, all the participants trying not to get too far ahead of themselves, but the enthusiasm was intoxicating. Nhung served tea and coffee in the main shop once the meeting had broken up, and Bart was left alone at the table sipping the last of his brew.

Thuy brought in a delicate teapot and refreshed his cup and served herself one.

"That went well," she said.

"Totally," answered Bart with a boyish grin. "And once we get that out of the way, the real work can begin."

Thuy smiled, which transformed her face into a thing of joy; Bart caught himself staring openly.

"Nhung says you're dangerous."

"She's right."

"Given that you're Hilde's friend I shouldn't be surprised but you're ... so small!"

Thuy grinned and put a small throwing knife into the table a centimeter from Bart's hand. He hadn't seen her move.

"Oh ... sorry."

Thuy laughed and retrieved the knife, which disappeared up her sleeve. She wandered back into the shop.

***

Tom Parsons was teaching Bradley how to rig the shade canopy for the charter boat and Will was watching from the dock. Thuy joined him.

"Miss Pham."

"Captain. I have a favor to ask."

"Ask away, ma'am. No promises though."

"Fair enough. Do you see that red post over there near the fuel bowser?"

"Yes, ma'am."

Thuy drew and threw her knife in little more than a shrug and the blade struck the post at eye height with a soft *thwack*. The post was fifteen meters away.

"Whoa ..."

There was a small popping noise and Thuy was gone and then back in several heartbeats, her knife in hand.

Will's eyes were very wide.

SHEHKRii
– The FLAME –

"Bradley has it in him to do that. And much more. I'd like to help him on the Path, which leads to that future. But only if you're agreeable. His father is gone and you are both grandfather and father, are you not?"

Will swallowed, "Yes. Lost the boy's dad six year ago in a big blow. Nearly killed my girl, Lucy. But she's tough. Made it through the bad time … Can he really do that?"

"Yes."

"What's the price?"

Thuy smiled, "Joy beyond your imagining."

Will swallowed. "Done, then."

CHAPTER 11

EDINBURGH
SCOTLAND

"THAT'S THE PAYLOAD? IT'S ridiculously small!"

"Rather the point, Henderson, don't you think?" said Neil Carlisle. He hated fundraisers and tended to use his 'Eton' voice to deal with the verbal jousting that inevitably arose.

"Yes, but how do we know it works; in vacuum, I mean? The launch is only weeks away," responded Henderson.

"Professor …" said Peter Tan in his heavy Cockney. "Your boys have poured over it several times already and given us the green light. How much leverage do you think you still have?"

"Well, it's not a done-deal, Carlisle. You know …"

Neil suppressed a grin. The banter continued and Neil kept an ear to it but let Peter take the lead despite Henderson's blatantly rude attempts to ignore him. Hilde's friend was a true gem. Unflappable was the best description Neil could come up with. Just being in the same room as Peter Tan lifted your spirits despite Neil's aversion to these functions.

He was due to give his presentation in twenty minutes. It's what he was looking forward to.

He'd known about the Ethical Profit Group for some time but hadn't in his wildest dreams expected to get access to them any time soon. Despite the oxymoron in their name, the group had a solid track record and more importantly access to long-term funding. They seemed immune to political interference as well, which was almost as important. Henderson, despite his pompous attitude, had prevailed against several American oil barons over the last few years.

"So," said Peter finally, "what really gets your goat, Professor, is you can't see inside the CPU module. Have I got that right?"

A snicker of laughter ran through the half dozen people standing around the table, with the small transparent box in its middle. The module at its center was a pristine tube of smooth black stone.

"Well … yes," conceded Henderson.

"It's the guts of the thing and will make all the difference. And it's proprietary," cut in Carlisle, slipping back into his normal Londoner voice.

"We've been over this before, Matthew. Get over it. Secret-herbs-and-spices and all that. Your share of the profits is substantial and I assure you, this is just the beginning. However, if you piss me off anymore, I'm willing to go elsewhere, even if it costs me."

Henderson grinned. The use of his first name was something of a red flag in the rules of such occasions and Carlisle's notoriously short fuse was well known.

"Had to try, Neil. Wouldn't be good form to just roll over."

Carlisle's eyes rose to the ceiling and back as the others laughed softly.

"Done then, ladies and gentlemen," announced Peter Tan, with a quiet authority that surprised all but Carlisle. "Final signatures tomorrow morning at Professor Henderson's rooms at the university. Agreed?"

Murmurs and nods.

Henderson extended his hand to Peter, "Good form, Mr. Tan. Very good form."

"And you, Professor."

Carlisle muttered under his breath and walked away to the refreshment table while the people who had come with Peter packed up the 'module'.

"It's going to destroy quite a few business streams for some very big American companies, Mr. Tan."

"Indeed, Professor. But we'll do it slowly and most of them will come to us for licensing. You might want to anticipate that."

"Oh, I will. They're not going to believe the accuracy, though. Weather prediction with ninety-five percent certainty across eight measures and out to ninety days."

"Easy enough to demonstrate."

"Yes, but you know the type of corporate blockhead we'll be dealing with … Ah, there's the signal. Time for Neil's big moment, eh?"

Peter Tan smiled. Henderson couldn't lose his latent sarcasm and the tone of his last statement suggested Neil might blow it.

SHEHKRii
– The FLAME –

Nothing was farther from the truth. Neil Carlisle had been on the path to this moment since he was born. It was likely this speech would end up in text-books; not so much for the oratory but for the shift in attitude which it represented. Generations to come would hang their hats on the principles Neil would set in motion tonight.

And if the oratory slipped a little then Peter was not above lending a little hand to smooth that over. There was also the matter of the woman at the back of the room. She was desperate to get away and report. Her fear of failure to do so, was palpable. Peter had one of his team tracking her. Something to look into after the talk.

Definitely!

***

Neil adjusted the microphone volume. He'd had a sound check a few hours ago and knew what he needed.

"Ladies and gentlemen, thank you for your time this evening. I do understand the privilege you've afforded us and believe we will not disappoint you.

"To cut straight to the chase, then. When you leave tonight you'll find at the exits, bowls of flash drives. Please take one. They contain two files. One is a copy of this presentation. The other is a technical assessment of the satellite venture, which Professor Matthew Henderson is sponsoring through your group. You're already aware of the financial viability of that proposal. What the files give you is the raw data and the business projections beyond the current agreement. We believe you'll be very interested in further commitment based on the information."

He took a sip of water and made some adjustments to the laptop on the lectern. A graphic image of a cutaway Earth appeared on the large screen behind Neil, mirrored on the laptop.

"Now, to the heart of the matter. Much of what my group offers is based on scientific re-interpretation of ancient observation. The only point we have to prove is that all knowledge is valuable. We do not discriminate. There is no ideology in play.

"This would be admirable in a philosophy class, but the realities of scientific application are that we are interfered with on multiple levels; corporate, political, production ... all these factors warp scientific effort and application.

"Unfortunately, it's easy to allow this to happen since short-term goals, funding and instrumentation are all day-to-day problems which obscure long-term planning, or anything really, that might be seen as the big picture. What we are offering you this evening *is* the big picture."

Neil tapped a key and the image behind him changed. Layers of different colors spread over the graphic, adding detail and creating relationships.

"This," said Neil, "is Planetary Management Theory ..."

***

SHEHKRii
– The FLAME –

The Q&A after the presentation had been vigorous, but Neil had handled it all smoothly with considerable help from Henderson, who, as moderator, had corralled those most intent on going off at tangents.

The two men had risen to the occasion admirably. There was a buzz in the room now that refreshments were served, which Peter felt was even better than anyone had expected.

The agitated woman was moving to the exit, the first escapee, noticeably so.

Peter signaled one of his team to switch and he moved away to shadow her.

***

Susan Mantell was desperate. She had to get word to Scribe. If she failed … it wasn't worth thinking about what he would do to her!

Her idiot ex-brother-in-law, Carlisle, had been on The Council's watch list for weeks. They were going crazy searching for him. Then out of nowhere he was tonight's mystery speaker. Sponsored by that prick, Henderson. Her embedment in the EPG had finally paid off after years of enduring their loony meetings and stupid ideas. Her sister's brainchild at first, it had been Scribe himself who insisted she join. She assumed it was punishment for some past infraction of hers.

Or her husband.

Scribe never explained.

She fumbled for her chit to retrieve her smartphone at reception and headed for an alcove in the foyer; somewhere she could see anyone approaching.

The number rang.

And rang.

A recorded voice chimed in and Susan ground her teeth.

"… leave a message at the tone. Beeeeep."

"This is Susan Mantell. I've found him, Carlisle …"

***

Peter took the phone from her hand, while the other rested gently on her neck. He placed the phone on his thigh and put a small black stone on top of it. A holographic image formed above the stone displaying the number called and the address.

The phone issued a scratchy sound and a live voice came on the line.

"Susan, this is Miles. Where are you? Answer me, Susan."

"Mrs. Mantell is indisposed at the moment, Scribe. You'll have to try a little harder, I'm afraid."

"Who is this?"

"Really! Is that the best you can do; ask the obvious."

"Well …"

"Not many options, I suppose. I'm a friend of Dr. Carlisle's. One of many protectors. You'd do well to withdraw, you know. You're outclassed here."

A stony silence, then, "We'll see about that. You don't know who you're dealing with."

"And yet I know your name, Miles Prendergast, the self-styled Scribe, leader of The Council. What would Eminence say to such a blatant failure of security?"

Peter cut the connection, bored with baiting the man. He removed his Stone and his hand from Susan's neck. She shook herself, yelped a little squeak and bum jumped a half a meter away from the tall Asian man seated beside her.

"Who …"

"Scribe is not happy with you Susan. I'd start running now."

She stood and sidled away to the door. With a final glance at Peter she fled.

Henderson joined Peter.

"Was that Susan Mantell?"

"Yes. She's a spy for a religious organization, which doesn't like your activities."

"Really!"

Peter handed Mantell's phone to the man.

"You might find some interesting information there but disable the tracking quickly before you do. And Matthew, protect your back. Susan's people play dirty."

Henderson looked at the phone and nodded.

SHEHKRii
– The FLAME –

GERRARDS CROSS
BUCKINGHAMSHIRE, UK

Jasmin Bhari sipped the last of her coffee and glanced around. Hilde's friend Sophia was paying the bill. The café in the high street was typical of any of the newer types that had sprouted over the last ten or so years. The faux Elizabethan facades of the old town were typical and so comfortable to her.

Nostalgia intruded violently and she was twenty-five years younger, staring down the barrel of a diabolical future.

Her sister had just returned from Pakistan and was no longer the same person. Jaz had another name then, one she shuddered to remember. But her sister, Shireen, had been the light of her life. The big sister and hero every little girl seemed to crave.

Now she was gone. Most of her anyway. In one of very few quiet moments which their parents allowed, Shireen whispered to her little sister. "Get out as soon as you can!"

Jaz's world shattered. She'd always expected to navigate the path between tradition and the modern world and with her sister's help, get to the other side with the best of both. The fear in her sister's eyes and the puffiness of the old bruises on her face made it clear that navigation was not an option.

So, the terrible year had started.

It had been total, unrelenting fear. She'd not slept properly and lost weight steadily.

SHEHKRii
– The FLAME –

But it had all been so necessary. She wasn't a fool and knew her family well. They mimicked integrated respectability, but behind closed doors her father was king and her mother his chief enforcer, backed up by her brothers who were worth ten times any daughter. Jaz realized she had been a fool to think she could find any compromise. Her sister's face haunted her the whole time she was planning her escape.

She had been hoarding money for several years, but now she took every opportunity to scrape and beg any coin that came her way. Her hundred pounds grew to nearly five in that time, which was just enough as it turned out.

While her mother began interviewing prospective suitors Jaz established an open file with the women's refuge in a nearby town. It took six months to convince them she was a candidate for total removal, and another three to realize that underneath the organization was a group who could do more.

Then at the eleven-month-point her mother had informed her she was going to Karachi to celebrate her fifteenth birthday. No other explanation was given, but she knew what it meant.

Leaving her friends at school had been the hardest. Some of the teachers, too. Mr. Burns and Miss Tosselini especially, they cared, really cared, and made learning such a delight. Mr. Burns had told her she had serious capacity. Whatever that meant, he said it with such pride, she couldn't help but be flattered and encouraged.

SHEHKRii
– The FLAME –

The refuge had her exit strategy ready and two days before she was due to go to the airport she went to school as usual, logged out at the front office and climbed into the waiting SUV to be whisked away from everything she had ever known.

She was numb.

She was determined.

Within two days the other, quieter group had taken over. It was a year before she had learnt the real reason.

It had been her brothers.

They were already on a watch list, having made a series of suspect overseas trips in recent years. MI6 had been part of her interview process and while she felt she knew little, they seemed very grateful for what she told them.

The women's group she had fallen in with was called the Network, after some fictional criminal organization run by a woman. They specialized in deep cover false identities and the backup necessary to make them work. They were also focused exclusively on domestic violence victims and migrant families.

So, she went from a first-generation Pakistani-Muslim to a third-generation Punjabi Indian raised loosely in the Low Anglican faith. The rote lessons were boring but she finally learnt what Mr. Burns' 'capacity' meant. She had near photographic memory and a differentiated mnemonic schema; a natural memory palace. Very rare, or so they said.

SHEHKRii
– The FLAME –

She breezed through embedding her cover story and discovered a whole new world. One of fascinating friends, generous lovers and dedicated support. And she was far away. Her family home in Birmingham was replaced with a shared flat in Brighton.

She was nineteen and a half before it all was seriously threatened.

She'd hardly noticed the years but her family had apparently gone certifiable when told she had been voluntarily withdrawn. The lawyers from the local Islamic Centre had scoured every nook and cranny looking for her; Cultural Imperialism they called it all.

Her brothers had been more effective, reasoning that as a female she had so little real intelligence she would have to have had help, and they terrorized several women's refuges until forcefully told by the police to back off. They didn't reach the one she'd actually used, as it was farthest from her home.

But they didn't give up. Somehow, they got access to her school friends' email accounts, and while she'd only ever used a fake identity via secure protocols, somehow her brothers showed up in Brighton one sunny August weekend trying to trace the account. The Network had warned her and she'd spent weeks cooped up and wearing a disguise. When they'd left, she relocated to Cambridge and disconnected all of her contacts. That had hurt deeply.

But her new identity grew and she discovered university. And Neil.

SHEHKRii
– The FLAME –

Her graduating dissertation on socio-political influence-matrices had also brought the intelligence services back into her life. Through MI6, the CIA had tried to recruit her. She'd refused but kept the contacts alive. Her work independently and in tandem with Neil had taken over her life. His dedication gave her skills purpose. She felt more alive than ever. Eventually, he had put enough funding together to bring her in full time.

Then her brothers returned.

They were working in Scarborough at a local university college and she was glancing out a window into the quadrangle. There they were; scoping out the locals. She had watched, fascinated. They were good; too good. She called her old contacts as she watched.

And resigned the day after. It was the hardest thing she had done in years, leaving Neil. And Liam and Bart.

But utterly essential. Her brothers had somehow hacked the Network and the organization was on high alert. They didn't have her identity but enough of a profile to look in the right places.

She went to Langley and used those contacts to finally learn the truth about her family. The Americans were wholly supportive and helped purge the Network of the hack. In return, she learnt the scale of the evil she'd escaped. Her family was a funnel for finance in and out of the U.K. That was the suspicion, at least. Nothing had ever been proven. The CIA suspected it was her mother who was the organizational genius. Skills inherited apparently.

SHEHKRii
– The FLAME –

And her sister was dead. Or so they suspected from the patchy intelligence available. Jaz cried for days.

Her brothers on the other hand, were very much alive but had not inherited their mother's intelligence.

They were simply thugs, but very effective ones who never offended on home soil. 'Contract problem solvers' to the fringe Islamic world was how the CIA described them. They sounded her out about infiltrating her family again but she would have none of it, and to their credit they left her alone after that.

Two years away and she felt safe enough to return to Neil and the boys. They'd moved on in terms of their activities, and she was confident they were off the family radar.

Now she had new protectors ….

***

"Are you ready, Jaz?" asked Sophia.

The daydream broke and she was herself again. "Yes, sorry! Lost in thought. Do you want to drive?"

"No, you can. I hate English traffic, so aggressive."

Jaz laughed. That was a given; hustle or die was *de rigueur,* in her opinion. She fished the keys out of her bag and headed for the nearby rental.

Sophia watched her charge.

She'd kept her distance as Jaz slipped into deep memory retrieval. It was beautiful to watch and very, very informative. The woman Jasmine had made herself into was a rare achievement. Hilde would have to be informed if she didn't already know. Probably did, given her particular sensitivities. They were an interesting lot, Hilde was shepherding. Switching between Joe and Neil's groups was proving to be a challenging assignment; an unexpected turn of events given the last few years and a welcome change.

Jaz was at the car so Sophia skipped over the last few yards and popped the passenger door. Their chore today was mundane, little more than office logistics but not having to kill anyone for a few days was pleasant enough.

CHAPTER 12

MONDRAGOE,
BASQUE COUNTRY,
SPAIN

LIAM CORMAC LOOKED OUT the loft windows toward the knoll, which dominated this part of town. As a city boy, he found the view both daunting and thrilling. Working for Neil had taken him to some out-of-the-way places, but he always came back to the city.

Things had changed now. This place was a new anchor. He shouldn't feel comfortable here but he did!

Strange times, he mused.

Someone trotted up the stairs and he turned to greet Hilde Nordstrom.

"Good mornin', Hilde. How are you?"

"Well, thank you, Liam. Are you ready?"

"I hope so. Should we wait for the others?"

"No, let's get started ahead of them. I'd like to show you the new 'mouse'. A crowd would be distracting."

"Mouse?"

"Yes, come."

She waved him over to the central cluster of laptops, which dominated the loft. It was a cool set-up, the best he'd ever seen. A circular ring of workstations dominated by a flat black center table. Six large rotatable screens were hung from the ceiling and could be configured to be either single or group displays. And they could be split into multiple sections.

Hilde indicated a chair and touched a panel that withdrew the screens upwards.

"Hey, don't I need them?"

"Next level, Liam, next level." She remained standing and placed a black half sphere at his right hand. It was the size of a cricket ball and very shiny. Liam tried to slide it over the desktop but it wouldn't move.

"OK, I give up. How does it work?"

Hilde placed her hand gently on the back of his neck. "Don't get any ideas here, Mr. Cormac, but I'll help you through the learning curve. The mouse is static. You have to learn to move it with your mind, so to speak. Place your hand on the stone and imagine what you want it to do."

Her hand was soft and cool and Liam blushed as he automatically imagined it elsewhere on his body. He was as tall as Hilde but whipcord thin and didn't for an instant think he was a physical match for her. Not given what he'd seen her do. But her touch was thrilling and comforting all in one.

"Concentrate, please."

"Yes, Ma'am."

Liam split his mind into several bits. This was an old trick, multitasking 101. He felt his hand over the mouse, stone; he wasn't sure what to call it now. Another part of him imagined what he wanted to see on his console screen and suddenly the cursor was moving. He manipulated it to open a file and right-click suddenly became obsolete. *What else?,* he mused and began to explore.

Hilde kept her hand in place. Liam's reaction to her touch had been pleasantly sweet. And his mind was agile. She'd not had to lead him through the initial learning hump in anything other than a minor way. He didn't need her touch but she left her hand in place anyway.

"Now," she said after several minutes, "imagine the large screens are still there and you want to throw something up on them for others to see."

Liam frowned. He intuited something as she spoke and suddenly the central table was alive with images. He focused harder and the jumble settled and the file he had on his small screen was a three-dimensional hologram floating in space before him.

"Holy crap!"

Hilde laughed softly. "A frequent comment."

His mind surged, sure and in control and the scans Neil and Jaz had made of the nearby knoll a few weeks ago, roared to life, active, alive, pulsating with the geo-tectonic energy of the intersecting leys high up here in the Pyrenees.

Biopulses, Liam corrected himself. The new terminology was still embedding but he didn't care. He focused more and the image shrank and expanded reaching into the upper atmosphere and deep into France and Spain. He imagined the weather pattern overlay and it inserted itself.

Now, he wondered, *what if* ...

SHEHKRii
– The FLAME –

The table became a weather dance rushing through each day in a few seconds, weeks of atmospheric change visible in less than a minute.

"Phew!" he said quietly, leaning back a little.

Hilde went for a wild ride.

Liam's mind craved order and searched for it unconsciously, keeping at bay a desperate loneliness, which sprang from having a brain so agile very few could keep up with it. Childhood had been a bittersweet mess plagued by rejection due to his 'otherness' and the unbridled joy of learning. But his discipline was not just powerful, it had depth, and as he saw more, he imagined more and chased it with fervor and detachment, craving to understand.

Hilde caressed his neck a little. What a pleasant surprise! She knew the nature of the man merely by looking at him, but this added layer was a thing of beauty. Did she dare complicate her assignment by getting involved? Something to ponder.

She removed her hand.

Liam was still working. He called up conventional data and compared it to the projection.

"Holy crap!"

"Repetition is not an attribute."

"Sorry, but look at this. The projection matches perfectly. This thing can predict the weather down to the last isobar."

"Yes. We're already building a business model based on that. What else can it do, do you think?"

SHEHKRii
– The FLAME –

He pushed back in his chair a bit more. "What do people need …."

After a few more seconds, he leaned forward and took hold of the stone again.

Hilde walked over to the bureau and prepared Liam a coffee. As she returned to see what he was up to, other people entered the loft. With a simple gesture, Hilde let them know she wanted caution and they moved quietly to avoid intruding on Liam's concentration funk.

***

The others were a strange lot. Liam smiled at the understatement.

He was taking a break and making his second coffee of the day. And steeling glances at the group he was beginning to think of as 'his crew'.

Hilde referred to herself as *Shehkrii*: 'pathfinder' in some antique language, Bart said. The group she had brought in to work with him was a mix of these and their friends and relatives. Those who were not like Hilde called each other 'unreturned'. Bart had said something about that, too. His new friend Casey was 'unreturned', apparently.

It all sounded just a little cult-ish to Liam, but no one took themselves seriously and he relaxed into the group almost immediately. They were serious players in *tech* terms and he had only to start a sentence and five different options were thrown up on the central holo-viewer before he had finished.

It was brainstorming on a mega scale.

After less than half a day's effort he had three business streams in detailed development. Once Jaz saw these reports she would turn them into agri-business prospectuses and they'd all be very busy for years.

But this was only the beginning. He finished adding milk to his cup and went back to his desk, eager.

***

Hilde watched Liam watching. His enthusiasm was delightful and engaging. He was adapting quickly. Of Neil's team, they had expected Cormac to be the most resistant, but he had surprised them all.

Inclusion was the key. Liam craved the satisfaction, which came from contributing. In all other circumstances, he was somewhat detached and reserved; a lonely soul who kept to himself unless working. Neil Carlisle's group had provided Liam with a home for ten years. Now his family had suddenly expanded and he was alternately wonderstruck and ecstatic.

She found it charming.

***

Liam had a generous bedsit elsewhere in the office complex and was wondering how long he'd get to enjoy the relative luxury before being dragged off to some other part of the world. The place was not big by any means but oh-so-cool. He really liked it.

He finished toweling off in the ensuite, opened the door to find clothes and found Hilde, sitting on the bed in a sheer next-to-nothing robe. She uncrossed her legs, rose and stepped towards him, the robe falling away with very many more curves on display than he had imagined.

"Body armor," she said.

"What?"

"I wear lightweight body armor. It tends to strap one's bits in."

"Oh."

She pressed herself against him, moving aside his rapidly rising penis, and nibbled at his ear, her hands sliding around his waist and gripping his cheeks, gently pulling their nether regions together.

"This is a surprise," he said, groaning a little at the pressure below. He slid his hands up from her waist and caressed the side of her breasts, draping his fingers across the nipples.

Hilde groaned too and turned her attention to his mouth, cupping her hands around his head and driving her tongue deep, twisting it around his.

They shuffled to the bed and she turned him so he fell on his back and was astride in one swift maneuver. Leaning forward she brought her breasts to his mouth, which he licked and kissed while she took his member with her left hand and rubbed its end across her clitoris, her temperature rising. She pushed him in, driving down. As the vaginal stimulation kicked in she sat back slightly to improve the angle of penetration.

"You don't mess around," he breathed as he matched her rhythm, arching up so his penis slid smoothly in and out. He felt for the right angle and maximum pressure on the walls of the tube clamped around him.

"Why wait," she cooed, "we're going to be here a while."

They were. Several hours of varying intensity, exploring each other and creating more than physical intimacy.

Liam found he could match her orgasms easily and it became something of a game between them, to see how long they could each hold themselves on the edge of climax before crashing in together. He discovered erogenous zones he didn't even know he had. And spent quite a bit of time trying to find the same ones on Hilde. She was both willing teacher and enthusiastic student all in one.

Eventually he lay back on the bed, spent. And happier than he had been for longer than he could remember. The background pressure of loneliness he'd carried unconsciously for so long was gone. He wanted to cry and starting, couldn't stop.

Hilde held him close, his head cradled on top of her breasts. She blended her rhythms to his and felt the shudder of emotion ripple through his body as he finally let go of the reserve he'd created so long ago. She pushed happiness into him, vibrating her emotional self to take over his, making him feel as satisfied and glad as she was. After a few moments, his sobs stopped and he sat up.

"Well," he said, snuffling, "that was very masculine."

"Very human," she replied and kissed his mouth gently. The saltiness of his tears aroused her again and she reached for his member, stroking gently.

"Oh!" he breathed.

RASOVO, BULGARIA

Vasily Radu approached Vizier cautiously with as neutral a mind as possible.

"Bad news, Vasily?"

"Yes, Vizier. Some good but mostly bad."

"Speak."

He swallowed. "Grigor Patrascu is dead. We don't know by whom. His skull was crushed. The Lutz mongrel still lives and has begun moving erratically. He is obviously alerted to some danger. On that score, we have some good news."

"Yes." Vizier's voice was flat and emotionless, a sure sign of anger.

"Ah … One of our contractors in England witnessed a fight outside a tavern in Tilbury, not far from our facility there. Lutz was involved. He took a few quick photos on his phone. There is another player involved; Braithwaite of their Organized Crime Directorate. Lutz has powerful allies, it seems. But this gives us an advantage for future surveillance and tracking."

Vizier rose and paced. "Have you checked the Tilbury operation for tampering?'

"Yes, Vizier. There are no signs of it and our security cameras are clean."

The other man grunted. "Regardless, downscale and insulate all operations through Tilbury."

Vizier had been dining at his desk when Radu entered. He picked up his fork. As he stared at it intently, the utensil began to vibrate and bend, turning molten as Vasily watched in awe. Vizier dropped it to the floor.

"Activate our people inside British Intelligence. I want something suitably atrocious, preferably involving senior officers. Chaos will cloak us, at least for a while. In the meantime, hunt down everyone associated with Lutz and this Braithwaite and slaughter them. Wives, children, those closest will do. Am I clear, Vasily?"

"Yes, Vizier."

"Good. Get out."

Radu scuttled away.

SEVILLE, SPAIN

"This is spacious, Viv."

"Si ... yes, Jaz. We wanted room to grow. The designer has given us a modular fitout so it's just plug-and-play as numbers increase."

"Wonderful."

Jaz walked out onto the strip balcony and glanced up and down the street.

"Nice outlook. The entry's a bit pokey, though?"

"Defensible," said the other woman.

Jasmin's eyebrows rose and she caught herself about to respond. *Yes, that was a factor.* She, of all people, should know that.

"Yes."

Vivian Lutz was booting up a laptop at one of half a dozen workstations in the center of the office. She tapped a few more keys and the space came alive. The ceiling fans rotated quietly, the balcony louvres adjusted to aid the airflow, lights came on over the desks and the glass doors at the top of the stairs swung closed to create a highly visible ante room.

"The glass is crystal polymer," said Viv. "A bazooka wouldn't get through."

Jaz laughed, "A bazooka would flash fry anyone fool enough to use it in that box."

Viv laughed also.

They worked steadily for an hour, organizing office supplies, connecting workstations and generally setting up the place to suit Jaz's expectations. There was an almost unconscious synch to how Viv complimented Jaz.

When they were done, Jaz made tea and they relaxed on exquisite timber chairs on the balcony.

"That should do us for about a year," she said. "Not sure what to expect after that. There's so much in the wind at the moment."

SHEHKRii
– The FLAME –

Vivian Lutz didn't answer straight away. This was not the first time she'd been involved directly with her husband's family enterprises but it was the first with a 'civilian' in tow. She liked Jazmin Bhari but wondered if she had it in her for the long haul.

"What do you think of Nathan?"

"Oh ... 'scary' would be the best word, I think. What about you?"

"I've known him since I first married. He came to the wedding at my mother-in-law's request. It was like meeting the father you'd never known.

"But, 'scary' is still about right."

Jaz laughed. "Let me tell you a story about 'fathers' ..."

Impulsively, she laid out her whole history to this stranger. It was intimately detailed and with each passing minute Jaz felt as though the most unbearable weight had been freshly lifted from her shoulders. When she finished, tears were flowing freely but she hardly noticed.

She felt whole for the first time she could remember.

Viv reached over and placed her hand on her arm. Nothing more was necessary.

A buzz intruded from the front door downstairs.

***

From the balcony Vivian watched the last of the staff leave. The shop across the road had a glass panel, which gave a perfect reflection to their front door. It was a habit from a previous life.

She had no more doubts about Jaz. The woman's story was horrendous and yet she'd not just survived but orchestrated that survival and the person she'd become. Fortitude was hardly the best word for what flowed through Jasmin's veins but it was there in oceans full.

Then there was the staff issue.

Jaz ran her team tight and at multiple levels. You were on-point all the time, which should have been draining. With Jaz in charge it wasn't. Not that this staff would wilt; they were very specially chosen, but even so, Jaz had them jumping.

Mischievously, Viv wondered if it was time to introduce Jasmin to Joe's mother, M'La.

That would be interesting.

Now, however, Jaz was off to Scotland for some reason. Vivian hoped she returned soon.

LONDON

Eddy leaned over the back of the couch and kissed Charlie full on the mouth, lingering.

Disengaging she said, "Red or white?"

"White please, with a dash of water."

"Blasphemy!" said Eddy as she padded naked to the open kitchen of Charlie's apartment to retrieve the wine.

Charles glanced behind and drank in the view. He had gotten very, very lucky. He was not looking at a woman on the high side of fifty although he knew her exact age. She could easily have been twenty years younger. She certainly acted that way. Since his divorce, he'd kept his sex life casual and tended towards younger, vigorous women.

It made breaking up that much easier.

Eddy, on the other hand, was experienced and aggressive. Playful, too. *Please don't mess this up*, he prayed silently.

"How do we handle this back at the loft, Charlie?"

He laughed. "They already know, I'm sure. I don't recruit dummies."

"No, you don't. Let's just ignore it and see what they do. That could be fun."

"And Joe?"

"Same, same. I've rarely been able to make him blush."

She returned with the wine, handed him his glass and sat opposite, completely at ease with her legs folded under.

"So," she said, "I'm wondering where all those scars came from and how a man of fifty-five can still have abs. And you're wondering why my tits and ass haven't sagged more."

Charles choked on his wine and sputtered all over himself.

"I didn't notice any sagging," he answered defensively.

"I see you and Joe's friend, Bijan went to the same charm school."

"A gentleman never … you know?"

SHEHKRii
– The FLAME –

"Ha! My answer is Paleo and high intensity training; forced on us thirty years ago by Joe's father, Victor; long before those things even had names, I think. Victor tended to do that, take control of the lives of his friends. The benefits are … interesting."

"I'll say," replied Charles, staring pointedly at small but, in his opinion, perfect breasts."

"Lech!"

He laughed. "OK. SAS training for my part, the lite version, at least, and the scars are mostly from knife fights. The Belfast boys liked their blades."

She nodded and elegantly placed her wine glass on the wooden arm of the sofa. Unfolding herself from the seat she leaned languidly over the gap between them, bending down and slowly licking the wine from his stomach, caressing his scars with her tongue.

CHAPTER 13

MILL HILL
LEEDS, UK

HILDE SAT AT THE BACK OF THE CAFE comfortably enclosed in wood paneling and tweed. It was a good angle to watch the waitresses as Bijan entered. The poor man just couldn't help the reactions he caused as every female in the place turned and the staff started toward him.

He was handsome in that classic sense, which always turned heads, but the man's aura was far more impressive. And woman got that almost instantly.

Bijan waved to her, which had the desired effect, the waitresses balked. Hilde was well aware of the effect she had on her own gender. At one point nine meters tall, the same as Bijan, and broad-shouldered she tended to scare them away.

Sitting, he said, "Hilde. How are you."

"Very well, Bijan, And you?"

"Good. A touch excited, actually. It's been very sedate the last few years, babysitting for Paul in Sydney. I was quite relieved to get Joe's call. What are you doing here, though? I thought you were escorting scientists or something."

Hilde laughed. "Or something. Nathan asked me to crossover for a few days. My scientists are covered. What about you? What have you discovered?"

A waitress approached, alternately hormonal and frightened. She held her order pad in front like a shield. Bijan ordered tea and fruit and she sidled away.

"It was interesting. Joe's brief and the cover story supplied by his new friend Braithwaite put me in the managing director's office straight away. I was given the royal tour. My credentials at Kharazmi University didn't hurt either."

"You still teach the swords?" she said, surprised.

"When I can. It's a visiting professorship of sorts. Anyway, I saw most of their Bradford operation with the exception of the cyto-toxic containment facility. The director's reflexes gave him away. We need to see inside, of course."

"Of course. And computer facilities?"

Bijan laughed softly. "Their servers would do justice to several government departments. They need an inspection as well."

His order arrived, as did the waitress's phone number slipped under a napkin. *Feisty,* thought Hilde as Bijan subtly showed her the note with a resigned expression and slipped it into a pocket.

"Astrid says 'hi' by the way."

"How is your daughter, Hilde?"

"Doing very, very well. Still in Sydney studying art and loving every minute. And dropping hints about you and I."

"Persistent!"

"She does it to annoy me. You're the one that got away! She loves that expression."

"Give her my love."

"Not likely!"

"And congratulations. I noticed your glow. I hope he's treating you well?"

"Ha. More the other way at the moment, but I have hopes. He is a gentle man."

"Those are rare."

They chatted for another fifteen minutes then left. Hilde slipped her arm through his as they exited just to annoy anyone watching.

"Tease," said Bijan, quietly.

"Absolutely. Now, I hope you have transport because I caught the train up from London."

"Blue Vauxhall, fifty meters down on the right. Any thoughts on how we play this?"

"A few. I was going to suggest parking several kilometers away and working our way in randomly. Then conceal and observe. It's the middle of the week so hopefully we won't have to wait long before we can enter."

"Sounds good to me."

***

"That's interesting," said Bijan.

Hilde didn't answer, she was not happy. The funeral home compound was ablaze with floodlights and two-man security teams, six of them. The cyto-toxic facility was fully occupied, and a large truck had reversed in, leaving its nose protruding from the loading dock. It was nine in the evening and the sun had only recently set.

Hilde touched the black stone necklace under her shirt and after a few moments Joe answered. The conversation was brief.

"So," said Bijan, "nothing scheduled. Ah … who's this coming out of the treatment building?"

A group of five walked briskly to the main office. Ten minutes later two of them exited, collected their car and left.

"The inspectors," said Hilde. "The ones whose families are held hostage for the seal of approval."

"So it would seem." Bijan's tone was flat, deadly.

They waited till ten minutes before eleven. The compound had cleared half an hour before, but the dog patrols were ongoing. No human security remained. As one they moved, trotting across the vacant lot, which had concealed them and the narrow road between. They vaulted the three-meter security fence with practiced ease.

The dogs ignored them, their senses dulled by Hilde's intrusion and control.

She took the cyto-shed and Bijan, the office. Ten minutes later she joined him.

"Anything?" she asked.

"The three who went out tonight were scheduled for late tomorrow morning but were moved up. They all died earlier today. There's no reason given in the records for the change. I've contacted Eddy and her people have checked the names and they appear to be legitimate. And you?"

"Nothing obvious," answered Hilde. "But the sick room attached to the workshop could do triage in a major hospital."

"I've infected their servers. Eddy will be able to analyze all their data and monitor future activity. I have a suggestion, if you're willing?"

"Yes?" said Hilde, one eyebrow raised.

"I'm curious to see what Eddy is up to. Also, Joe is trying not to show his concern, but I suspect there is much more going on than simply prying loose information on The Twelve for the Keeper. I'd like to be more involved."

Hilde considered the matter. Bee's instincts were legendary. He had a knack for getting at the heart of things. And they were both babysitting at the moment after years of more frantic activity. It was a well-earned rest she had, shepherding Neil Carlisle and his crew. Bijan was doing the same in Australia, keeping an eye on Mark Todd, the fractured nemesis of their friends Paul and Diane Gareth. It was pleasant enough but …

"I think I can spare a few days. And I've never met Eddy Bryce so, yes, let's help out a little."

"Excellent!" said Bijan as he rose from the chair he occupied and snatched a jet-black stone from the top of one of the office computers.

GLENELG
SCOTLAND

"Wow. And it's about bloody time."

"Sorry," said Neil.

Jaz snorted. "So you should be. Bloody secrets!"

As they exited the car, the manor house door opened and two people approached. The woman was middle aged and quite thin. The man was ancient but walked towards them with authority despite a slight dependence on his walking stick. Jaz was sure he was well over ninety.

Bowing slightly, the old man said, "I'm John, Lord Ellsworth, last of my line. It's a pleasure to finally meet you Miss Bhari."

"What! Sorry, Lord Ellsworth. You know me?"

"Indeed. Young Neil speaks of you often and always well. Please, call me John," said Ellsworth.

"Does he, now?" answered Jaz with a certain sharpness in her tone.

The other woman chuckled and Ellsworth said, "My pardon, this is Brigid, my estate manager."

Brigid nodded. "I understand we're expecting a third. When do you think he'll arrive?"

Her accent was vaguely American.

"Not sure, Brigid," answered Neil. "Nathan said to start without him, though."

"Very well. Let's get his lordship inside before his joints freeze. Some tea to warm up as well, I think."

She hustled them all inside. Ellsworth was surprisingly agile.

Jaz took it all in. The dour exterior typical of much Scottish architecture was betrayed by a thoroughly modernized interior. Old materials re-worked. It felt light and fresh. Brigid placed orders for refreshments with other staff as she took them through to a balcony overlooking a cavernous circular library lit from above by a huge steel and glass canopy.

"Wow," breathed Jaz.

"Absolutely," said Nathan Chalk from the center of the space, a spidery circular staircase, which serviced the cavern.

"How," said Brigid, reaching for a handgun tucked under her tweed coat.

"No need, Brigid," said Ellsworth, "I've been hoping for this. Welcome, *Makh t'heh Panku-khan.* The old ones spoke of you before they passed on. And Neil only recently. My home is yours."

Nathan inclined his head, "Well put, John. You honor them all."

"I have tried."

"Ah ... what the *effing* hell is going on here?" asked Jaz.

The men laughed as Brigid said, "Language, Miss Bhari!" Jaz grinned.

The tea arrived and Nathan crossed the bridge connecting the stair to the rim and directed them all to a lounge area nearby.

"A quick summary, then you can give Jaz the tour, John."

The lord nodded.

"When we first met Jasmin, I mentioned the last of the Druids, the *Druheidá,* died over eight hundred years ago. Lord Ellsworth is in the line of their retainers, the keepers of their knowledge. Unfortunately, such knowledge is best transferred verbally. So much is lost in writing it down.

"The last *Druheidá* scholar struggled with that particular problem all her life and eventually came up with the idea of instruction manuals. Those are here as are encyclopedias of everything she could think of from herbalism to astrological measurement. And guides on how to seek out similar information from other areas of the world. The *Druheidá* travelled widely but their last stand was here in Britain."

Nathan inclined his head to John who took up the tale.

"Over the centuries, we've collected anything related to that central resource especially companion works, which verified the core information. So you see before you eight centuries of specialized knowledge. Our index system is unique, of course, and takes a while to get used to."

Jaz was thunder struck. "But why keep it secret? This is fantastic."

"Books burn," answered Brigid.

"Seriously?"

"Yes, Miss Bhari. I was a nun in my youth and recruited by The Council. If they had a clue this place existed, we'd be all hung from the rafters and burned to a crisp. The level of hate out there is simply not measurable.

"You know about The Council, don't you?"

Jasmin nodded.

"So," said Neil, standing, "when I published my Ph.D. dissertation, John contacted me and brought me here ... eventually. The idea was to create parallel verification without exposing the library. Our progress over the years has been in no small part because of the insights in these books."

Jaz nodded. "I can see it. Your 'what if's' ..."

He grinned. "I hurt myself several times keeping a straight face with you lot."

"Brigid," said Ellsworth, "Why don't you show Jasmin around. She's fit to bursting already."

Both women laughed and rose. Brigid ushered Jaz to the central stair and they descended into the library.

"A new beginning, Neil. I'm so glad for you."

"Thanks, John. For us both, I think. But, you don't need this place, Nathan, so why are we here?"

"Nothing is wasted, doctor. You can now bring your team here and make better use of John's legacy. With the help I'm offering, all that knowledge will click together much, much better. There are references here which will give you access to work done in Europe and Asia. It will expand your associates.

"I said this was a path best walked with company. The group just got a lot bigger. Some of the weight carried by John and his people can now be lifted. They certainly deserve that."

"Indeed," said Neil, raising his cup to Ellsworth.

Nathan rose and walked to the balcony, skipping lightly over it using one hand on the rail. He didn't fall but drifted out to the center of the atrium.

Ellsworth gaped and stood.

"I have a gift for you."

He extended his hands slightly and in each was a smooth black stone. The library started to glow, a soft golden color, which intensified till neither Neil or Ellsworth could look directly at the man floating in the center of it.

Suddenly the glow was gone and Nathan was back on solid ground handing them each one of the stones.

"All that is here in this place is now copied into the stones. Back-ups, if you will. Get Cormac working on that Neil. I think he may be able to do some interesting things with it."

"How?" asked Ellsworth.

"Things are worse than anyone ever thought, John," said Nathan. "I'm Plan B, unfortunately."

He walked back the way they had come, leaving the two men stunned.

***

Jaz found Neil on the rear terrace sipping more tea. Ellsworth was nowhere to be seen.

"Neil, this place is outstanding. I should hit you for keeping it secret."

Neil snorted. "You should. And Liam and Bart certainly will."

She sat and touched his arm.

"When I came back from the U.S. I told you my history. I trusted you with my life. Why couldn't you trust me with this?"

He looked down. "I should have. But I was seriously low when you came back. My divorce had just wrapped up and I was cleaned out in more ways than one. I kept telling myself I had to deal with that first. It was easier to push everything else away, including you. I'm sorry. You deserved better."

"Yes, I did. And you're going to make it up to me."

He looked up and saw the sparkle in her eye, the expectancy. He'd suppressed his attraction for Jaz for so long it should have kicked in automatically now, but the hope on her face was like a shot of cold water and he smiled back.

"We should talk about that," he suggested."

***

Brigid joined Ellsworth in his study.

"She's extraordinary, John. I think she may have mastered the index already. What's wrong?"

SHEHKRii
– The FLAME –

"The Keeper of the Flame is gone. We've gained an incredible thing today, my dear. He's more powerful than any of the *Druheidá* of old. Much more powerful."

"Which is good. But you're scared, John. I can tell, you know."

John laughed softly. "We're a good team, Brigid, but we're going to have to be better."

He handed her the stone. "Guard this with your life until you can get it to the Archive. It's the entire library. A gift from the Keeper."

She took it and slipped it into a pocket.

"How did you know who he was?"

"Look up Eanraig the Slow's 'Pronouncements on Possibilities'; late Ninth Century, I think. He spoke of a vision sent by the Earth Mother; of a son of terrible power who she would birth upon us if we didn't serve her purpose well enough. A final solution. Plan B."

"It's that bad?"

"Indeed, it is."

"How then, are Dr. Carlisle and his too-clever-by-half little *girly* going to help?"

"I think the capitalists of your homeland might call it 'value adding', Brigid, my dear. You've known Neil as long as I have. You've seen his skill set. And now, we've both seen young Jasmin and how she enhances all that. Imagine both of them with many, many helpers …"

"Ah … yes! But that will attract attention, which exposes you. I won't have that."

Ellsworth smiled. "Won't you now? Unfortunately, when I took Neil into our confidence those few years ago, it was the beginning of more risk. I knew it would come to a head eventually. Now we have to prepare."

"Why did you do it; with Carlisle? I've never questioned it. I trust you, but …"

"Secrets kept too well are wasted. When I read his graduating dissertation, I knew he had what it would take to use what we protect. I have no regrets."

Brigid laughed. "At least that's one of us."

Ellsworth smiled. After what he'd seen the Keeper do, he suspected regret might be a thing of the past. Hard times were coming but harder people were about in the world too. And they had his back. He felt fifty years younger.

LONDON

They looked remarkably like their father. Peter Tan watched the Braithwaite boys approach, blissfully unaware of any danger. While they were eighteen months apart in age, a casual glance would have assumed they were twins.

Intensely discussing something, neither had seen the black van slowing behind them.

As they came abreast, Peter spoke. "Gentlemen."

The boys froze, suddenly alert, which was when the van pulled in quickly and its door slide back. Three masked men leapt out.

Sophia had been trotting unseen beside the van and skipped forward from its rear, swatting all three to the footpath before they had taken more than two steps. The bodies hit the ground with an unnatural limpness.

The boys gapped.

Peter and Sophia drew small, silenced handguns simultaneously and fired, Peter killing the driver and Sophia the backup abductor still in the van.

"Gentlemen," said Peter again. "Your father sends his compliments. Would you keep walking forward please and we'll escort you to safety?"

They glanced at each other and nodded to Peter. And began walking. The eldest said, "It wouldn't do us any good to run, would it?"

"In general terms, no. But a little cardio never hurts."

They laughed despite themselves.

"You're really from our dad?"

"If I mimicked his Irish accent, would you be convinced?"

They laughed again, relieved.

Sophia brought up the rear.

THE BRITISH LIBRARY
LONDON

Eminence and Reverence swept into the basement. Everyone else jumped. Mayhew stormed over to Brony.

"Sister! Why haven't you reported for over a day?"

"Eminence. We've been busy …"

Mayhew drew breath but Fitzsimmons touched his arm and the vitriolic retort was withheld. Reluctantly.

SHEHKRii
– The FLAME –

"I understand, Sister, you've made some progress?" asked Fitzsimmons.

"Yes, Reverence. Significant progress. But we are still very much 'operational' and reporting has been deferred. I take it some of our success has been passed on to you?'

Fitzsimmons grinned and glanced at the other man. "Yes. There are ears everywhere. What can you tell us, as of now?"

"One moment, please."

Brony rose from her chair, turned and called to another person on the other side of the room. "Bernard, call in back up for Team One and send someone into New Bern to find the people we left there yesterday."

"Yes, Sister."

She sat back down and faced the two standing men. The excitement of the last thirty hours had enervated her and she wasn't afraid of them as much as usual.

"My apologies. Our progress has not been without difficulty."

"Problems you can't solve, Sister? Scribe's faith in you would seem to be misplaced."

Brony stared him down and Reverence raised his eyebrows.

"Peter," he said warningly.

"Very well. Report Bronwyn."

"Yes, sir. At Scribe's instruction, I activated my personality profiles of Carlisle's team. Early yesterday we learned of a bulk shipment of exotic tea for a town in

SHEHKRii
– The FLAME –

North Carolina. A local café had sold all its stock to Bart Smith and ordered its replacement, as it turned out. Our team arrived within seven hours only to find Mr. Smith and some associates leaving. Our people split up to follow him and investigate what he was doing. We've had live operations ever since and have been stretched a bit thin."

"Have you secured him?" interjected Mayhew.

"No, Eminence. On my recommendation, we maintained tracking in order to find the others."

"Daring," said Fitzsimmons.

"Risky," countered Mayhew.

"And by taking this daring risk, Sister, what have we achieved?" asked Fitzsimmons.

"Much, Reverence," answered Brony.

"We followed Smith to Wilmington International and the team held back. He should have shown up on facial recognition and we would have had his travel details. He didn't and we lost him there."

"As I said, risky."

"But …"

"But, I instituted a rapid manual search of all the airport video surveillance and we reacquired him several hours later. He was on his way to Gatwick.

"Facial recognition again failed there, but we were monitoring all live feeds and found him and the Nordstrom woman simultaneously. She appeared to be there to meet him. We've had a long tail team on them ever since with parallel video surveillance. There have been three loss-and-reacquire incidents.

"Notably facial recognition is not working at all. This is a major concern. I have a technical team looking into it as we speak."

Mayhew paced. "What went wrong in the town where you first found him?"

"We left two people to back track Smith's activities. They haven't reported in."

"So, what's your strategy, Sister?" said Mayhew with a sneer.

"Our strategy," answered Scribe, from behind, "is to use Mr. Smith to lead us to the others. On his own he has little value."

Brony had watched Scribe approach and was enormously proud of herself for not giving him away.

"Scribe," acknowledged Fitzsimmons.

"On this matter, Eminence," said the senior man, "we will leave Sister Bronwyn to pursue her instincts. They have proven themselves worth the trust so far.

"In other matters, however, we need to make some decisions. Sister, how go our Scottish inquires?"

Brony swiveled to her workstation and called up a report, which she flicked to the large screen above her desk. The slideshow format started.

"Some progress there, Scribe but as yet, inconclusive."

Reverence gasped. "Stop. Go back."

Brony complied.

"Where is that? When is it?"

"Glenelg, Scotland. South of Fort William. Two days ago."

"What is it, Keith?" asked Scribe, using Fitzsimmons' first name.

"That woman to the left is Sister Catherine Mulvaney. She's one of our very few turncoats."

"Explain," said Scribe in the commanding persona which aroused Brony.

"She was a nun; forget the order, but she's brilliant. We had high hopes for her but twenty-odd years ago, she broke ranks and released a huge amount of financial material to the press. She disappeared. We never could find her. The whole mess took nearly a year to manage."

"And you know her how?" asked Mayhew.

"I had to clean up that mess, Peter. I know a great deal about Sister Catherine. We leaned on her family at one point and she shot at me!"

"I beg your pardon," said Scribe. "She what?"

"She stalked me and put a round into a tree I was standing next to. She learned to shoot doing missionary work in Africa. Quite the marksman apparently. I received a letter the day after saying she'd deliberately missed. I backed off a little. But by then getting damage control done was more important than tracking her down.

"It will be no coincidence that you've turned her up here, Bronwyn."

"Well, well, well," said Mayhew. "This is interesting. Progress at last."

Brony ground her teeth at the slight.

"In which case, Peter," said Scribe, "you and Bronwyn will concentrate on finding this renegade. Sister …"

"Yes, sir."

"Delegate the monitoring of Mr. Smith. You've done well and others can follow up. Work with Eminence to find this Mulvaney person. You're authorized to use a tactical team and whatever surveillance you need. This will be connected to Dr. Carlisle and is most likely much more than a mistress. Are we clear on our priorities?"

"Yes, Scribe," they all answered in unison.

"And I think it is time we played our card in regard to the Bhari woman. That effort may complement our efforts with Smith.

"Keith, I'll leave that to you. You may want to involve Mahdi. If her family were to discover her whereabouts for example …"

"Yes, Scribe," said Fitzsimmons, "I think we can get a quick result in that area."

Brony swallowed. She was bursting to know Jasmin's backstory but they were talking about murder, she was sure.

Good, she thought to herself.

SHEHKRii
– The FLAME –

CHAPTER 14

SHOREDITCH, LONDON

CHARLES BRAITHWAITE trotted up the stairs to the operations loft, his body tense and face neutral. Eddy heard the urgency in his steps and glanced over as he entered their working space. She saw the tiny hesitation as he spied Bijan and Hilde, but he kept coming to stand next to Mats and Brent.

"Code Red Three, gentlemen. I want your reports in five minutes."

The analysts twisted in their seats to glance at their boss. They turned straight back and got to work, studies in concentration. Eddy saw Charlie's shoulders relax a little.

"Charlie. What's happened?"

He turned and walked the few paces over to them, extending his hand to Bijan then Hilde.

Introductions out of the way, Charles said, "Joe rang me an hour ago. My sons were targeted just before lunch."

He glanced at the new couple. "He tells me your people dealt with it. The snatch-team is dead and disposed of. They had pictures of me and Joe from our little adventure in Tilbury the other night. Someone got lucky."

Eddy reached out and touched his arm. He took a long breath and let it out.

"Thank you," he said, looking at Bijan.

"You are welcome, Sir Charles. Did Joe mention his own situation?"

"No."

"His family was also attacked, in Seville. His mother dealt with it."

Hilde grinned fleetingly and Eddy hiccupped a laugh. "All dead?"

"Of course," answered Hilde, "M'La does not tolerate discourtesy."

Charles grinned. "I definitely have to meet her."

Bijan's eyebrows jumped up. "Careful what you wish for."

Hilde laughed outright and turned to get herself a drink from the sideboard. Eddy watched her go, marveling at yet another of these amazing people who orbited around Joe. The woman was imposing in so many ways, but seemed very comfortable around Bijan, almost flirting at times, which the Persian deflected with practiced ease.

"Charlie," said Eddy, "your ex-wife?"

"Joe says she's protected but there's been no incident."

Eddy nodded.

"Mark!" said Brent.

Charles turned and walked back to his men. Hilde returned, sipping fruit juice.

"You've touched a nerve, Eddy," she said. "I'm glad we came down."

"So am I, dear. Once the boys have their heightened alert in place we all need to review the material you sent last night. It dovetails with something I've been chasing down separately and, quite frankly, if what I suspect is true, we need the extra help you can provide."

They waited quietly for a further five minutes before Charles returned and the operators took a break.

"OK. That's sorted. We have increased security at all levels and Joe has agreed to formally list this operation as an Interpol joint venture under the drug trade umbrella. We'll have about a week before I have to make any sort of official report. After that there will be compromises."

Eddy nodded and activated her tablet. "Let's use the screen. There have been developments, Charlie and a week may be all we need."

"Sir Charles," said Bijan, "given the photo identification of you, how is it your family was tracked so quickly. I don't imagine you are in the phone book, so to speak."

"That's what has me the most concerned. It should not have been possible, which suggests your mysterious Twelve have their fingers inside the security services."

Eddy manipulated the screen and an MI6 report popped up. "This was intercepted seven hours ago, ostensibly from Al Qaeda, but with linkages that tie it to Patrascu's activities. It's an encrypted directive to deep cover agents here in Britain. SIX know the format from previous records but can't break the encryption on this one. It's an old-fashioned cypher and without the key it's *gobbledygook*. The very clever Mr. Mersey, however, has had a moment and discovered part of that key."

Charles glanced over at his analysts and Brent Mersey raised a glass to his boss in acknowledgment.

"I knew I kept him around for some reason," said Charles with a grin.

"Yes, well ... it turns out the Twelve are using the literary works of their oldest enemy as a code key. Perversely poetic, somewhat."

"Omar Khayyam," said Bijan.

"Yes," replied Eddy. "Joe's briefing gave us some history on the Twelve and how they were driven out of Persia a thousand years ago, mainly on the efforts of Khayyam. Mr. Mersey has a penchant for conspiracy theories, it seems, and made an intuitive leap. Khayyam's *Rubaiyat* is only part of the solution, however, so the transcription is garbled. The gist of the matter is they've ordered an attack on a security target. To do that they must have people inside with significant access."

"Hence, my details getting out," said Charles.

"Yes. And given hints in the message and the priorities between the branches of the security services, the leak is most likely in SIX not FIVE. The target, however, could be anyone. We need to warn SIX in particular and the security community in general."

"Good luck with that," said Eddy.

Charles glanced at her. "Colleridge?"

"Yes. I'd be sending an informal warning to Andrew Pearce with the strong suggestion to pass it on to MI5. Then Colleridge can't do an impact analysis and delay notification. Given the Twelve's actions of the last week, I strongly suspect this play is already in motion."

Charles signaled Brent and Mats and they hurried over. "You heard all that?"

"Yes, sir."

"Make it happen officially. Drop the hint we got the SIX material in parallel from Interpol. Be vague about everything else. Send Sir Andrew a private communique from me saying I'm working with Eddy and Joe on this and it's red hot.

"Go."

They returned to their desks and got to work.

"Now," said Hilde in a quiet, deadly voice, which made Eddy jump, "the other matter."

Charles laughed. In her moment of surprise Eddy had instinctively moved towards him and he had extended a hand to support her. It was a brief, reflexive gesture which confirmed them as a couple to anyone watching.

Bijan cleared his throat politely.

"Yes, well..." said Eddy as she adjusted the large screen yet again from her tablet.

"We've tracked the last five months of funerals at Bradford against standard identity confirmation and donations from a variety of charities. The red highlights are definite deceptions and the pink are ones that seem suspicious but don't have outright confirmation."

"Holy...there's twenty-seven people there," exclaimed Charles.

"And that's only one of four facilities here in Britain, with another eleven in Europe; all are either funereal or medical in nature and use containers large enough to conceal a body."

"What else, Eddy?" asked Bijan.

"This," she said and another chart sprang to life. It was police missing persons lists cross referenced to the funeral home and personality profiles compiled by the investigators.

"This is what I hinted to Joe might be happening. Patrascu and others are profiling a specific personality type and hunting them. It's the most sophisticated, selective human trafficking I've ever seen."

"And all for torture and death; to get their brain tissue?"

"Yes," said Hilde, stepping toward the screen, "fragile personalities but strong minds; easily addicted but able to cope with the effects of addiction; breakable but survivors. To do that to another human being over and over ... Eddy, I'm in. Whatever you need, it's yours. I can delegate my other responsibilities."

The air around them seemed to chill suddenly.

"Agreed," said Bijan.

"Right then. In that case, you need to see this." Eddy adjusted the screen once more. "We've been monitoring Missing Persons reports. The time lag with this sort of information is an issue, but twelve hours ago, this young woman was reported missing. She was probably snatched thirty hours before from Shipley. One of the suspect funeral packages from Bradford left for the Continent thirty-five hours ago.

"Her name is Nadira Tareen. She's second generation English from a Pakistani family who've lived here since the sixties. She's twenty-five and a graphic designer. Her family is going insane with worry."

"Where's the truck now?" asked Hilde.

"Southern Germany heading toward Salzburg. They're obviously using two or more drivers to get there that quickly; should be in Zagreb in eleven hours."

"So, they have one victim in transit and have cleared their schedule; expecting more soon," mused Bijan. "What options do we have to act?"

"We've discussed this before," answered Charles, "if we show our hand, the scrutiny becomes counterproductive, even damaging. But I can't sit by while one young woman goes to her death and at least several more are packaged for the same fate. We have to rescue Miss Tareen and close down Bradford."

"I agree," said Hilde, "but … how to do the latter without losing advantage."

Eddy suddenly began tapping her tablet. The other three looked at her then the screen.

A document from the Bradford facility popped up. The heading was 'Prospective Employees Register'. An overlay in red began attaching addresses to each name. Those on the current missing list flashed slowly. Matches!

"Brilliant! Malicious intent, by any definition. And therefore, actionable," said Charles.

"Yes," said Hilde in her quiet, deadly voice, "and we wait for the first of these to be delivered for 'packaging', as Eddy politely puts it, and then pounce, using the missing persons records as legal cover. I'll arrange for Bradford to be surveilled. You, Sir Charles, will need trusted personnel to carry out the raid. Any suggestions?"

"Yes. There are people I can rely on. But what if we have more like Morvan present?"

"We'll take care of that," said Bijan.

"That's the second item dealt with, then. What about the first?" asked Eddy.

"That's my job," announced Joe as he joined the group. Hilde stepped forward and embraced him. "Johan, it's been too long."

"Indeed, Hilde. My best to Astrid."

"Of course."

"How..." asked Charles.

Joe held up his stone. "We're a good team, Charles. Care to go again?"

"No," said Eddy.

Charles grinned. Eddy hit him in the arm softly.

He kept grinning. "Seriously, Joe, I want to do it but it has to be quietly, and quick! How do we get transport?"

Joe turned and eyebrows raised, stared at Bijan who for once looked a little caught out. "Oh..."

Hilde and Eddy burst out laughing.

RASOVO, BULGARIA

SHEHKRii
– The FLAME –

Vasily left Vizier's suite quickly. Danev's twisted smile followed him. The old fool was terrified and rightly so.

I have killed so many messengers, mused Aleksandur Danev; Vizier. *But I need Radu. He is a truly devious Servant and safe from my wrath so long as he remains useful. Even after, since his family is so entrenched in the organization.*

Yes! Family is so important. A thought had risen; a very interesting thought involving family.

Vasily had brought more bad news. Well, some, at least. Their attacks on the families of Lutz and Braithwaite had failed. It was maddening, but clearly there were other forces arraigned against them who were protecting their enemies. Vasily, in his deviousness had placed surveillance personnel behind their kill teams, but these too had been ambushed so they still did not know who opposed them.

The strategy however, was obvious. It was defensive. So, a small group, but with superb intelligence. Well then, there were a number of ways to combat that situation. But for the moment he would let other matters proceed and see what benefits resulted. Things were progressing nicely with the campaign of disruption inside British Intelligence. Soon ... many deaths to muddy the waters.

Yes, then ... we shall see. Nothing must disrupt their current endeavors.

In the meantime, family.

He opened a drawer in his desk and removed a satellite phone from its charging dock. One button press was all that was required to connect him.

"Uncle! Greetings, Vizier. How may I serve you?"

"Nephew. Lucian, I am pleased to advise you of an advancement in your current project."

"Advancement, Uncle?"

"Yes, yes, my boy. You have done well, setting up our American operations. We look forward to moving that enterprise into fully functional status very soon. However, I believe the day of reckoning may be closer than expected."

"Yes, Uncle. A glorious day, indeed. What must I do for you?"

Vizier smiled. "Prime the pump, nephew. The Chechens most likely but I leave that to you. If the glorious day comes unexpectedly we must be ready. And Lucian …"

"Yes, Uncle?"

"You are well supplied with Nectar, are you not?"

"I am."

"Stick to your dosages, nephew, and success will be ours. You will take your place at my side soon."

"I live for that day, Uncle."

"As do I, beautiful boy. Stay strong."

He cut the connection and returned the phone to its drawer.

Grandnephew, really, not that such things mattered. The boy was the son he had always longed for. A sharp, unforgiving leader of men, unhampered by morality or hesitation. Danev had cultivated him since he was a child when he had found him torturing other children.

Such a find.

His mind returned to the Nectar. And Kerenski.

The Russian fool was undoubtedly correct. The Herd were a specific lot. It was maddening not to be able to simply take what they needed. Hunting for it was infuriating. But Kerenski was gifted and that could not be wasted. Once the system of acquisition was perfected, however, then the doctor's impertinence would be rewarded. The punishment would take days.

Perhaps he would invite Lucian to watch. Yes, it would be good to share such an experience.

His mind wandered into the intricacies of pain and how to maintain it without diminishing the neurological impacts.

***

Vasily went back to his office quickly, keen to start backtracking the failed attacks on both Lutz and Braithwaite. It was infuriating, these failures and terrifying to have to report them to Vizier.

He was crossing a courtyard back to the front building of their complex when one of the guards rushed up.

"Honored Sir, we have a problem."

Vasily looked up. Behind the guard came one of several local officials whom they paid and someone new. An officious looking, middle-aged man and an assistant. The local, Dorin, looked alternately embarrassed and afraid.

Vasily focused. The air around the group started to appear in patterns, then colors. He read intention and personality in a glance.

Muttering under his breath, he stepped past the guard and raised his right hand.

The newcomer collapsed to his knees, clutching his guts and pitching forward onto the cobbled pavement.

Vasily turned to the assistant. "Your superior is mistaken about anything to do with this place." He looked down at the writhing man and twisted his hand slightly. The official screamed like a stuck pig and soiled himself loudly.

"If you do not wish to suffer worse you will do exactly what Dorin tells you. Comply and you will be rewarded. Now get this trash out of my yard."

He turned and walked away, irritated that his train of thought had been interrupted. He would call his brother, Aurel. Speaking his mind to family always cleared his head and let him think clearly again.

The guard and Dorin lifted the moaning man gingerly and dragged him back to the front gate.

BRADBURY, U.K.

SHEHKRii
– The FLAME –

Charles had established Hilde's credentials with the tactical response team. She was a somewhat vague consultant with the Swedish *Polisen*, which was true in principle, once. Beyond that the team didn't care, because she ran them like they'd known each other for years, and if there was one thing combatants valued it was a leader who knew what they were doing. Hilde radiated that confidence like a drug.

And she had warrants issued by MI5 thanks to the indirect influence of Andrew Pearce.

"Incoming, Ma'am," reported the squad leader, Captain Wrigley. "Two vans with a bike on long tail. ETA, forty seconds."

Hilde grunted. Her own team had reported the approach a minute earlier. *Now,* she mused, *we see who the serious players are.* She concentrated and let herself swim in the sea of consciousness. Where Bijan had his knack for judgment, this was hers; a knowing of the human psyche that was fine-tuned.

There was one monster among them, a passenger in the second van, which was now entering the compound. An ugly, ravening mind keen to cause pain, but now restrained and focused, watching his team and keeping them in line with the hint of punishment. Watching also, for the telltales of anyone who came too close.

So …

"Captain, hold all positions. We have a bogey, which I'll take care of. When you see the leader fall, initiate the take-down."

"Ma'am! Are you sure? We have everyone in our sights now"

"He's a specialist, Captain. You wouldn't make it past the fence."

"Yes, Ma'am."

***

"They're all conscious now," said Brent.

Eddy let out a breath. "Thank God!"

"Captain Wrigley is getting formal statements but the initial reports seem to be the same for all three; knocked out with no warning and nothing till they were revived."

"What now?" asked Mats to no one in particular.

"How so?" said Eddy.

"Well, we've rescued the abductees, captured the gang and their leader, and no one's the wiser thanks in no small part to Miss Nordstrom. We could use all that as leverage for greater access to the Islamic community and paly the long game. Or we could prosecute the hell out of the funeral home and start a few riots."

Eddy looked uncomfortable.

"The latter, I think," said Bijan.

"Excuse me. I would have thought ..."

Bijan held up a hand, his expression hard.

"Few of these infiltrations go unnoticed. The communities accept they are being held hostage and choose to do nothing. The younger members who have the will to make changes leave because it's that or have their families targeted. Until the process is reversed, there will be no change from within.

"My recommendation is that you expose the schemes but go softly on the businesses involved. Work the extortion angle sympathetically. With the information at hand you should be able to retrieve or protect the people most at risk. Once established it's a matter of that protection remaining reliable enough for people's courage to catch up.

"The charities financing these things though, them you should purge aggressively. And we'll help you with the information streams, which will prevent the financiers slithering out of harm's way. Sir Charles has to report to your superiors in a few days, I think? I'll show you how and we'll have both a detailed document and an achievable action plan for him when he returns."

"Returns. Yes, there is that," said Eddy.

Bijan stepped close and placed a hand on her shoulder. "Try not to worry, Eddy. They are both in good hands."

SHEHKRii
– The FLAME –

CHAPTER 15

GLENELG
SCOTLAND

HE WATCHED.

It was what he did. Everywhere.

Here in his home and in faraway places.

Like Afghanistan. On and off for decades.

Helping those people had been so gratifying. But there was only so much you could do when people didn't want to be helped. So, you fished for the ones willin' to take a chance. And helped 'em.

Now, however, he was home and watching the locals.

Sort of.

A funny lot they were, too. He'd not known much about the Laird and didn't mix in those circles anyway; sprightly old sod, though. And the woman with him was a hard case. Very organized, she was.

But he kept his distance and watched. It was what he had been asked to do and he had no problem with the askin'.

***

Brigid glanced around. She had a strange sense of being observed. The estate staff was packing up the van after taking delivery of this month's supplies and everything was normal.

SHEHKRii
– The FLAME –

But …

She shrugged it off, checked the manifest one last time and got them on their way. John was at the pub and she started walking that way to meet him. The town car was there also and the two of them could take their time returning. John liked to mix with the locals when he was in residence and she couldn't complain. They were a small community here on the coast but very agreeable. Especially to foreigners like herself. She was local color in their eyes.

Oh, if they only knew what color.

I'm getting maudlin, remembering the bad old days, she mused. Must be that strange man, Nathan Chalk. His visit had stirred up old fears. What if the Council found her? What if they found what John was guarding?

She couldn't entertain regrets, though. The last twenty years had been so good. She didn't want to lose that; wouldn't lose it. She had been so lucky stumbling over Lord John Berwick Reginald Ellsworth all those years ago and would defend him to the death.

Brigid laughed softly to herself. *I'm winding myself up. I need some tension relief.* It had been a while since she'd indulged sexually. That usually sorted her out. There were friends in York who'd happily help, gentle lovers with no strings.

The Church used sexual guilt so skillfully and obsessed over every nuance, a spider's web of hang-ups. Once you were free of that it was like living on another planet. She smiled again, musing over who would best suit her current need.

***

The tide was in, the loch full and the sky clear over the hills. John Ellsworth drank it all in, getting much more satisfaction from the view than the beer he'd just shared with the publican and a few locals. The energy of the place was like a fine liqueur. Brigid would scold him for shimmying over the stonewall of the car park and walking to the water's edge, but he looked forward to it.

She was a treasure. The fates had landed her on his doorstep at a crucial time and he was determined to keep her safe. Especially given the tremendous favor she'd provided him.

He had always been a thorn in the side of the local bishop, unwilling to toe the Church's line or sweep their many sins under the carpet. Making himself a target was, however, a calculated risk. It kept the enemy close and allowed him better warning if ever his family's legacy was threatened.

He had, however, underestimated the venom of the bishop.

Brigid had sorted all that.

Brigid! Her third given name, very appropriate. He had refused from day one to call her Catherine. That person was gone. Had to be, really.

SHEHKRii
– The FLAME –

She was on the run when their paths had crossed. Brigid was in York to listen in on the Anglican bureaucracy, reasoning that if the American Catholics were after her, then an alert from The Council would be likely in Britain. And security less stringent.

Instead, she had overheard a scheme to honey trap him. The bishop was vindictive in so many ways.

She found him through a journalist and after some negotiation laid out the scheme. With the journalist's help, he had been able to turn the tables and discredit the bishop to the point of resignation.

It had all worked out swimmingly, but Brigid was intent on moving on.

It took weeks to persuade her to stay. Understandable, given the circumstances. But in those few weeks he had realized what a find she was and determined to keep her at his side. His own resources provided a new identity and she slotted into his life like she'd always been there.

"Old man! What the hell are you doing out there? I'm not getting wet if you fall in …"

John turned, smiling.

ZAGREB,
CROATIA

Charles Braithwaite stood back from the ancient building's corner, alternately elated and as close to afraid as he was willing to admit. The people Joe had brought were the problem, especially the two he was looking at now. Peter Tan and Sophia Theophoulous.

He shivered.

They were close to their target location after half an hour of careful infiltration, most of which, for Joe and himself, had been simply moving when told to do so. Except for five minutes ago when they had come across a sweeper team a hundred meters out from their destination.

Which was when Charles had seen Peter and Sophia move!

Joe's mysterious *tech* and quasi-ninja skills were one thing but these two were entirely another. No human being could move that fast or jump that high. These two did it with a casual grace which chilled Charles to the bone.

Peter Tan turned and looked at him. The eyes penetrated his soul and Charles began to get very, very angry.

"Give him your Stone, Joe," said Tan from ten meters away, yet Charles heard it as though they were standing very close.

"What!"

Joe handed Charles the little rock which he'd used to such good effect at Tilbury. At first, he felt deep cold then spreading warmth as he gripped the Stone, unable to let it go.

Then things changed.

Sophia spoke from the same distance but her voice was like a lover's whisper, coiling around his ears, a breath upon the neck.

SHEHKRii
– The FLAME –

"People such as yourself, Charles, are in tune with their instincts much more than most. It is essential for your survival, no? The Stone allows you to take the next step. To not just trust your instincts but to see what they react to. And much of that is based on the world around you. Until now you have only looked at the world. Give yourself to the Stone and truly *see*."

Charles wanted desperately to let the thing go but could not. He stared at his hand, concentrated on it, felt the Stone's warmth, its touch, tried to understand how this could be happening. Suddenly there was an emptiness in his hand and he looked up, startled.

The world had changed. The colors ...

Charles slumped against Joe, momentarily boneless. Joe held him and gently took his Stone back. Charles straightened, turning to look around, his face a mask but his eyes alive with the delight of a child.

"How?"

"Friends in high places," answered Joe. "No time to play, Braithwaite. Adapt, utilize." This last in a hard, commanding voice, which Charles understood implicitly. He nodded to Peter, glanced at Joe and grinned fleetingly.

Peter Tan's mouth twitched a small smile and then he turned to face their target as the truck they'd tracked from Bradbury pulled out of its enclosed loading dock and swept down a side street, empty.

Peter touched his shirt below his throat and said, "Understood, Paul. I'll deal with them now."

He moved and was a hundred meters away at the warehouse in a few heartbeats. Sophia followed, leaping two storics up and through an open window.

Charles watched in wonder, following the lines of force around the couple, understanding subliminally the natural processes they'd used to perform miracles. He moved to follow.

"Wait," said Joe, simply.

"Why?"

"Peter and his team have to deal with the predators. Sophia and hers will provide a distraction. Otherwise the collateral damage would be excessive."

A few gunshots rang out; small caliber, Charles noted.

A sniper appeared on the roof and took aim at them.

"Joe, move!"

"No time. Track the bullet."

Strangely, Charles knew what he meant. As the sniper pulled the trigger he saw the slight nudge to the right, which would send the bullet off center. He saw the angle of the barrel, the downward trajectory and moved, twisted just enough to feel the bullet scream past his chest.

Before the man could fire again, a slim, blond woman appeared behind him, reached down and flipped him over the parapet.

Charles watched the fall, detached, failing to flinch at the impact. When he looked back up the woman was gone.

"Dianne," said Joe, "always direct."

"Yeah," breathed Charles.

SHEHKRii
– The FLAME –

Sophia appeared in the window she'd jumped through previously and signaled them. A few minutes later Charles was looking at an operations center that would do justice to his own department. The blond woman who had killed the sniper was standing next to a seated man, both intently watching a large screen, which was scrolling at ridiculous speed.

The screen stopped and the man pushed himself away, stood and turned, the woman taking his arm.

"Joe! Good to see you again. It's been a while."

"Paul, same."

They stepped forward and embraced, the woman smiling and taking her turn.

Charles cleared his throat.

"Ah …" said Joe, "I don't think introductions would be a good idea, Charles."

The woman, Dianne, chuckled.

"I assume you two are on a watch list somewhere?"

"A few places," said the man. "Call me Paul and that should do." He extended his hand and they shook. Charles heard the Australian accent fully and suddenly knew exactly who he was talking to. His eyebrows rose briefly and the woman chuckled again. She stopped when Sophia entered, leading a large Slavic man by nothing more than a hand around the neck. She gave a slight push and released him into the center of the room where he shook himself and turned, glaring.

"This," said Sophia, "is Aurel Radu, brother to Vasily. He runs this center."

"Bitch," spat Aurel, who spun in place and launched himself at Dianne.

Charles saw it all in slow motion. Radu was a big man and very fast, and no one else was moving. He started to reach out in frustrated reaction as the man was almost upon the slim, middle-aged woman.

The slim, middle aged woman who now moved just a little bit faster than her attacker. Stepping in and grouching, reaching up with both hands to take him by throat and crutch, she stood, turning and using his own momentum to drive him head first into the floor. She stopped millimeters from the floor still holding a man who easily weighed well over a hundred kilos and was now alternately gurgling and whining from the very firm grips, which held him in place.

Charles closed his mouth and lowered his hand.

"Do we need him?" asked Dianne in a flat tone.

Paul looked at Charles.

"Yes," he said. "I'll use him as source material. Better than any report. Assuming he'll talk, of course."

"Oh, he will," said Peter Tan, joining them. "Put him down, Dianne, if you would."

She casually tossed Radu into the space he'd left and at Peter's feet. He crouched down and placed a hand on the groaning man's head. Radu went stiff, trembled and slumped limp to the floor. Peter stood. "What do we know?" he asked.

"Quite a lot," answered Paul.

Indicating the screen behind him, he went on, "This is their primary satellite. Home base is a placed called

Rasovo, a thousand kilometers west, in Bulgaria. Zagreb is the main distribution and marshalling center.

"We have enough to shut down their European operations, including the U.K. I've kept the internal monitoring systems operational, but that will only be effective for a day, at best. After twenty hours, the other facilities will know something's up.

"Joe, I believe you should make some calls if we're to maximize the damage we want to do."

Joe nodded, looking at Charles.

"There's reference to American and Chinese centers but they're not directly connected. Both seem to be relatively new and small in scale. The rest is nuts and bolts. The really important material is the number of hostage families in play. I'm recommending we get directly involved with that. There are hundreds of people at risk and they're all on dead man's handles. We need to do something massive in the next few hours."

The concern in his voice was evident. Dianne took her husband's hand.

Charles was still not fully reconciled with what he was seeing and what he knew from intelligence reports about these two, but Paul Gareth's obvious concern for the hostages was something that resonated with Charles at a fundamental level. Bombs and hostages were things he felt were profoundly wrong and he wanted to destroy anyone who used them.

The 'shoot-on sight' orders for the Gareths could wait.

***

An hour later, Charles pushed his chair back from the makeshift *comms-center* Paul Gareth had set up. The man was an organizational genius on a level Charles had never experienced. He stood and walked to a quiet corner to think, waving to Nadira Tareen who had been revived and sat quietly in a corner sipping tea, looking slightly bewildered. She, at least, was no longer a concern.

Paul and Dianne Gareth were, however. They were on most international watch lists as arms dealers and lately, eco-terrorists. The affectionate, highly moral couple he'd just met belied all of that. And Joe, a senior official in Interpol knew them intimately. Then there were all the others, the very scary others who could do things that were simply not possible. At least, things that weren't possible yesterday.

He was getting a headache.

"Explanations time, I think," said Sophia, standing beside him when only a second ago, there had been no one sharing his corner. The throaty sensuality of her voice vibrated through him and he thought instinctively of Eddy.

"Please."

"Well, as I showed you before, the world is not what you thought. If you don't expand your frame of reference, you'll be stuck in the past. Until now, you've been one of Britain's fiercest bulldogs, a brilliant protector. Your watch just extended. If you can accept that alone, you'll cope."

SHEHKRii
– The FLAME –

Charles absently scratched his stubble. "I get that bit. I'm not quite there but I think I can make it with a little time. It's the details though … what you can do!"

"Yes, glorious, isn't it. I remember my Return … anyway, let me put it this way, within every single human being is the capacity, the imprint, to be as we now are. By luck and design, we've found the means to access that capacity. Given the scope of what we can do, our frames of reference are not limited by loyalty to country or convention. Paul and Dianne for example …"

"Yes. Especially them."

"They protect the fringe peoples of Asia and destroy the worst of the predators as well. Don't research them through your security servers, because it will be noticed and you'll suffer because of it. There are other means if you're still curious. You're no stranger to the grey-on-grey world of politics, Sir Charles. We're just a new color you have to add to your spectrum."

Charles laughed softly. "That's very poetic for someone who could be the best assassin I've ever met."

"Now, now. We don't want to fence, do we? I'd win, of course."

He grinned. "You haven't told me much, you know. I could be upset about that if I was of a mind."

"True, but it's the spirit that counts, no? Talk to Joe when you have the time and will be free of interruptions. He's lived his whole life this way and look at what he's achieved."

She glanced over at Joe, who was speaking to Peter Tan.

"Watching M'La's son grow," she said quietly, "has been one of my life's greatest pleasures."

Charles found himself momentarily embarrassed at the intimacy of her comment. He cleared his throat softly.

Sophia turned her gaze on him, luminous eyes aglow. "You are such a gentleman! Eddy is lucky to have you."

He blushed for the second time in thirty years and Sophia walked away, a soft chuckle trailing behind.

Charles decided a coffee would be a good idea and stated toward the kitchen. He wondered if the strange plane they'd used to get to Zagreb would be taking them back to London; maybe this time he would get a decent look at the thing. The sooner the better, he mused.

He had to talk to Eddy about all this.

RASOVO
BULGARIA

The doors of the laboratory burst open and the entire room shook as Vizier stormed in. Reflexively, one of the technicians swore and glanced angrily at the old man.

Vizier rounded on him immediately and gestured with a hand. The technician gurgled and clutched his head, falling to his knees. Vizier twisted his hand and blood burst from the man's eyes and nose and he pitched forward with a squelching noise as his face hit the tiles.

He did not move.

SHEHKRii
– The FLAME –

Stepping forward, Kerenski said calmly, "How may we help you, Vizier?"

Danev glared at him, reluctantly returning his hand to his side.

"You have heard?"

"Yes. Vasily informed me a few minutes ago."

Radu stood frozen at the door to Kerenski's office. He had sent underlings to inform Vizier of the fall of their Zagreb factory.

Vizier sneered. "Coward. Come here."

Vasily complied.

"Elaborate, Vasily. I have not permanently injured your secretaries but they were less coherent than I would have liked. What happened?"

"It was Lutz and Braithwaite, Vizier …"

"I know that!"

"Ah … they, they raided our computer system. Completely gutted it. All the leverage I've, we've established with hostages … it's gone. The people have been removed and Interpol is seizing all our major assets. Some of our people have escaped but very few.

"It is a disaster, Vizier. Our enemy is … terrifying. Some of our people saw things, impossible things." He trailed off, mute, pleading.

Vizier ground his teeth.

"Doctor. If your supply of subjects is curtailed what impact would that have on the research?"

"We slow to a crawl. Without test subjects, I cannot refine the profile."

"Vasily, shut down everything west of Zagreb and keep watch for any investigations heading in this direction. Exterminate anyone who gets close. Use the Seniors. Call them in from wherever they are.

"Also, up our intake from Gong Li; triple it. And Marouk. Keep them on a very short leash, Vasily. Send Servants to oversee each. They may take Seniors also. And you doctor, you have forty-eight hours to modify your assessment criteria so it may be applied to a conscious captive in transit. When the slaves arrive, I want them already sorted.

"Vasily."

"Yes, Vizier."

"Do not disappoint me. Now … I have a phone call to make."

He turned and gestured at the doors, which blew off their hinges as he stormed back through them.

Vasily waited a full minute then left.

Kerenski waited a little longer. "Medevco."

"Yes, Doctor."

"Exit strategy?"

"In place, Doctor."

"How quickly can it be activated?"

"You have but to say the word, Doctor."

"The Work?"

"Continuous backup to multiple archives. There is no problem there, Doctor."

"Excellent. Let us get back to it then."

"Yes, doctor. Cautiously back to work …"

SHEHKRii
– The FLAME –

Kerenski laughed.

CHAPTER 16

LONDON

ANDREW PEARCE WAS GRUMPY and resisting the urge to indulge his distemper.

It was bad enough having to attend one of Colleridge's American style breakfast seminars with an internal alert in place but they had also separated him from Wethers, so he didn't even have her snide humor to distract him.

She seemed to have secured better seating, however. He was watching her, two tables towards the center of the room engaged in animated discussion with a severe-looking blonde woman he didn't recognize. Wethers was even smiling occasionally, a very un-Wethers thing to do if you didn't know her well.

But Pearce did know her well and the ensuing friendship was one he valued greatly. Lieutenant Colonel Constance Wethers was ex-SAS, one of very few women to rise high in that particular boys' club. Apart from truly impressive combat skills she was also an organizational genius, which was where Pearce valued her most.

Heaven only knew what she would do when he retired. She simply did not suffer fools and had put Colleridge's man, Kennedy, on his backside more than once. Figuratively and once, literally. Oh, what joy to see, that had been.

Colleridge had begun his morning lesson and Pearce automatically tuned his voice into the background.

SHEHKRii
– The FLAME –

He focused on the other woman: tall, pale and Scandinavian, would be his guess. She seemed to sense him looking and their eyes locked. Pearce glanced away reflexively and then back but she had returned her attention to Wethers.

He was determined to find out more. The look he had seen was one of total authority. Not just supreme self-confidence, but absolute conviction. She was dangerous and his first instinct was to warn Wethers.

Now Constance was laughing at something the blonde woman had said. Totally un-Wethers-like.

Which was when Pearce saw and heard two things simultaneously.

It was over in seconds.

He saw the armed security guard on the other side of the room bring his weapon to bear, cocking the breach as he did so. The sound of the same thing happening was all around him.

The blonde woman stopped mid-sentence and stood, spinning in place quickly, her arms whipping out, a pistol in each hand. Pearce heard five shots in rapid succession. The dull thumps of bodies hitting the floor echoed around the room.

There was absolute silence and he sensed the crowd take a collective breath, ready to scream.

But the blonde woman spoke first. "Sit. Down."

Pearce felt his backside cement itself to the chair and a chill ran up his spine.

SHEHKRii
– The FLAME –

Passing a pistol to Wethers, she said, "You have my back, Connie. Eight shells left in that magazine."

To his eternal pride, Pearce saw Wethers take the gun without hesitation and follow the blonde, adopting the standard sweeper pattern as they moved towards one of the exits.

***

Hilde placed a hand on the head of the guard she had not killed. Standing, she spoke to Wethers but loud enough to carry to Pearce. "They have back up one floor down, three men and a woman in SRR uniforms. Two other squads are attacking the main servers here and another two are hitting the back-ups in Swindon. Who can you call?

Wethers considered. SRR uniforms on all of them, probably. A general stand down order would only disadvantage her people.

Lockdown? No, it simply froze a bad situation in amber.

A light bulb went off and she smiled.

***

"Brilliant, Wethers. Truly brilliant."

"Thank you, Sir Andrew. I quite liked it."

Colleridge, followed by Kennedy stormed into Pearce's office. "What's your *effing* game Pearce? Get out, Wethers …"

SHEHKRii
– The FLAME –

The very loud cocking of a handgun silenced Colleridge, and Kennedy said timidly, "Sir …"

Hilde had moved from a corner of the room adjacent the door and had her weapon resting on the man's shoulder angled towards his face.

Wethers grinned.

Pearce resisted.

"You were warned, Colleridge, but went ahead with your ridiculous business-as-usual agenda, regardless. If not for this young woman we may all be dead."

"Who is she?" spluttered Colleridge. "She's not authorized."

"She's part of an Interpol taskforce. The one which warned us about infiltrators. The warning you tried to sideline. The Cabinet is now asking about that so why don't you toddle off and call your sponsors. You're going to need them."

Hilde tapped Kennedy sharply on the side of the head and stepped away. Kennedy spun in place dropping low to leg sweep the woman. Hilde kicked him in the thigh spoiling the move. Kennedy gasped in pain and rolled away. He came to his feet at the door and began to draw his weapon.

He was stopped by a second trigger click as Wethers extended her arm, bringing her Kimber Micro within centimeters of Colleridge's nose.

"Leave," said Pearce. 'Now."

Both men withdrew. Hilde closed the door.

SHEHKRii
– The FLAME –

"Typical," said Wethers. "Bulldoze the opposition before cooler heads can prevail.

Hilde laughed. "Surely, incompetence this obvious will be punished."

"No." answered Pearce. "He's covered himself sufficiently. And the people above him are of the same ilk. I'm seriously considering moving my retirement forward."

"Colleridge would take that as a 'win', sir," said Wethers.

"Yes. So, we will persevere, Wethers. But I'm more concerned about you, Constance. The day after I leave, Kennedy will come after you."

Wethers laughed, an ugly sound.

"Don't concern yourself, Sir Andrew," said Hilde, "Connie will prosper. I'll see to it. Someone with her mental facility should not be wasted. Calling up a biohazard evacuation and then having the perimeter guards isolate all SRR personnel worked very well. And minimal casualties when the infiltrators tried to break away.

"Talent like that will find its place."

"I'm standing right here!"

"Good hearing, too."

Pearce laughed loudly, tension suddenly welling up and leaving all in one refreshing rush. "What are we to do, Miss Nordstrom?"

"Nothing for the moment. Eddy's warning will now be taken more seriously. Whatever political influence you have should be brought to bear. Connie should also institute defensive procedures as she sees fit. Mix up the protocols. I have watchers placed to provide oversight. You should be safe for the moment."

"And after that?"

"We'll see. Much will depend on what Charles Braithwaite reports once he returns from Zagreb."

***

"Sir, I have some news."

"It had better be good news, Mr. Kennedy, because the Minister has just reamed me a new one."

"Oh!" Kennedy hesitated.

"Well?" Colleridge snapped.

Kennedy took a seat. "Sir. That alert from Interpol, which prefaced the attack yesterday … it had Charles Braithwaite's name appended and …"

"Yes, I know that, Kennedy. The Minister *pointed* it out and asked, *pointedly*, why we didn't take it seriously, given bloody Braithwaite and his impeccable reputation. So, what's *your* point?"

Kennedy's grin was vicious, "He's fucking Edwina Bryce."

Colleridge strained his eyebrows and said, "Is he now …"

SHEHKRii
– The FLAME –

GLENELG
SCOTLAND

They had spent three days in Fort William chasing down Carlisle's movements and Brony was not in a good mood. The bloody man had been too clever by half.

Eminence hadn't helped by calling her every two hours for reports.

Nor, by insisting she take the whole tactical team of twelve with her. They stood out like the proverbial. And the locals were, predictably, not cooperative hence the three days. Brony was certain Eminence had sent her just to be rid of her.

But now, she had Carlisle or at least his destination.

They were in Glenelg, a blink-and-you'd-miss-it, little blot on the map and making no attempt at deception. The team's two vans were taking up half the local inn's carpark and the rest were marked off for the helicopter Eminence was using to land in the next few minutes.

Now they were sure of the American nun's location, he had elected to swoop in and take charge. Brony couldn't fathom why Scribe tolerated the man. She wondered if she dared say so to Miles.

The helicopter's noise started to intrude and she stopped her musings and left the van to meet its occupant.

He stepped out with a little flourish of his overcoat, which spoke volumes about pride. Brony filed that one away. The machine powered down and Eminence strode over to her.

"Well! Where is she?"

SHEHKRii
– The FLAME –

"Good morning, Eminence. I trust your flight was pleasant." She heard him draw breath and rushed on, "Catherine Mulvaney is in residence on an estate about ten kilometers east. It's an untitled property attached to Lord John Ellsworth's holdings. He's from York, by the way."

"Yes, I know the family. Thorny lot. What's the nature of the place?"

"Ah, it appears to be a summer residence, quite substantial. We've had drones doing long-range surveillance. There are a half-dozen staff and several out buildings near the manse, which has been noticeably extended. I have snipers at long range."

Eminence nodded. "Well done, Sister. There's hope for you yet. Drones you say. Let's get a better look, shall we?"

"Yes, Eminence. This way."

***

Eminence gasped.

"Closer," he ordered.

Their best drone was directly over the glass and steel roof of the main house. Brony operated the device to drop it lower and increased the magnification of the video camera it carried.

On a table, the image of several books enlarged dramatically on her screen.

Eminence groaned softly, "Fucking mother of Christ, it can't be …"

SHEHKRii
– The FLAME –

The technicians nearby shuffled nervously. Brony bit her lip.

"Orders, Eminence?" she asked quietly.

***

The library was burning. Her home of the last twenty years was gone.

Brigid Perkins wanted to scream and cry but could not afford the time. John was struggling and the staff were in similar condition. Two were missing and they weren't clear of danger yet.

She looked back down the valley through the trees to the smoking ruin of her home.

Half an hour after they'd detected the drones, the assault team had come in at speed. She'd had sixty seconds of warning and immediately responded, but the bastards hadn't hesitated and the front of the house was destroyed by grenade launchers before the vans had skidded to a stop.

The quad bikes had earned their purchase price at that point, as she and John sped away just as gunfire erupted within the house. Four more staff on the other two bikes raced after her and they were clear just in time, keeping to heavily wooded trails planted for just this reason.

But the drones were still aloft and she had a nervous feeling about breaking cover.

The brakes were on hard before she could think, and the bike slid dangerously as a thickset young man stepped into the trail and held up his hand. She desperately held onto Lord Ellsworth, whose grip was no longer strong.

"Who, the hell …"

"Miss Perkins," said the man in a thick Glaswegian accent, "The Keeper has set me as your protector. I have friends nearby."

Brigid felt herself wilt in relief. She drew breath to speak.

"Wait, please. We're dealin' with the snipers and the drones. Do you have your escape route well in mind, Miss?"

"Yes. We know the drill …"

The young man was smiling.

"What?"

"Your accent, Miss. I had no idea you were from California. I have friends there. Lovely place."

"Really! Do we have time for this chit chat?"

"Always time for civilized conversation, Miss. Now … yes." He turned his head slightly as though listening.

"You can proceed. Their outliers won't bother you. I'll cover your trail."

Brigid glanced back, "They're heavily armed. At least a dozen." She turned back to regard the youngster. He shrugged and was suddenly holding two very large handguns with extended magazines.

"Not to worry, Miss. Dealt with worse than them a few times. Please proceed now. The Laird is a bit fatigued so not too much of a rush, if ya please."

SHEHKRii
– The FLAME –

He stepped aside and the group moved smoothly forward. Brigid glanced at him as she passed and he inclined his head with a stern expression, which made her think he was much older than he looked. Suddenly, he was gone, leaving a soft popping sound in his wake as Brigid turned back to the trail.

***

"You over-reacted, Eminence."

"Hardly, Scribe. The material could not be allowed to exist. As it is, Sister Bronwyn has seen it and I am concerned about that. At least the others remain ignorant."

There was only the two of them in one of the vans, with Scribe on a secure screen. Brony cleared her throat.

"What did you see, Bronwyn?" asked Scribe.

"An extensive library of mostly antique books, sir. Druidic subject matter predominated, but there were related materials. At the lower levels, there was an artifact vault also."

"You are a keen observer, Bronwyn. And a valuable member of The Council. Eminence's acrimony is misplaced so do not fear.

"Peter, I will not caution you again. Treat Bronwyn well. And instruct her on the significance of Ellsworth's collection. You've both done well today, but this is not the time for personality politics."

Peter Mayhew was red with anger. He took a steadying breath and his color subsided.

"As you wish, Scribe."

"Good. Bronwyn, there can be no skerrick of the library left for examination. There may also be digital records. I'll leave their eradication in your capable hands. Keep Eminence informed at every stage."

"Yes, sir. I'll see to it."

The screen blinked off.

"Well," said Mayhew, "Enforced truce, it seems?"

"Yes, Eminence."

"So be it, Sister. Now, the library. What do you know of the Vatican vaults?'

The oblique question took her by surprise. "Ah … nothing in detail. I've seen the précis provided by Reverence when I was inducted to Senior Operational status a few years ago. It's extensive and esoteric. Seems a waste of effort, personally, but …"

"We agree on that last. They have to keep digging more basements. Hoarders simply can't stop!

"Unfortunately, much of their collection is extraordinarily dangerous. Its publication would cut our flock in half. Ellsworth's library would do worse."

Brony gasped, "How?"

"I saw the index. It demonstrates everything we've ever appropriated from the Pagans and paints them in a far better light than even the Romantics tried to. It would have been our undoing."

He sat down deflated.

"They must have backups," said Bronwyn. "It would be gross stupidity not to. We *have* to find them."

"Agreed. Recommendations?"

Brony began to think furiously.

A nearby screen pinged and she turned to acknowledge the incoming message.

"Sir."

"Yes, Sister."

"We've found Carlisle."

Mayhew's vicious smile sprang up immediately and Brony found herself aroused. She blushed furiously and Mayhew began to laugh.

LONDON

Mats and Brent jumped up to greet Sir Charles as he and Joe topped the stairs.

"Welcome back, sir. You too, Joe."

"Thanks, I think!"

Charles laughed. "What have you three been up to in my absence?"

Eddy walked up and embraced Charles. Stepping back, she said, "Follow ups mostly, not as exciting as setting half of Europe on fire, like you two."

"Smoldering rather than on fire, I would think," said Joe.

Eddy laughed as they returned to the room proper.

"The French are having a fit. But that report of Bijan's, which you authorized while in transit, seems to have kept a lid on things. Very little has made the press, at least. Yet."

"Speaking of Bee ..." asked Joe.

"Not sure," answered Eddy, "he left a few hours ago; said something about being needed back in Australia. He also said he'd take care of the Twelve's Chinese operation."

Mats brought Charles a cup of tea. "There's something else you might want to see," he said.

"Yes?"

"Those follow-ups Eddy mentioned. We've been tracking the Twelve's American operation. It looks nasty."

"Really; do tell." Charles gave Eddy a speculative look. She smiled back.

"Mats is right, 'nasty' is a good word. Brent, would you project the matrix, please."

"Done."

They all turned to the large tactical screen.

"This, lady and gentlemen, is the skeleton of a repeat of what we've just shut down in Europe. The focus is not so much funereal repatriation, but rather cyto-toxic waste disposal. It's got no ties we can find to any of the financial entities here, but the profiles are the same.

"The interesting thing though is the timing. This set-up appears to be in its early days. We don't think they've started abducting anyone yet, but they have bought some significant property in Manhattan and Brooklyn. We've identified the U.S. inspection personnel involved and are trying to profile them but at arm's length, it's going to take a while."

"I might be able to help," said Joe, standing and facing them. "I should probably keep mobile. The Twelve still have a contract out on me and I know someone in the C.I.A. who can help."

Charles sipped his tea. "You'll be protected over there?"

"Oh, yes. Very well protected."

"Good. It would be nice to be ahead of this thing rather than simply reacting. My suggestion, use 'alternative' transport. If they know you're in the U.S. it won't take much to panic them."

"Agreed. Think I'll get going; that way I can spend a few hours at home in Seville before landing in New York."

He rose and embraced Eddy. Nodding to the other men, took his leave.

"Priorities?" asked Charles.

"Well," said Brent, "we have an opportunity to recruit a few people. Bijan's strategy with the Bradford community and the successful return of Miss Tareen have popped a cork, so to speak. He was right, give the younger ones some security and they will step up."

Eddy listened. Her team was whole again and she was happier than she could ever remember.

NORTH WALSHAM
NORWICH, UK

Bart operated the remote-control console, alternately watching it and the sled at the end of the platform. It started to move.

Then it accelerated, tearing past them in a matter of seconds.

SHEHKRii
– The FLAME –

"Feckin' hell! I mean, wow!" said Rhys Davidson. "What's the power to weight ratio again?"

"Thirty-seven to one. The sled weighs nine hundred and five kilograms."

Davidson ran a hand through is hair. "Why haven't we seen anything like this before?"

"It's new and we don't want to be swallowed up by the corporates. Our investors are looking at a forty-year program. Your situation is ideal for them."

Bart brought the sled back to the platform and the custom crane-truck on the freight side of the platform started lifting it off the tracks. He signaled to the stationmaster that they were finished with the test.

"But we're a bunch of amateurs and volunteers. I can't see the opportunity you want." Gesturing around, he added, "We barely keep this little stretch of track operational. And profit is just a dream."

"We can change that. The solar cell and turbine rig needs long duration testing to justify further investment. Your rolling stock is easily adaptable to our drive system. We get test data and you get to offer a local freight service. British Rail needs to handle the signaling. That's the only hiccup to be ironed out.

"If we can get the first phase up and running, you'll be pleasantly surprised at the number of small ethical investors who'll line up to help."

Davidson scratched his nose. "I've signed the confidentiality agreement, by the way."

"Good. Ten years from now there'll be an off-shore wind and wave power plant in the Western Eddy just off Cromer. This area will get a huge economic boost."

"And we'll be the only railway available to move people and freight. Ten years isn't long."

Bart ground his teeth. This was taking more effort than he wanted to make.

"Rhys, mate, how hard do I have push to get you over the edge?'

Davidson grinned. "Not too much more, mate. But I'm not the only one you gotta convince, you know. The volunteers, they don't like change."

"Which is why we want to keep all this in-house. Your chief stick-in-the-mud is Owen Walton, right?"

"Oh yeah!"

"Well, he's got a nephew on his sister's side; name's David. He lives in Cambridge but is about to move home. He's one of our technical people and I can guarantee, Uncle Owen is about to get a new hobby."

Bart nodded towards the sled, which was now being strapped down on the truck.

"OK, then," said Rhys.

They found the car Bart had rented and drove back to Rhys's office. He was one of a number of local surveyors and had a small staff of eight. A huge map of Norfolk dominated the end of the open plan office. Someone had drawn a thick, irregular red line around the whole county.

Walking in with Bart, Rhys saw this and said, "Hey! Who the feckin' hell did that?"

"That would be me," said Hilde Nordstrom, stepping up from behind.

"Oh," answered Rhys. He'd met Hilde earlier in the day and had drawn the obvious conclusions.

"Boss, boss," interrupted one of the staff, "You've got to see what she drew. You're the railway man, right?"

Bart grinned at her.

"I've given the staff our IFP," said Hilde. "They're all quite enthusiastic about the opportunities. None of them will betray the enterprise and we can leave Mr. Davidson to stew over possibilities for a few days. The others need us back in London."

"Oh, I thought … OK. I hope I'm going to get a break soon. The last few weeks have been non-stop."

"I'll drive. You sleep. We seem to have lost our tail again, so the journey should be quite sedate."

"Yeah, right."

CHAPTER 17

MARYLEBONE
LONDON

NEIL CARLISLE SAT IN A CORNER nursing a cup of Bart's favorite tea and felt ... *what! Like a teenager after his first kiss?*

He and Jaz had finally ... made love, bonked their brains out! He wasn't sure what to call it but by God, she had stamina. And he was out of condition.

His body and his mind were both feeling very mellow.

Unfortunately, they were going to have precious little time to explore their new normal. Things were starting to gather momentum. Things being the new ventures which were popping up all over. After nearly a decade buried in Plymouth, he was travelling more than he was writing.

Maybe he could do both.

This morning was supposed to be a coordination workshop. The building was an old, solid masonry thing, refitted as serviced offices. They had the top floor and more of Hilde's people were due soon to manage the meeting and make happen whatever Neil and his team decided. It was a significant change, having a staff and not having to make do all the time. He was getting very used to it. Jaz was in her element

Bart arrived and Neil stood to greet the young man. It had been weeks since they'd seen each other.

After a few moments, they all adjourned to the kitchen.

"What took you so long?" asked Liam.

"We picked up a tail at Gatwick," said Bart. "Hilde was pissed. She said facial recognition wasn't working ..."

"What?"

"Yeah, I know. Apparently, we're invisible to that sort of program. Don't ask me how."

Liam frowned. He could see how it might be done but ... that could be chased later.

"Anyway," said Bart, "we kept losing them and the little leeches kept picking us up again. Hilde said she'll look into it soon. I think she's worried."

"So," interjected Jaz, "we've been comparing notes and we know what we've been doing. What have you been up to?"

Bart scratched his chin, "Well, after we left Spain ..."

It took nearly an hour to recount his travels and more of their 'staff' arrived, introduced themselves and moved out into the open office area.

"... So, the rail project looks like it'll happen across the next eighteen months and we can start prepping for the off-shore power plant immediately after."

"Wow," said Liam, "seriously, wow! We're a corporation."

"Obviously," added Jaz.

"Yeah," said Neil, "but are we directors or just very active figureheads? I still baulk at the scale of all this."

SHEHKRii
– The FLAME –

"Fellow travelers on the same Path," answered Hilde as she joined them. She reached out and caressed Liam's face as she stopped next to him. He smiled but also turned beetroot red. The others just gaped.

Which was when the laser dots appeared on all their chests.

Hilde took Liam and Bart to the ground instantly. She was about to go for the other two when Neil moved, crashing into Jaz to knock her aside. A bullet ripped across his back and shoulder. The 'staff' reacted with the extreme speed typical of the *Shehkrii* and were gathering up Neil's team and dragging them to the outside walls for protection.

Hilde stood in full view of one of the large windows and touched the torc under her shirt. She spoke briefly in the guttural language Liam and the others had heard on several occasions. The tone in her voice could melt glaziers. She was covered in laser dots but did not move.

A fusillade of shots rang out and Hilde blurred, stepping out of the way and back again as the bullets tore apart the back wall of the office.

The same guttural voice spoke from her torc and she answered briefly.

"All clear," she said and stepped over to Neil to check his injuries. The young man with him and Jaz said something about 'painful but repairable'.

Liam and Bart knelt to help.

"Get him up, please," said Hilde. "We'll have to vacate immediately. The Council will have back-up on the way. Jaz, stay with him. He'll have medical attention shortly. Angus will shepherd you until then."

Jaz glanced at the young man who had helped, nodded, and together they lifted Neil up and gingerly walked him away. He seemed dazed but not much more. The three of them were shadowed by three others from the 'staff', who had gone from looking like casual office workers to something resembling a military protection detail. They all had guns.

"With me, please, gentlemen,"

"Yes, ma'am," they answered jointly and smiled at each other.

"What's going on?" asked Bart as they left the office via the rear stairs.

"Something unanticipated. We've heard chatter for over a week that the Council were actively searching for you. But we were confident our countermeasures would make you invisible. I suspect Brony has been creative. There's a fountain of spite in that girl and quite a bit of intellect.

"Something will have to be done."

They reached the ground and a car was waiting. Ten minutes later they entered a large shopping mall car park and changed vehicles. No one had spoken.

Hilde's torc glowed and she touched it with two fingers.

"English, please. I have Liam and Bart with me."

"As you wish, Hilde," said a voice the two didn't recognize.

"We interrogated the team leader. They've been tracking you by intensively watching the camera feeds from any available surveillance system. Dr. Carlisle and his team are identified as are you, Hilde. The group which attacked you were London S.F.C. The range of influence involved here is quite impressive. We will need to deal with that."

"Agreed. However, let's wait a little longer. I'm sure there will be more to deal with shortly. The shape of that may help us."

"As you wish. We're decommissioning the London office, it's compromised, obviously. I'll keep you apprised of alternative facilities."

"Thank you. Once Dr. Carlisle is stable, bring him to the shop in South London."

"Done."

Hilde touched the torc again and the conversation was over.

"Shop?" asked Liam.

She smiled, "Yes, it's quite quaint. A dress shop. One which has a rear warehouse we can drive into. No chance of random identification. We'll change cars again, though."

"What just happened, Hilde?"

"We were the victims of our own over confidence. With the cloaking effect on facial recognition we enjoy, we assumed our coming and goings were invisible. Somehow, Brony managed to locate you, Bart in North Carolina. We lost the tail of course but she reacquired you and me at Gatwick. It's been cat and mouse since then. I should have taken it more seriously."

"Maybe, maybe not," said Bart. "The harm's done. How do we deal with it?"

Hilde glanced at him, a small grin played across her face.

"We wait. Once we see their next move, I can map out a more appropriate response."

"Massive, I hope," added Liam.

"Oh, yes."

***

"Dress shop" was a relative term. Bart couldn't stop blushing. More like a high end, alternative design studio, there was an eye-catching amount of the female form on show. The place seemed to be a drop-in center for aspiring models and couturiers in equal numbers. He thought they were in Walworth but wasn't entirely sure given the torturous ride they'd just had.

Fortunately, they had adjourned to offices on the third floor fairly quickly. Three hours later, Neil and Jaz joined them. As did Nathan Chalk.

"Well, we've had a little kerfuffle, haven't we?"

Neil laughed and then winced.

"Sorry, doctor. I'll try to restrain my wit.'

"No problem."

"And I have news."

"Good news, I hope," said Jaz.

"Depends. Through their puppets, The Council have had you and Hilde declared terrorists. Our existing computer tricks will mitigate that, but the effects will be short lived. We need to counter attack now. It must, however, be subtle. We cannot afford to be identified. Yet."

"Follow the money," said Jaz.

"Interesting, Miss Bhari, very interesting. Hilde ..."

"Yes, Keeper." She touched her torc again and issued what sounded like orders but which had a strange, rhyming cadence.

"Oh!" said Bart as he stepped away from a spot on the floor. The slight gaps between the timber floorboards had begun to ooze black liquid. It quickly congealed upwards becoming a square-ish, glossy black slab.

"Excellent," said Nathan.

Bart stared at the thing. He should have been freaking out but after the last few weeks this was ... unsurprising.

Hilde stepped up to the slab, placed both hands on it and said, "Liam, Jaz. Join me, please."

"Okaaay!"

The top of the slab glowed gold for a few seconds then erupted into a holographic jumble of code and images.

"Liam," said Hilde, "think of this as a larger version of the 'mouse' you've been using. I'm going to deal with the security issues. I want each of you to dig into the Council servers and tell me what you find."

Nathan and the others watched for several minutes as Hilde, Liam and Jaz manipulated the information net projected by the Stone. Eventually, Hilde stepped back and the others followed.

The smile on Jaz's face was vicious. "I have a suggestion."

"We're listening."

"Well, Hilde's countermanded the terrorism alerts somehow but they can be reinstated. We really need to knee The Council in the balls …"

There was a ripple of laughter around the group.

"… And the best way to do that is twofold: go for the head and go for the money. Eminence and Mahdi are immediately vulnerable based on what I've just seen …"

"Yes," said Liam, "turns out Eminence, I can't believe that name, has got his fingers in some very dirty pies. If we simultaneously drop a few files on the tabloids and MI5, he should be in custody within hours."

"And Mahdi has been playing both sides of Islam for decades. There are several videos which will get him killed in a week."

"And the money?" asked Nathan.

"I can deal with that," said Hilde. "There's an opportunity here, Keeper, if you approve."

"Yes?"

"When Eminence destroyed Ellsworth's library …"

Neil gasped and groaned simultaneously and Jaz said, "When? Are they alright?"

"… Yesterday and 'yes'. As I was saying, when they attacked Glenelg, we insulated Ellsworth and his estates by setting up a blind trust in Zurich. His finances are protected. We can augment that trust with The Council's hidden monies and give Dr. Carlisle a boost which could save decades. Isn't there a saying about 'birds' and 'stones' which applies here?"

Nathan chuckled softly, "Traceability and consequences?"

"With Jaz's help, I believe we can control both. I'd also like to involve Liam. He's shown a certain complexity of thought lately, which will be useful."

"Agreed. Timeframe?"

"A day at most."

"Very well. Hop to it, you three. Bart, m' lad, you've not met John Ellsworth or the indispensable Miss Perkins. Take Neil in tow and we'll visit them while the others work. They're down in Winchester. A friendly face should perk his lordship up a bit. The last few days have been a touch tryin'."

***

"...MAJOR SCANDAL HAS ERUPTED IN THE HALLS OF THE ANGLICAN CHURCH. PETER MAYHEW, UNDERSECRETARY TO THE ARCHBISHOP OF CANTERBURY HAS BEEN TAKEN INTO CUSTODY ON MULTIPLE CHARGES OF MONEY LAUNDERING, BLACKMAIL AND ORCHESTRATING THE DEATHS OF AT LEAST FIVE POLITICAL RIVALS. THIS SENSATIONAL DEVELOPMENT

SHEHKRii
– The FLAME –

COMES ON THE BACK OF THE SUPPOSED TERRORISM RAID ..."

"Turn it off," snarled Scribe.

They were in the basement again, under the British Library.

Brony complied.

He paced for minutes, muttering occasionally.

The other operators squeezed into their chairs and kept as far away as possible. Brony sat and waited. The last thirty hours had been devastating. They'd been so close and almost taken Carlisle in central London. The snipers were supposed to wound, not kill but they'd failed miserably and then Carlisle had vanished. Eminence had been furious and stormed off to get the terrorism alert in place. She'd returned her team and their vans to the depot then found her way back here.

It felt safe, deep in the ground, away from any scrutiny.

A day later it no longer felt that way.

"Any word on Mahdi," snapped Scribe.

"No, sir. He missed his allocated window."

"Alright! Clear the room. Sister, you stay."

They were quickly alone.

"Miles," said Brony, daring to use her cache, "what is it?"

He threw his hand in the air and began to walk around erratically in little circles.

"Mayhew is an idiot," he shouted.

SHEHKRii
– The FLAME –

"The fool of a man had no filters. He could not be convinced to hide his excesses. And this …" he gestured at the screen, "… is the result.

"Knocked over like a house of cards."

Brony reached out and touched his shoulder lightly. "Miles. We can fix this. *I* can fix this."

He rounded on her, taking her upper arms in a fierce grip and pulling her close. The mint returned.

"Yes. Yes, you can, Bronwyn. But what I need from you now, Sister, is much different."

She smiled into his eyes, feeling his heat, her own already risen. Leaning in, she kissed his mouth tentatively.

Scribe responded, tenderly at first, then with more vigor. He began to tear her clothes off and she responded, rising to the urgency of his need.

They stumbled to a nearby lounge and he penetrated her without any foreplay, rutting deeply, one hand on her hip and the other squeezing a breast hurtfully.

Brony drank it all in, the culmination of her career. Rough play was nothing new. Truth be told it helped assuage the tendrils of guilt she felt whenever she indulged in sex. But this was different. This was Scribe and it was holy.

He flipped her over and entered her from behind. Brony arched her back and tilted her head towards him, turning to see the look on his face.

He was smiling but there was strange caste to the look. It was expectant, ecstatic and just a bit manic. His hands slid forward around her throat and his rhythm increased.

His fingers closed tighter and Brony began to pant.

"Yes, Sister. On the edge of life and ecstasy. Exquisite, isn't it?"

"Miles, I ... I can't breathe."

He turned away as he reached climax, his hands spasmed, crushing the life out of Bronwyn Petersen just as her own orgasm began. Scribe pumped away into dead buttocks vibrating on impulse only, the life gone from his latest victim.

Just the way he liked it. She was worth something, a good soldier. And he had taken it away.

Scribe pulled out and cleaned himself, sated. Picking up some of her clothes, he threw them over Brony's corpse then dressed. Sealing the room, he called his personal security; they knew what to do and the evidence would be ash by tomorrow.

MURRAY HILL
N.Y.C.

Joe landed in McCarren Park early the next morning. Hakim Jackson was waiting with a nondescript car and breakfast. The skimmer was gone within seconds.

They ate quietly then set off. The traffic was light and Hakim headed toward midtown while Joe reviewed the file on the front seat.

"So," he said, "the townhouse at East 36th Street seems to be the main facility."

"It's the most expensive piece of real estate and the one with the most personnel. They've just finished renovating so there've been multiple deliveries. Ideal cover for just about anything."

"True, but nothing technical. No similarities to the U.K. setup."

"Not on the surface. But if they were aiming for a shopfront, which was medically orientated this would be ideal. Maybe the warehousing comes later. They've got a small bond store in Greenville but it's more exposed than you would expect."

"Hmm … how close can we get to the townhouse?"

"No problem. I've had blanket surveillance in place since yesterday and an observation point across the road."

Half an hour later, Joe was listening to a Chechen dialect he didn't understand.

"Housekeeping," said Hakim with a shrug. The other two people in the apartment smiled and continued to monitor the screens. It was a conventional set up; motion, infrared and audio/visual sensors. Hakim placed his Stone over a console and the voice began to translate.

All very mundane stuff. Joe found a seat and tried to reset his imagination. *What have we missed?*

"Sir!"

Instantly he was out of the chair and joining Hakim behind the operator. The monitor showed two mini-buses arriving at the mews entrance to the target townhouse. Ten men and three women disembarked with light luggage and entered in relatively short order. While not all universally grim it was a dour bunch. Hakim reached over and dialed up the audio slightly. Joe recognized Yemeni Arabic. The translations were all ordinary.

Joe was about to return to his chair when he saw another mini-bus pull up depositing a further eight people, all men. Two of these were shown an obvious deference and quickly ushered into the townhouse.

The translations suddenly became much more interesting, Arabic again.

> *"All present and accounted for effendi."*
> *"The weapons are ready?"*
> *"Yes."*
> *"Good. Marshal in the basement. We will begin shortly."*
> *"Yes, effendi."*

Instructions were issued in several languages.

One of Joe's people reset controls and an infrared 3D image took over one screen and scrolling translations, the other. Hakim touched his shirt just under the collar and Joe saw a familiar glow. He spoke softly in the guttural language Joe had grown up with. A few minutes later the leaders addressed the group.

> *"Brothers and sisters, we have been given the keys to the gates of Heaven. Tonight, your families will feast in your honor and your names join the rolls of the holy saints sitting at God's feet. Take up your weapons and go forth. You know the plan; you have practiced and are perfect.*

SHEHKRii
– The FLAME –

Terrorize for a few minutes and draw the police back here where we may kill so many more.
  "Allahu Akbar!"

The audio was drowned out momentarily as the group returned the salutation thunderously.

Seconds later heavily armed, armored men and women began a controlled exit in disciplined fire teams, leap-frogging out of the mews and splitting in two directions up and down 36th Street. No shots had been fired but the few bystanders who were about started to scatter.

A soft alarm went off next to Joe.

"Sir! Radiation spike."

Hakim leaned in a little to look at the infrared image and saw a man in the basement opening a crate, which flared with heat and hard radiation.

"Crap!" he said and started giving orders in the old language. Joe rushed to the window to observe, expecting gunfire to erupt any second. Hakim joined him.

"When …"

"Wait …."

Seconds ticked by as the teams took up holding positions and made ready to fire.

A single, very loud gunshot rang out and all the armed men and women dropped as one.

"Go," said Hakim beside him, and he saw the familiar blur of the *Shehkrii* appearing from elsewhere in the mews and cannoning through the townhouse door and windows.

"Let's go," said Hakim.

SHEHKRii
– The FLAME –

As they crossed 36th Joe looked in both directions and saw police barricades being erected and enough uniforms to keep people back from all the bodies.

Smooth. Hakim seemed to have a knack for anticipation. And resources.

They entered the townhouse and quickly descended to the basement. Two women were present, one standing over the opened crate peering in and the other holding one of the leaders by the back of the neck. Two bodies lay nearby.

"Hakim," said the one at the crate, "we have a problem."

Joe stepped over with Hakim and looked at the timer on top of the small stainless steel device. It read seven minutes and fifteen seconds and was counting down.

"He got to it just ahead of us. Another three seconds …"

The captive laughed. "It's only two megatons but we are all martyrs now."

"Clear the building and those adjacent. Hold him outside. Joe, let's go."

Joe was stunned: *I'm going to die!*

CHAPTER 18

WINCHESTER, U.K.

Neil stared harder. "How is that possible? We're weeks ahead of schedule."

Bart smiled. "Liam put in some extra time last week. Stress tested the whole system and it passed. Planetary Management Theory is now live and hack proof."

"Seriously?"

"Yep," said Liam, "the site is hosted across multiple servers, which rotate randomly every thirty seconds. No way anyone can trace it, and the firewall is absolute. We tried everything. Terra just eats 'em for breakfast."

"What about contributors? We want people to interact with the site."

"No problem," answered Liam, "we've got …"

The conversation flowed back and forth for twenty minutes.

"Brilliant," said Jasmin, "within a year we'll have an online community in the tens of millions."

Neil stepped away. Once Jasmin saw a path forward he knew better than to play agent provocateur; she would shred his arguments if he tried. And she was right. The community they were building would grow exponentially courtesy of some high-tech wizardry that could never get out.

SHEHKRii
– The FLAME –

Ellsworth would be so pleased. The old boy was resting but he had to see this. Maybe, once they had a schematic.

Then there was The Council's financial trail. Jaz said it was under control but they didn't have everything just yet. Soon, she said.

Ellsworth would need to see that, too.

Hilde had entered their new rooms and was speaking to Nathan. He walked over to ask a question.

"… Well, thank you, Keeper. I've just been informed we have reacquired the Heir."

"Really. That's fortunate. Where?"

"Langley. Andrew Moses spotted her. They've changed her face."

"Ah … and Andrew's assessment?"

"She has hardened herself. Her grief is a shield."

"Sad, no?"

"Yes. I hesitate to think how I would react if Astrid was taken from me."

"Indeed. Inform Hou. I would value her opinion on the matter."

"As you wish, Keeper."

Hilde grinned at Neil and left.

"May I ask …"

"Of course. What do you know of Sun Tzu?"

"Um … ancient Chinese military strategist?"

***

SHEHKRii
– The FLAME –

Jasmin sighed with satisfaction. They were working together again and it felt so good. Liam and Bart were fully briefed, and within days she'd have the first draft to start shaping into something much more potent. The last few weeks organizing this place had been draining despite the promise it held. They were buried in an older part of the town, a nondescript terrace amongst many more of the same. But what a facility; more an operations center than anything else.

And the equipment! Gods above and below, I hope I can keep the Americans out of this, she thought. *And others.*

She shuddered. If her family found her now, she might actually survive. But the lifelong fear wasn't dead yet. The nightmares were less frequent though.

Bart interrupted her.

"Jaz, you asked to see this when it came in."

She took the tablet and began scrolling. The attack they had started on The Council was running full tilt. The financial structure was incredibly complex and raiding the multitude of accounts they found was initially worrying. She hadn't wanted to give away what they were doing. Liam came up with a strategy and the tablet now let her know the progress they were making. The numbers were staggering.

Then there was the information. Despite what they'd already done to Eminence and Mahdi, the rest of it was a prosecutor's wet dream. The Council had its claws into corners most people didn't know existed. Most of which were populated by politicians. It would have been depressing if it weren't so damned juicy.

She had to tell Neil about all this. Now, where was he?

***

"That's extraordinary! And she's the last of the line?"

"Not exactly ..."

Neil stepped back involuntarily when he saw the expression on Nathan's face change.

The other man gestured and suddenly a tall, black man was facing Nathan.

"Yes, Hakim. What's the problem?"

"Keeper, I'm with Joe in New York and we've just stumbled on a nuke smuggled here by the Twelve. It's been activated and we have less than five minutes ..."

Neil felt the man's fear; a nuclear bomb in New York City! The death toll ...

Nathan was moving and Neil followed instinctively. They were in the rear courtyard in seconds. Jasmin had joined them. The image of Hakim had not disappeared.

"Hakim, keep Joe close and clear the area. I'll be there in thirty seconds."

Jasmine opened her mouth to speak but was cut short by the intensity of anger that radiated from Nathan.

"Damnation and broken plates! I'm going to gut the Twelve for this. A bleedin' nuke!"

Hilde appeared from nowhere. "Keeper, What's wrong?"

SHEHKRii
– The FLAME –

Turning, his eyes ablaze, he said, "Hilde, protect yourself and these two. Full spectrum. I'm going to do something spectacular. NORAD will go ballistic. Warn the others when I'm gone."

"Yes, Keeper. As you say so shall it be."

Neil's head snapped around at the reverence and power in her voice. She strode over to them, the personification of the ancient Valkyrie, implacable, unstoppable.

She stepped behind Neil and Jasmin and held them each with a hand on their respective shoulders. There was sudden coldness in the air and Neil felt his cheeks sting. He returned his gaze to Nathan Chalk, who stood in the center of the courtyard, his arms slightly extended and his face raised to the sky.

Cobblestones started to pop. A broken piece sped toward them but ricocheted a meter before it hit.

The cobbles boiled as golden light erupted from below to engulf the other man. It spun in patterns and churned upward disappearing into the grey English sky. Celtic and Runic patterns Neil realized, an engine of graphic energies. They were suddenly engulfed in a blinding glow which surged over them and then was just as suddenly gone. Absolute silence was broken by a few cobbles that fell back to Earth.

The center of the courtyard was glass.

Neil felt Hilde's hand fall away and turned to see her stepping back. She was crying but the look on her face was one of ecstasy.

SHEHKRii
– The FLAME –

"The power ... by the Mother, I never realized ..."

She flopped onto her backside and wept like a child.

***

The café wasn't much but the coffee was good, a South American blend, and Eddy had taken a liking to the owners. Just off East Road, it was a five minute walk from Charlie's OPS center. The little cul-de-sac between it and the pub captured the warmth and excluded the wind and she found it a nice respite from the pressures of the work they were doing.

Charlie was meeting her here shortly.

The couple who approached now, however, were so obviously security service she smiled reflexively at the ridiculousness of the situation before becoming very worried.

"Edwina Bryce. You're to come with us," said the woman, while the man maneuvered behind her.

"On whose orders?"

The man tapped her on the shoulder, "Never you mind, Granny, just get on yo' fuckin' feet."

Eddy stood and he took her upper arm in a cruel, vice-like grip, shoving her forward. With the woman in front, Eddy was quickstepped towards the pub side of the cul-de-ac.

An arm shot out of the recessed doorway of the pub, striking the woman under the nose. She collapsed and rolled forward, unconscious. Charles followed the arm and seemed to embrace Eddy, turning as he did so.

Suddenly she was free, the male captor was clutching his groin and Charles was bringing his elbow down on the back of the man's neck. He turned, taking in the surrounds and then focused on Eddy, stepping up to take her gently by the elbow.

"Are you alright?'

"Yes. Now I am."

Several people were moving around them, handcuffing the couple and lifting them up. Charles directed Eddy back to her table. By the time she sat down there was no one around.

"That was quick," she said.

Taking a seat, Charles said, "Thank you. It needed to be. Those were Kennedy's people. Ex-Special Branch, now 'contractors'. I was warned half an hour ago but couldn't get here soon enough to divert you. And we suspect your phone is being monitored."

The café waitress brought out two coffees.

"Thank you, Rose. You hit that man rather hard, Charlie."

"He's a thug. Name's Morrison. There are better ways to scoop people up. He enjoys frightening his marks. So now, he'll sit in a hole for a few days and sweat. After that, both of them will be bound and gagged and dropped on Colleridge's doorstep."

"You're upset."

"Damn it, Eddy, you could have been seriously … yes, I'm upset."

He sipped his coffee and took a long breath. "And now I'm over it. Sorry."

"Thank you. I knew Colleridge was stupid but this is … you know … infantile."

Charles shrugged. "I'm not surprised but measures will have to be taken. Will you excuse me for a moment while I make a call?"

"Of course."

Charles touched several numbers on his cell phone. "Yes, Home Secretary, sorry for the intrusion. We've had a little incident and …"

Eddy was impressed. Charlie was really well connected. She'd have to make it up to him, the effort he had gone to and the intense concern he'd shown. Yes, when this was all over and done with, some very intense making up was in order.

NEW YORK CITY

Hakim rushed Joe to the front of the townhouse. He stepped away, took out his Stone and spoke, "Nathan, I need you."

Joe felt the itchy vibration of Voice at full spectrum, a sensation he'd experienced only once before when his mother had done something similar.

An image of Nathan Chalk snapped into reality in front of Hakim and he told him in a few short sentences what was happening. Joe couldn't hear the reply but

SHEHKRii
– The FLAME –

Hakim turned as the image vanished and moved Joe a few meters away.

The air suddenly lost all heat and Joe was hugging himself for warmth without realizing it. Golden lightning sprang up in front of them, reaching into the sky. It spun and spiraled creating a rumbling vortex and then was gone.

Nathan stood where the lightning had sprung from, the air crackling around him and his expression an ugly mask.

"How long, Hakim?"

"Three minutes, two seconds, Keeper."

"Get at least fifty meters away. I assume you've evacuated as best you can?"

"Yes."

"Wait for me. Gas main, I think. A cliché, I know, but …"

He was walking quickly to the front door as Hakim lead Joe away a short distance.

"But it's a nuke, Hakim."

"I know," said the other man, swallowing hard. He took out his mobile phone and dialed a number.

Joe listened, dumbfounded. He only half heard the conversation.

" … Yes, Director. An emergency situation. We believe it will go up any minute now. Evacuations are underway but it will require a major response …"

But it's a nuke, said Joe, half to himself.

SHEHKRii
– The FLAME –

***

Nathan pondered the device. Its spectral signatures were not sophisticated. A big bang and everything within two kilometers would be vaporized, including the UN. It was superbly shielded and modular in design. The Twelve must have had this in the works for months, if not years. Something will have to be done soon, he promised himself.

The last few seconds ticked off and the device detonated.

Simultaneously, a sphere of electromagnetic and gravitational force formed around the crate. The bubble glowed through every color of the spectrum and then went ultraviolet as it expanded out, engulfing most of the townhouse and several meters of the adjacent buildings.

The fires within reached fifteen mega kelvins and produced vortexes of thousands of kilometers per second. The townhouse didn't so much vaporize as fracture into subatomic particles modern science had not yet identified. Anything touching the edge of the sphere turned to powder.

Zero point three four seconds after it detonated, all that remained of the bomb and the townhouse was a pebble of matte black, carbon-like material resting in Nathan Chalk's hand as he floated in the air where the basement had been.

The adjacent buildings and the rear of the townhouse began a partial collapse, sliding into the hole.

Nathan moved through the air until his feet found purchase and he walked up to Joe handing him the pebble.

SHEHKRii
– The FLAME –

"Give this to your mother with my apologies. In my arrogance, I nearly broke a promise to her. This is to remind us both not to be so trusting.

"Hakim ... Joe and I will be returning to London. The bistro on the corner makes an excellent expresso. I think we'll have a cup or two and then depart. Please arrange a skimmer at St. Vartan's Park in about an hour."

Hakim's voice was barely a whisper, "As you say, Keeper, so shall it be."

"But it was a nuke," said Joe.

"That it was, *boyo*, that it was."

***

Lucian Danev waited.

And waited.

And nothing happened. It had all been perfectly timed. The mushroom cloud should be rising like Allah's triumphant hand over New York City now.

The small freighter was fifteen kilometers off shore, a private ship fully under his control but they could not wait much longer or there would be suspicion.

He looked out the window again then reactivated his hack into the traffic cameras around 36th Street.

Police and emergency services. Barriers everywhere!

He dialed back several minutes and then swore, reflexively striking his thigh at the blasphemy.

He saw his brothers and sisters swarm out magnificently; pride swelled.

SHEHKRii
– The FLAME –

Then they all fell together as though a switch had been flipped on their lives. There were blurs of motion nearby but they were too fast for him to follow.

Two black men crossed the street and entered the mews leading to the headquarters. A few moments later the feed was wiped out in a haze of static. It took ten seconds to reset. He could not see the building from this or any angle and then there was a rumble and the image staggered only to right itself again.

Some seconds later one of the black men and another older Caucasian came out of the mews and turned down the slight hill towards 3rd Avenue. The white man stopped momentarily and looked at one of the cameras, looked at him and he flinched back. The old man had seen him, he knew it in his soul.

He must report to Vizier at once.

Before the grizzled old man came after him.

CHAPTER 19

WINCHESTER, U.K.

They'd done it!

Starting in London and then finishing things off here in Winchester with the extra staff.

What a ride!

Jaz ran a hand over her head, absently smoothing her hair. It was something Neil did when they were in bed. Apparently, he loved her hair.

Men! Who knew.

Then there was Liam. And Hilde. No one had seen that coming. Not even Liam, or so he protested when she'd quizzed him. He couldn't stop smiling though.

But these things were small change compared to what they'd just finished doing.

Seven point three billion pounds!

They had that in a Swiss bank. More importantly The Council didn't have it. Any more or anywhere. The money had been squirrelled away in dozens of bogus financial entities. Now it was all in one place. Their place.

Her mind reeled at the possibilities.

Seven point three billion pounds!

She started writing a mental list every time she thought of the figure.

Someone cleared their throat.

Jaz turned in her seat to see Hilde entering the room followed by … her sister and two young women. There was no mistake despite the years.

SHEHKRii
– The FLAME –

She rose and crossed the gap, embracing the older woman without hesitation.

"Shireen. How …" she looked at Hilde.

"We've been looking for a while. Despite your liberators telling you long ago that Shireen was dead, we had doubts. It was not easy. But she was willing."

Jaz held her sister at arm's length. "After all this time …"

Her sister grinned. "Stockholm Syndrome? Never! Let me introduce you to my girls."

***

It seemed like hours later. Hilde showed Shireen, Gharra and Meesha to the door and their escort took them to a safe house.

Jaz was stunned. Despite the horror story of her life, Shireen had never given up hope. Her son was lost to the cultural poison served up by his father, but against the odds she'd kept her daughters unwed and educated.

And secretly subverted them to an enlightened mind-set, ready to escape if the chance arose.

It had. Finally.

Hilde returned.

"Thank you."

"You're welcome. They will need a lot of help adapting. In my opinion, England is not the place for that. I will be returning to Australia soon, I think. You should give serious thought to convincing them to come with me.

It's a less stratified society, easier to fit in across many levels."

"I'll think about it. I might join them."

Hilde laughed. "You'll be too busy for anything except frequent holidays. However, your family reunions are not over.

"Your brothers are coming."

TILBURY, UK

They came in as Customs agents; it was a frequently used deceit. Taymur and Almeida moved with easy grace and the confidence of many successful kills.

Until they saw her.

They froze.

The pictures which identified their apostate sister were in their pockets as were the ones of her protector, the freakishly tall blond woman who stood beside her now.

"You've read the file I gave you and know what monsters they are. If we let them live …" said Hilde.

"I know. I should do it, though. You've done so much and this is really about me and the mess I left behind."

Hilde smiled. "I was going to suggest that, but you anticipated me. I'm impressed."

Jaz said, "Really?"

"Yes."

Hilde produced a small caliber pistol from somewhere and handed it to the other woman. It had a fat, stubby silencer.

SHEHKRii
– The FLAME –

Jaz walked towards her brothers who suddenly found they couldn't move. Anger then panic crossed their handsome faces. Jaz wondered if she should say something, make it formal.

Instead, she simply placed the muzzle under Almeida's chin and fired twice. He was the torturer.

She turned and looked at Taymur, saw the terror and did the same. He was the rapist.

She gave the gun back to Hilde and said, "Can you have them delivered to my parents. Wait a few days until the bodies are ripe. That way they can't have a proper burial."

"As you say, so shall it be."

LONDON

Eddy handed Joe a cup of tea.

It was a day since the New York incident, as they all called it, and Joe had been back at the loft for a few hours. Charles was due any time now, having been summoned to a high-level briefing in the City.

"Thanks, Eddy. And stop frowning. I'm fine, now. Just needed time to put it all in perspective.

"I'll bet. I can't imagine …"

"Yes. My mother doesn't gossip but I have heard a few stories about the Keeper over the years. To see him in action, though … words just aren't enough."

"I know that feeling," said Charles who'd arrived unnoticed.

Eddy turned and embraced him fiercely.

"Oh," said Charles.

Joe smiled. It was so good to see Eddy happy. The last of his lethargy fell away and he rose, ready for whatever came next. It occurred to him he didn't actually have a clue what that was!

"Perhaps, I can help," said Peter Tan, joining the group, accompanied by Connie Wethers.

Brent and Mats rose, surprised, not having seen the couple enter the loft.

Charles held up a hand to calm them and then handled introductions.

"Colonel," said Eddy, "lovely to see you again."

"Mrs. Bryce. Unfortunately, I'm the bearer of bad news. Sir Andrew sends his compliments, regardless."

"What's happened?" asked Charles.

"You have," answered Connie. "Colleridge's failed attempt to kidnap Mrs. Bryce was sanctioned from above and the rather public humiliation you visited upon him was not received well by his supporters. They can't touch you because of the taskforce but they are determined to restrain Mrs. Bryce. Whether it's out of spite or simply to gain leverage is unclear."

"Damn," said Charles.

"Maybe I can help," said Joe.

"Unfortunately, not," said Peter. "The British Foreign Office has formally asked Interpol to step aside while they clean house in the wake of Bradford. If you push back it will be counterproductive."

"Taskforce?" said Eddy.

"Oh, yes, that," said Charles. "Our success plus Bijan's strategy in the aftermath has opened up a world of opportunity in the Islamic community. A whole lot of people are keen to reset the clock and they have significant community support. I've been asked to manage a taskforce to take advantage of that. The Home Secretary wants long-term outcomes, not just good P.R. I'm going to be busy for a while.

"And there's been something going on with the Anglican Church hierarchy, too. Haven't got to the bottom of that yet."

Peter laughed softly.

"Yes?"

"Not relevant now, although it would help for you to know in the long term. Now, however, you need to regroup."

"Indeed," said Wethers, "Sir Andrew has some suggestions."

"I'm listening," said Charles.

"Well, Mrs. Bryce has friends in Australia. My new friend Hilde Nordstrom is also heading back there soon. Sir Andrew feels that distance and the protection of people like Miss Nordstrom would give Mrs. Bryce a time-out, which might placate those who want to make an example of her."

"Removes a piece from the board without loss," added Mats.

Eddy gave him a radiant smile and he nodded.

SHEHKRii
– The FLAME –

"It makes sense," said Charles, looking at Eddy, "but I don't like it."

She smiled. "Neither do I, but I can't think of anything else."

Wethers cleared her throat. "Sir Andrew will provide a rear guard of sorts. He would like to coordinate that effort with you, Sir Charles."

"Of course."

"And us?" asked Brent.

"Have just been promoted," said Charles, "You're both on the taskforce with me; Chief Technical Managers. Pay's better, too."

"Cool. Wish Eddy was part of it, though."

"Yes, well," said Joe, "for the moment, that's not going to happen. Maybe later. We make a potent team and it would be a waste not to keep that going. I have really enjoyed what we've done. Except for New York, of course. Which raises the question.

"Peter, what about the Twelve. We're still in danger there, aren't we?"

"Not for the moment. You gutted them and they've closed ranks. Your protections will stay in place, however, until further notice. We interrogated one of their senior people on a ship off New York. He was the coordinator for their American operations and the CIA is shutting that down also. It will be done behind closed doors. The Twelve will be quiet for a while. You can relax on that score."

Joe let out a breath. It was good to know. He wanted to spend time with his family and then get back to work. The gains they'd made in the last few weeks offered many opportunities. The European network used by the Twelve was open to intensive investigation which might ultimately lead them to Vasily Radu, the organizational genius behind all this.

"Charles," he said, "How long to wrap up here and transfer over to the taskforce?"

Charles looked at Brent and Mats.

"Couple of hours."

"Well then. Why don't we tidy up then all have dinner somewhere private? Peter, Colonel Wethers, you're very welcome. Where's Sophia, by the way?"

Peter looked at Wethers, eyebrows raised, question asked.

"Why not," she said. "Any friend of Hilde's …"

"And Sophia has returned to her duties in Australia," added Peter.

"There's a lot happening down that way, isn't there?" said Joe to no one in particular.

***

Scribe rose early, refreshed and took a light breakfast. His instructions the night before had been attended to and a car was waiting to take him out of London.

The first hour of the trip was spent by phone, alternatively bribing, cajoling and threatening a variety of very well-placed people. The results were not encouraging. Mayhew's arrest was bad enough but even that should not have occasioned the cowardice he was now having to deal with. Those he had the most leverage with were daring to challenge his judgement. It was not outright rebellion but …

One of the two secretaries he had constantly at his side gasped.

"What, Simon?"

"Sir. I was checking the Berlin Accounts and … they're gone. I mean, the accounts themselves still exist. We have seven interlocked trusts … but, sir; they're empty."

Scribe swallowed. "Check all accounts, Simon. Mathew, find Reverence and the other Councilors. I want them all at the southern safe house by the evening."

"Yes, sir."

JERSEY
ENGLISH CHANNEL

"We're fucked," said Reverence.

"That's not helping, Keith."

"Do you think, Miles, at this point, that I really care. The money is gone. Our supposed brother councilors have run for it and Mayhew is cutting a deal. And our previously compliant sponsors are not answering calls. *We're fucked*, hardly covers things at all."

"Have you given up completely, you spineless turd. Or is this just therapy?"

"Name calling already, that's jumping the gun, don't you think?"

Scribe snorted. "We've been well and truly reamed, Keith. Rolling over is not an option."

Fitzsimmons paced. "I wish Sister Bronwyn was here. She's been very useful."

Scribe remained silent.

Fitzsimmons looked at him. "You didn't?"

"What resources do you have access to in the States?"

"Miles, you fuckin' brainless dick. She was one of ours!"

"What resources, Keith?"

Fitzsimmons shrugged.

"As of this morning, not much. The Council of Bishops is furious with me. The media is knocking down their doors just like that pedophilia thing a few years ago. Without funds to leverage any threats I make, we're neutered. For the moment."

"Oh. You have a backup plan?"

"Maybe. Ah ... I've been skimming."

"That's not possible."

The other man laughed softly. "American financial regulation is notoriously spotty."

"And?"

"My cut comes off the front end. Before your accountants get their little *grubbies* on it."

"How much?"

"Ah ... two hundred and eighty-seven million. U.S."

SHEHKRii
– The FLAME –

"What! Keith … you're a genius. It's not much but where to use it?"

"Ah, it's going to take time, at least a week to get at it. Then we've got to ease it into a bullet-proof holding company."

Scribe stood up. "It doesn't matter. Simon, get in here."

Stony silence greeted Scribe's loud call.

"Simon."

"I'll go," said Fitzsimmons, "I need a drink anyway. Can't believe you don't keep hooch in the library."

He stomped off theatrically and slammed the door. Scribe grinned, his spirits lifting.

He had a momentary regret. He could certainly use Brony right now. She was clever in a spiteful sort of way, which usually produced interesting results. But he'd enjoyed stealing her life and felt that energy rise up anew. Should he indulge again so soon. Given their current circumstances, probably not.

But …

Where WAS Keith?

After half an hour of searching he knew he was utterly alone. It was a large house and he'd inspected every room.

He collected a shotgun and cartridges along the way.

The car sat starkly in the front of the house but he hesitated every time he looked at it. He would not expose himself out there even if he did find the keys.

SHEHKRii
– The FLAME –

Scribe returned to the library, gun in hand and tossed himself into a large comfortable armchair. He thought of trying his phone again but resisted; it was obviously blocked in some fashion.

He waited.

And woke suddenly hours later, grasping at the gun in his lap and blinking furiously at the still lit library.

It was almost midnight.

He cursed and rose painfully from his chair realizing the situation finally and resuming his seat. He dosed off, knowing he was safe for the moment.

In the morning, he dared try for the car. There were spare keys in the glove box but the vehicle refused to start. He was not surprised.

Returning to the library he found a single man facing the morning light through a window, his back to Scribe who brought the shotgun to bare and fired.

The noise was deafening but only the glass of the window shattered, the man remained unmoving.

"That was impulsive, Miles. I might have been your only hope."

Vaguely Irish accent in a deep authoritative voice.

"So … you're Chalk."

"That I am, *boyo*, that I am."

"Was this little piece of theatre supposed to intimidate me?"

"A pause for reflection. A courtesy wasted it would seem."

Nathan turned and regarded Scribe. He was a touch haggard but defiant.

"You have so much to lose, Miles. Let's see to that now, shall we."

Nathan turned back to the window and walked through. Scribe followed, not entirely of his own free will but it didn't seem to matter much and he was intensely curious. The gun fell by the wayside.

Nathan walked for several minutes until he came to the estate's edge, a clifftop looking back to England. It was a sheer drop with no protective barrier.

"Your staff are in Interpol custody and being very helpful. Fitzsimmons will be landing in New York about now and the FBI will take him in tow. His surrogates within that organization have already been outed, so it's a neat little parcel, all wrapped up. You're done."

"Why am I still here, then?"

"Yes, that's the question, isn't it? I had planned on letting The Council destroy itself over the next fifty or so years, but you just couldn't leave poor Dr. Carlisle alone, could you? Lashed out, confident in your own power, assuming success before you had it. And then there's Ellsworth's library. Eight hundred years of effort there, Miles. Eight hundred years! I wanted your death to be very, very, personal.

"And there's Brony, of course. Your cleanup crew haven't arrived. The Met have, though, and you'll be on the news tonight, I dare say."

SHEHKRii
– The FLAME –

Scribe ground his teeth and tried to turn away. He couldn't.

"I did this to Brony as an object lesson, but she failed to learn from it. Let's see how it goes as a punishment instead."

Nathan gestured with his hand, a sweeping motion of sorts and Miles Prendergast was thrown off the cliff edge out into clean air, a look of total shock and terrifying realization forming as his body dropped a hundred meters to the rocks below.

He screamed the whole way down.

CHAPTER 20

MONDRAGOE
BASQUE COUNTRY
SPAIN

HILDE HAD SAID HER goodbyes at Winchester. She'd embraced them all warmly; a very un-Hilde-like gesture. Except for Liam. Him, she kissed passionately and long, turning the poor man scarlet.

With a pointed, "Behave, I'm coming back," to Liam, she simply turned and walked out of their lives.

For now.

Shireen and her daughters had decided to go with Hilde, so Jaz expected to see them all reasonably soon. Maybe she'd ask Liam along!

Once Hilde was gone they'd all been bundled up and whisked away to the countryside where a strangely military-like aircraft had dropped out of the clouds and taken them back to Basque country.

Jaz was glad to be back but a little rattled. They had been just settling in at Winchester and she had so many things on the boil. Strangely, Lord Ellsworth and Miss Perkins had come also. She was glad of the company and had caught up on their terrifying adventures but this trip seemed unnecessary.

"You're winding up," whispered Neil as they approached the building where they'd first learned to fly the thistle drones.

"Why are we here?"

SHEHKRii
– The FLAME –

"Don't know: don't care. Those Council bastards shot me Jaz. Almost did the same to the rest of you. The physical pain is gone but emotionally I'm ... I really don't have the words. And that's before you throw in what we saw Nathan do. I need 'down' time."

She took his arm and pressed him close. She'd been trying to avoid feeling what he had just said but maybe having someone to share it with was better than pushing through it. They followed the others upstairs to the office-come-studio they'd' been in only a few weeks beforehand.

Nathan was waiting.

"Welcome back."

There were changes. They all gawked at what had been done to the studio. There were openings everywhere and a great big hole in the middle, an atrium connecting to other buildings. The glass roof on the top of it was a work of art.

"Nice," said Liam.

"Nice?" exclaimed Jaz, "It's perfect!"

People they knew from the decommissioned London office said their 'hellos' and showed them to a lounge on the perimeter of the building. Coffee and cakes arrived as they took in the view to the knoll where Neil and Jaz had flown the drones.

"This will be home base for the next few years for you all," said Nathan. "We had planned on that in about a decade but your adventures with The Council have altered the timeframe. There will be adjustments. Anything you need, ask."

SHEHKRii
– The FLAME –

"Thank you," said Neil. "What about The Council? Won't they regroup, fight back?"

"No. Their leaders are in custody and in disgrace. Their money is yours. None of you are on watch lists anymore and we can maintain that. And I killed Scribe yesterday."

"Oh."

"So, it's entirely up to you, but I recommend you take your time settling in here. Get to know the place. Angus, whom you've already met will handle language lessons for Bart and any of the mundane things that will help you get comfortable. When you're ready we can start planning in earnest. You are all going to be very busy for the next fifty years, so a bit of a holiday now is probably advisable."

"Fifty years ..." said Neil.

"Yes!" answered Liam with heat. "Neil, this is everything we've ever dreamed of. We can kick-start green projects all over the world and not just agricultural stuff. That's the base. From there we can seriously influence global production at every level ..."

"And," said Bart, "we have the resources to make it happen when we want it to. And deal with the big boys. You know the shit I had to ignore before you picked me up. We can not only fix that, we can make it *not-happen* in the first place.

"The people we've met ... it's like long lost family. We don't have to make do any more ...

"Neil, we can go back to Bodmin and finish what we started."

SHEHKRii
– The FLAME –

Carlisle glanced around at his team. The looks on all their faces were the same. Shining enthusiasm wasn't even close.

He grinned. "Yes, a holiday and then take over the world."

They all laughed.

"Excellent," said Nathan.

***

Lord John Ellsworth was taking the sun. The term was one he remembered from his youth at the beginning of the last century. So much time, so much change.

He had a seat on an old stonewall near the knoll. Brigid stood nearby.

"I've been meaning to ask," she said, "that title you give Mr. Chalk; The Keeper of the Flame. It seems a touch mundane, a cliché. What does *Makh t'heh Panku-khan* really mean?"

"Ah, it's complicated. Our records don't give any definitive source for the term but it has linkages to several ancient languages. *Panku* is Hittite for 'teacher', for example."

"Yes, I knew that bit. And the origin of 'khan' is lost in antiquity but 'leader' is at the core of it."

"Indeed. Have you heard the term 'the spark of humanity in us all'?"

"Yes. Usually when describing monsters; because they lack it."

SHEHKRii
– The FLAME –

"Yes, well ... if we're reading the records correctly, that spark was supposed to be much more by now. Not the dim flicker of hope we currently live with but a raging flame ..."

"And he's what, head coach, chief fire lighter ...?"

Ellsworth smiled. Brigid's sharpness was not feigned. She'd say that to Nathan's face.

"No. He's responsible for it all. Being 'Keeper' means that if the Flame of Humanity goes out so does he. It's all or nothing."

"Oh."

Brigid's raised eyebrows alerted him and he turned to see Nathan approaching.

"Keeper."

He stood.

"John. Can you feel *her*?"

"Oh, yes. I could die happy right now."

"Don't you talk like that," snapped Brigid. "You're not done yet."

"Indeed, John. Neil is keen to involve you here if you're agreeable. Once he and the others have rested a little."

"I'm ninety-seven years old, Keeper. I could use a rest, too."

"Ha! Lots of juice left in you, old man. And we can help with that. Since I discovered you and your legacy over thirty years ago, my people have kept an eye on you and we've had an indirect hand in your health. Now we can do more. But you must be willing, eh?"

SHEHKRii
– The FLAME –

"Oh, I'm willing, but there are limits."

"Are there? Speaking of which. Brigid, do you remember the young man who covered your exit from the library?"

"Yes. Cheeky young pup."

"Indeed. Well, he's down the street at the office asking to see you. He's quite taken with your brave heart and cool head, it seems."

"What! I'm almost old enough to be his mother. That's ridiculous."

Ellsworth struggled to hide his smile as Brigid's color rose.

"You'd better set him straight, dear," said John. "I'll be fine here with the Keeper."

Brigid gave him a withering look and stormed off; a little too theatrically, John thought, but she went, which was the important thing.

"Really?" he asked.

"Indeed. The rhythm of both your lives is changing John. Brigid has buried herself with you and the library. Time she spread her wings."

"Yes. I've worried about that since I rescued her from the Council. Your young pup better be tough, though."

"Oh, he is. Rest assured. And he's not as young as he looks. Now …"

"To the matter in hand …"

"Yes. Neil and his team are going to need your experience and contacts. You have a century of life to call on and all that implies. Are you willing to build the empire I need to withstand what *she* must do to set things right?"

"Always. To my last breath."

ITALY

Eddy soaked up the glorious view. The villa on the shores of Lake Como was just high enough to look out over the morning mist. It was like the world went on forever. She sipped her coffee. Johan's amazing mother had invited her to spend some time with them.

M'La.

Such a strange and terrifying woman. She and Victor were a good match. Seeing them together intensified her missing Charlie. But there was no other way for it at the moment.

She was on her way to Australia and sharing this brief moment with Joe and his family. His wife Viviana and their three children had come from Seville. The night just past had been filled with congenial noise.

M'La padded out barefoot onto the terrace and stood at the stone balustrade, inhaling deeply. She reminded Eddy of pictures she had seen of the Masai - African nomads of extreme beauty and eye-catching elegance. Six feet tall, her skin was the flat pitch black of coal tar and her eyes, the most vivid white with almost black irises. When she turned her gaze on you it was impossible not to be drawn into those eyes.

As Eddy well knew.

SHEHKRii
– The FLAME –

Glancing at Eddy, M'La smiled and nodded, then returned her face to the lake. Impossible to tell her age, thought Eddy. Her hands and neck gave away nothing, yet she had to be in her late fifties, at least.

"I'm seventy-three, Eddy," said M'La.

"How …" began Eddy, startled.

"*Abuela* is a good guesser," said little Paolo, from behind Eddy. "She does it all the time," continued the boy, who stopped to give Eddy a kiss on the cheek before walking to his grandmother for a hug. M'La lifted the six-year-old and sat him on her hip.

"Show me?" he demanded as only the very young can.

Extending a long graceful arm, M'La said, "Observe the mist as it rises from the water. Do you see the patterns?"

The boy laughed. "Yes, yes. Like Mama's curtains at home."

"And on the water itself, other lines as well?"

"Yes. Sort of. They're darker, aren't they?"

"Indeed."

Eddy rose to join them as the boy wriggled to be put down.

"What is it you were showing him?" asked Eddy.

M'La looked at Eddy for a long second and then returned her gaze to the lake.

"This is a special place. The energies of Terra are potent here because they converge. At the deepest part of the lake, about four hundred meters out, there is a place of exquisite peace and great potential. The wind and water react to that. You can see the patterns at times like these when the air is heavy with moisture."

Eddy stared out over the lake. She didn't strain to see but simply let the beauty of the place fill her up. Slowly, what she saw changed, not physically but perceptually and a majestic dance was revealed. The lake was alive - breathing into the morning.

Quick, indeed, smiled M'La to herself. *I have invested well with this one.*

Paolo returned at a run with a flower for his grandmother and the moment broke.

The rest of the family started to wander out. Viviana began setting the table in preparation for breakfast. Joe brought out a coffee service, kissed his son and his mother, then sat down as Eddy returned to the table. "So,' he said, "What are your plans?"

"Nothing much,' she replied. "I'll go to Sydney, do the tourist thing and try to relax. Gregory Palmer has been very good about the short notice. He even has an interview arranged for me if I like to take up the offer. A government department of some type, run by a woman named Relk."

Johan shifted in his chair. "Tina Relk?"

"Why, yes, I think so. Someone you know?" asked Eddy.

"If it's the same woman, then 'yes'. Tina is a lawyer. Or was. She worked for us about ten years ago in The Hague at the International Court of Justice. She was marked down for great things. A real talent. But then she resigned and moved back to Australia. More interesting though, is the man she works for now, Peter Jones."

"What does he do?' asked Eddy intrigued.

"We don't know," replied Joe. "Which is what makes it interesting." He grinned.

"I'm not sure I want to get back into the cloak and dagger brigade, Joe. Not yet," she said.

"One step at a time Eddy. The choices are yours," he said, touching her hand.

Victor strode out onto the terrace. "Eddy, what have you done?' he said, with some exasperation. They all looked at him and the piece of paper he had in his hand. Holding it up he said, "This is an Apprehension Order for you, Eddy. Issued to all stations by MI6, at three this morning."

"Oh dear," said Eddy in a small voice.

"Well," said Victor taking a seat at the table. M'La shooed the child inside and came over to listen.

Eddy glanced at the concerned faces and felt a twinge of guilt. "I hope this doesn't cause you any embarrassment," she began. "I'll phone the embassy after breakfast and turn myself in."

"Forget about that," cut in Joe. "What did you do?"

"Well ... before I left, I set up an independent background check on a number of senior people across the intelligence family. MI5 and 6, and a few others. Colleridge was one of them. I thought I might need some ammunition when I went back from my holiday.Someone must have twigged to it."

Victor sighed. He glanced sideways at her. "Was this spite or something else, Eddy?'

Sheepishly she replied. "A little of both."

M'La said to Victor, "You will not allow this."

"No, my love, I will not," replied the old man, and Eddy glanced at him hearing in those words the implacable force of twenty years ago.

"I won't let you get hurt, Victor," said Eddy with heat. "None of you."

"It won't come to that," replied Joe, calmly. "What do you suspect?"

Eddy took a breath. She glanced at M'La. The woman was watching her intently. Eddy drank in the depth of her gaze and found new strength and quietness.

Exhaling, she said to Joe, "Colleridge is an opportunist. Always has been. I don't believe he's completely above board or alone in his greed. The pattern of deceptions I found when I investigated his protégé, Kennedy, set me to thinking that others may be vulnerable in a similar fashion. But it's academic now. I don't have any choice except to return and explain ... and beg."

"Father," said Joe. "Eddy may have access to Peter Jones in Canberra."

"Really," said Victor, "what luck."

M'La listened as her family discussed and planned. She felt a focus to these events, which indicated *synchronicity*. What a lovely word it was. So apt. She regretted the chance that had been lost back in the fifties, to meet Jung. But, this turn of events was curious. Eddy was setting her course for Sun Wu Lin, who even now moved within the circle of this unusual man, Jones. Which brought them into Paul and Dianne's orbit. So much the better. M'La was intensely proud of her son and his choice of friends. She would not allow Eddy to be hurt.

She sensed Viviana watching her and glanced at her daughter-in-law. The younger woman smiled and tilted her head towards the house. Collecting the children, they went inside. M'La maintained an ear to the conversation on the terrace.

"No such thing as a holiday in this family," said Viv in Spanish.

"Indeed," replied M'La in the same language. "It looks like I will be leaving for the Far East a little earlier than expected."

"So, that's where you're off to. The children will miss you. So will I."

"When this is over, I'll return and we will take them to the west of Ireland. I have a friend with family there. They can run riot through the hills. And you can rest."

"That would be nice," said Viv with a sigh, as her youngest darted underfoot.

***

At Rome airport, Eddy and M'La waited in the cargo depot carpark. Eddy was officially an Interpol *protectee*. Johan had arranged it in the last twenty-four hours. The papers she carried were authentic and legal, but could not protect her from the sort of thuggery practiced by the intelligence services.

Victor had arranged transport to Australia on board a Red Cross supply plane. It was basic and not much else - so much for business class.

She would be met in Sydney by this Relk woman and Greg Palmer and placed in protective custody for thirty days. Enough time to sort out the mess.

But, getting into the airport through security, that was the trick. M'La assured her there would be no problems.

Eddy started.

M'La's neck was glowing. No, something beneath her blouse. There was a barely audible hum. The woman touched something through the garment and the glow and noise changed. She made a sound, waited, then another incoherent grunt. The glow subsided.

"My plane has arrived. We can go in now," said M'La. "Take my arm and don't let go," she instructed. "You'll see some strange things but don't speak and keep walking."

"Yes, dear," said Eddy.

M'La cocked an eyebrow.

"Sorry," said Eddy, vacating the car.

As they left the carpark and entered the security lounge, Eddy found herself almost light-headed. Despite her fitness level, the heaviness of body to which she had adjusted with age seemed to lift and she found a spring in her step she barely remembered. More noticeable though, was the change in her vision. People appeared to be transparent in a strange way. And surrounded by colors. She knew instantly who was angry or sad, what a person was about to do or had just done.

As the two women strolled smoothly through the lounge, security post and departure area, no one stopped them or even looked at them. People in their path of travel suddenly moved and were out of the way. M'La stopped when they reached the base of the access stair to the Red Cross cargo jet. Disengaging her arm, she said, "Here we are."

"What ... what was that?" stammered Eddy, who was rapidly getting her usual focus back.

"For a few moments, you saw the world as I do," said the tall woman. "I won't do it to you again, if I can help it."

Eddy shook her head gently. "Someday you'll have to explain it to me."

"Someday I will. Now off you go," she said, urging Eddy up the stairs. "If all goes well, I'll see you soon enough."

Eddy made her way up the stairs and presented her papers to the attendant. She looked back but M'La was gone.

EPILOGUE

AFTER AN INTENSE THREE months, Lin found herself at one of Langley's quiet corners staring into space, the huge curtain window and its wooded splendor beyond, tuned out of her perceptions. She stood with feet wide, hands behind her back. She was relaxed, focused inward, striving not to bubble over with hope.

A week's effort had been spent to verify what the last few months had hinted might lie beneath an ordinary exterior. The patterns had been subtle and unexpected. But, once alerted, her particular instincts had seen through the veil. While the discipline resembled the Master, there were deviations and variations, which set it apart. A gifted amateur, or a committee perhaps. A group effort would account for the discrepancies.

Somewhere, within the Australian government apparatus, there was a group using the skills of Sun Tzu and the weapons of trade and diplomacy to secure everything from corporate success to military infrastructure.

Not that there was an avalanche of achievement, quite the contrary. The approach was incremental and carefully disguised.

Should she tell Morgan? No.

But she must go there, find these people and bend them to her purpose. For all its power, the American intelligence machine lacked the delicate subtlety necessary in this situation. Morgan himself was the best of them and he had too many blind spots. Henry Katz might have been a better choice, but he lacked the power base and influence. And there was something about Henry that caused her to stop short of taking him into her confidence. A hesitation she couldn't quite define; a reluctance.

No.

She would keep this to herself and engineer a move to Australia. First, however, she had to have her security downgraded.

"Miss Keogh."

She turned.

"Yes, Agent Moses."

"Mr. Katz is here and would like a word, please. He's in the Planning Room."

"Very well."

Andrew Moses watched Lin's back as she left. The woman's control was superb but she was so wound up she'd kill someone soon just to relieve the tension. And probably wouldn't even notice.

Such a waste!

He hoped things worked out and Lindsey Keogh got some relief. He liked her.

And she was about to get a pleasant surprise.

She'd been angling for the trip for a few days, but whatever she was up to had just been overtaken by more urgent matters. At least Hakim was going, too. And Henry Katz.

SHEHKRii
– The FLAME –

Lin was about to find out they were all off on a little trip down under.

Things were getting interesting! Although, after New York, 'interesting' was looking a touch overrated.

SHEHKRii
-The Curse-

Journalist, Mark Todd, has pursued the gunrunner, Paul Gareth for nearly a decade.

Now, Todd is about to get his man.

Or is he?

What Todd has stumbled over is something far more sinister. Unfortunately, he's not alone.

Gareth is the target of the CIA and a secret Australian government agency.

In their quest to capture an international criminal and eco-terrorist they will uncover the *Shehkrii* … inheritors of a hidden human heritage that is the last hope for the survival of the species … the spark of humanity in us all that should have been a raging flame, but has instead become a dying flicker!

And they will know Terra.

Manufactured by Amazon.com.au
Sydney, New South Wales, Australia